A CONSTANT BLAZE

Last Flame of Alba, Book 2

Mary Lancaster

(Previously published as *Lady of Ross*)

Dragonblade Publishing, Inc. is an imprint of Kathryn Le Veque Novels, Inc.
P.O. Box 23
Moreno Valley, CA 92556
ceo@dragonbladepublishing.com

Produced in the United States of America

First Edition September 2022
Trade Paperback Edition

ARE YOU SIGNED UP FOR DRAGONBLADE'S BLOG?

You'll get the latest news and information on exclusive giveaways, exclusive excerpts, coming releases, sales, free books, cover reveals and more.

Check out our complete list of authors, too!

No spam, no junk. That's a promise!

Sign Up Here

www.dragonbladepublishing.com

Dearest Reader;

Thank you for your support of a small press. At Dragonblade Publishing, we strive to bring you the highest quality Historical Romance from some of the best authors in the business. Without your support, there is no 'us', so we sincerely hope you adore these stories and find some new favorite authors along the way.

Happy Reading!

CEO, Dragonblade Publishing

Additional Dragonblade books by Author Mary Lancaster

Last Flame of Alba
Rebellion's Fire (Book 1)
A Constant Blaze (Book 2)

Gentlemen of Pleasure
The Devil and the Viscount (Book 1)
Temptation and the Artist (Book 2)
Sin and the Soldier (Book 3)
Debauchery and the Earl (Book 4)

Pleasure Garden Series
Unmasking the Hero (Book 1)
Unmasking Deception (Book 2)
Unmasking Sin (Book 3)
Unmasking the Duke (Book 4)
Unmasking the Thief (Book 5)

Crime & Passion Series
Mysterious Lover (Book 1)
Letters to a Lover (Book 2)
Dangerous Lover (Book 3)
Merry Lover (Novella)

The Husband Dilemma Series
How to Fool a Duke

Season of Scandal Series
Pursued by the Rake
Abandoned to the Prodigal
Married to the Rogue
Unmasked by her Lover
Her Star from the East (Novella)

Imperial Season Series
Vienna Waltz
Vienna Woods
Vienna Dawn

Blackhaven Brides Series
The Wicked Baron
The Wicked Lady
The Wicked Rebel
The Wicked Husband
The Wicked Marquis
The Wicked Governess
The Wicked Spy
The Wicked Gypsy
The Wicked Wife
Wicked Christmas (A Novella)
The Wicked Waif
The Wicked Heir
The Wicked Captain
The Wicked Sister

Unmarriageable Series
The Deserted Heart
The Sinister Heart
The Vulgar Heart
The Broken Heart
The Weary Heart
The Secret Heart
Christmas Heart

The Lyon's Den Connected World
Fed to the Lyon

De Wolfe Pack: The Series
The Wicked Wolfe
Vienna Wolfe

Also from Mary Lancaster
Madeleine
The Others of Ochil

Twelfth Century Scotland

ROYAL KINDREDS OF SCOTLAND:
CENÉL LOAIRN

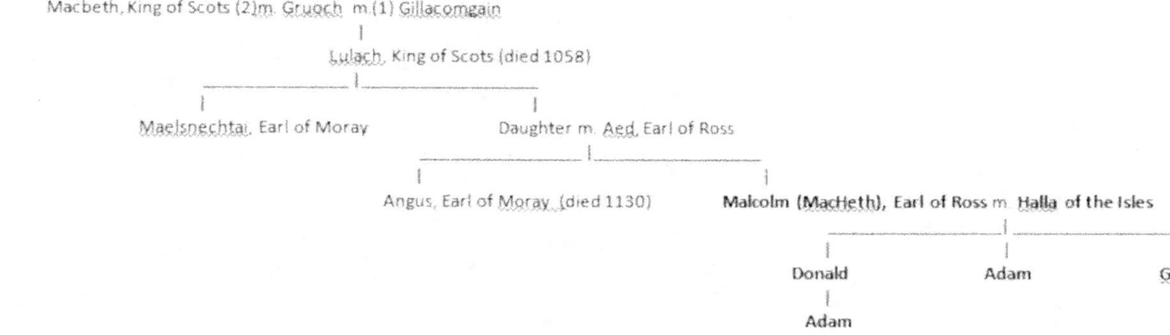

CENÉL GABRAIN

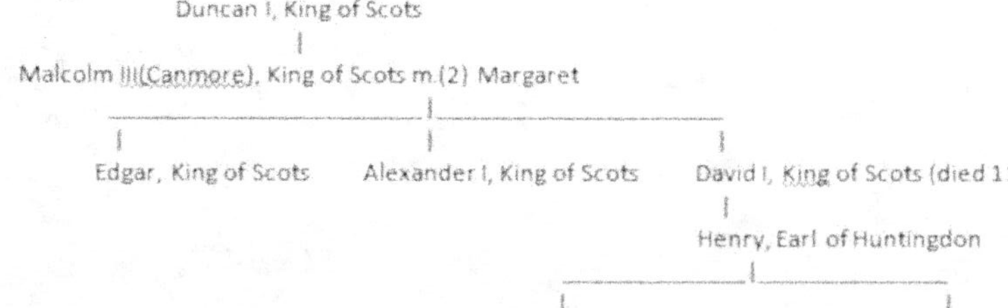

A Brief Note on Names

Because Gaelic, Norse, English, and French were all spoken in twelfth-century Scotland, my heroine is known in this story variously as Christian (English), Christina (French), and Cairistiona (Gaelic). But mostly, where there is a common modern equivalent of Gaelic names, such as Malcolm and Donald, this is the version I have used.

Scotland itself had many names at the time: Scotland in English, Alba in Gaelic, Scotia in Latin.

Though the matter is beyond my control, I have to acknowledge there are too many Malcolms in this book! Unfortunately, they are all historical characters and their appearance or reference necessary to the story. For clarity, they are:

Malcolm MacHeth, one time Earl of Ross, father to Donald and Adam.

Malcolm IV, current King of Scots.

Malcolm III, also known as Malcolm Canmore, late King of Scots, great-grandfather of the current King Malcolm.

And finally, the "mac" issue. Surnames/family names were still rare in twelfth-century Scotland. It was normal to be known as the son or daughter of one's father, e.g., Adam, son of Malcolm, or Adam mac Malcolm. On the other hand, Adam's family *is* also known by the surname MacHeth, probably a corruption of MacAed, because of their ancestor Aed, who linked them to the throne of Scotland. So I have given "mac" as a patronymic, i.e. "son of," a small "m," and MacHeth as a surname a capital M.

PROLOGUE

Ross, spring 1153

THE VICTORY CELEBRATIONS were well underway, presided over by the lady, glowing with new hope. Barely reined in by her presence, the men were raucous, jubilant, and rightly so. Smiling, yet restless, his whole being buzzing with equal parts euphoria and doubt, the youth made his casual way out of the hall alone.

He took his horse and his blanket and, still alone, rode beyond the stockade to camp under the stars. To light a fire where no one could see.

He and his brother and his uncle had already lit the bigger fire of war. They had raided deep into the territory of the King of Scots, battled and defeated his men. For the youth, there was huge relief in having acquitted himself well, in making his family and his men proud of him. And yet for part of one fight, he had been blinded by dreams. There had been moments, mercifully brief, when he hadn't even known which battle he fought, this one or the others playing out in terrible glimpses behind his eyes.

There had been no time for fear, but it had taught him that as a warrior, his life was likely to be short. And the price of war high for everyone.

The fire crackled into life and he lay down before it, wrapped in his blanket, and gazed into the spell-binding flames. He looked desperately for confirmation that the risk and the carnage were worth it, that the glorious blaze he and his brother had begun, could indeed bring his imprisoned father home. And win his family, finally, the kingdom of the Scots.

But the fire would not play. The dreams came so often when he really didn't want them and could not deal with them. Yet now, when he *needed* to see, they eluded him, even in the fire.

His eyelids grew impossibly heavy. Days in the saddle, nights under the stars, hard fighting between organizing, ordering, and keeping watch—they had taken their toll. But the leaping flames would not grant him the relief he sought.

As his eyes flickered, he imagined the shape of a crown in the fire. At first, he thought he made it with his imagination, and then, without warning, he hurtled after it, into the flames, only to find it had jumped further away. He was riding again, the crown bouncing along the road before him, through burning halls and dying men. But he could not catch it.

The MacHeths could not catch it.

When he woke at dawn, cold and stiff, he didn't know if he had dreamed in the fire or in sleep. But his face was wet and not with the dew.

CHAPTER ONE

Autumn 1156

DONALD MACHETH WAS not convinced that the monastery at Whithorn was the best place for a discreet meeting, and certainly not with the wily Fergus, Lord of Galloway.

Monks wrote to each other all the time, and the king was bound to hear of it all the quicker. Which meant, Donald thought with some excitement as he rode through the town on borrowed horses with his two followers and Fergus's messenger, that Fergus's plan to obtain his father's release was surely about to reach fruition.

Donald was glad, proud to be overseeing it. Since his return from the western isles in the spring, his brother Adam had been the one making all the plans. With maturity, Adam had learned to command as well as fight, using rather than hiding his strangeness, and Donald had to admit it sat well on him. Their mother and the men, his own and Adam's, obviously thought so, too. Donald loved his brother and had grown up both protecting him and trusting him. It came hard to realize Adam no longer needed that protection. Perhaps he never had. Perhaps it had always been Adam protecting *him* in his own, weird way.

Whatever, Donald didn't like the twinges of jealousy that had crept into his thoughts of Adam. Perhaps it was even what had changed his mind in Kintyre. For when Adam had ridden north to Ross and his bride, Donald, instead of sending Fergus's messenger south to Galloway as agreed, had sailed with him.

The messenger, who'd pointed the way, now fell back as they rode up the hill toward the monastery, giving Donald his place. So that when the men erupted from the buildings and the trees, they cut Donald and his two men off from the messenger.

Donald wasn't worried. He'd taken much the same precautions when Fergus's band had entered Ross earlier in the year. Fergus himself strolled across the road on foot, armed to the teeth as always but dressed as the great lord he was.

"Greetings, Donald mac Malcolm!" he called. "Welcome to Galloway, and to Whithorn."

Since Fergus was on foot, Donald dismounted. Which was when the whine of arrows rent the air and both of Donald's men fell to the ground without uttering a sound.

Blood sang in Donald's ears, fury for the death of his friends tore at his heart, along with shame because he'd allowed himself to be betrayed by the man Adam had warned against. He drew his sword free, urging the horses forward with him to give him cover until they got as far as Fergus's men, when Donald slapped the horses' rumps and lunged, killing one man instantly with his sword through the heart and felling another with his dagger in the stomach.

He'd dealt with four more, dead or incapacitated, before Fergus's men got close enough to disarm him and Fergus himself held a sword point to his throat.

"You'll rot in hell for this, you treacherous bastard," Donald panted.

"Treacherous?" Fergus said, gazing down upon him with curious sympathy. "My dear Donald, you are in my country for unknown reasons and wanted very badly by the King of Scots. What else could I do but my loyal duty to my royal ally?"

HALLA, THE LADY of Ross, dreamed of her husband.

No other dreams affected her this way, causing her to wake with restless anger and grief and dark physical arousal. Stupid, because she had stopped being angry with Malcolm MacHeth decades ago. What really distressed her now was that the dreams no longer came very often, and when they did, his face was blurred.

For more than twenty years, what should have been the best part of her life, she had lived without him. While he lay in the King of Scots' prison, she had brought up his children and ruled his earldom of Ross. And she'd fought every way she could to have him released. She needed to remember him to go on.

Or at least, so she had always believed.

Throwing off the heavy blankets, she rose from the big bed she'd first slept in as a young girl and paced to the window, throwing the shutters wide to cool her face and body in the chill wind. Before her spread out the ridged farming lands and the endless wild moors and forests of Ross, all crisscrossed with misty rivers and streams and lochs. Malcolm had made the isolated hall at Brecka his main residence because it was so hard to find, and he was so frequently pursued by the king's men. Behind it rose the steep hill from which Gormflaith, Halla's daughter, watched constantly for the return of the father she had never seen.

Halla leaned out, tilting her face into the damp wind, reaching for the serenity she had so painstakingly acquired. Malcolm MacHeth had never been a serene or tranquil man. But in spite of everything, she didn't want to forget his face, even though she knew the decades would have altered it, as they had changed hers.

She was thirty-nine years old. Most women of her age and rank would have no greater concerns than households, children, and grandchildren. Few had ever exercised the power she had here in Ross. She had already ruled much longer than Malcolm ever had, longer than his father. And she did it well, better than either of them.

Not for the first time, she acknowledged that it would be hard to give up such power when Malcolm MacHeth, Earl of Ross, finally came home. Or when Donald, their elder son, finally decided there was no longer any point in waiting and hoping, and took up all of the reins of rule himself. And when he married, his lady, whoever she might be, would take the rest of Halla's place as was only right.

Halla dreaded that day because she would have nothing to replace the huge responsibility she'd taken up so long ago. It was no longer possible for her to live like other women through her family alone. But she would adapt and change as necessary because she loved her children fiercely. She'd taught them to fight for their father's right to be King of Scots, just as Malcolm would have wished.

Without warning, she shivered. One of those violent, spine-tingling shivers that warned of a future when someone would walk over her cold, earthy grave. Halla dreaded that. She wanted to be pushed out into the sea and be consumed in flames with her longship.

But perhaps the danger was not hers. She shivered again, reaching up to slam the shutters. Her sons were with their uncle still, fighting and raiding. Or perhaps on their way home. Either way, she had no cause beyond the normal to fear for them.

And yet she did.

"IT'S DONE," FERGUS, the Lord of Galloway, told the young King of Scots, who was hawking in the Pentland Hills.

The king, a fair, handsome boy with a love of all things chiv-alric, rode with Fergus a little way apart from his courtiers, bestowing a genuine smile upon him. "Excellent! Where *are* the captured MacHeth sons?"

"Well," Fergus confessed, "I only have Donald. Adam didn't come, although with the bait of his brother, I could probably catch him, too. On the other hand, I don't want a war in Galloway if I can help it. Donald is probably enough for our purposes."

The king was still smiling as he gazed into the sky. His hawk had caught a sparrow. He held out his gloved hand, and the hawk flew toward it. "Then perhaps it's time I visited Roxburgh. You'd better bring your prisoner there to join his father."

"*Your* prisoner, Your Grace," Fergus said graciously. He wheeled his horse around and found the Lady Mairead of Kingowan almost in front of him, gazing upward at the soaring, hunting hawks.

Damn her, the woman moved like a snake, silent and inconvenient. But he knew how to deal with women, even dangerous ones. Especially when they were as comely as Mairead with her fair, flawless skin and fiery red hair mostly hidden beneath her almost decorous veil. Fergus, retreating from the royal presence as the rest of the court advanced, urged his horse even closer to the apparently distracted Lady Mairead.

"Lady Mairead," he murmured. "I was just thinking of you. Can we escape this dullness, do you think?"

Yes, there it was, the betraying blush and flutter that meant a little dalliance would not be unacceptable.

"Slip away into the wood as you pass," she breathed with unmistakable promise.

He watched from the corner of his eye as she began to walk her horse casually in that direction. Fergus's blood heated. She was, in fact, a fine-looking woman. Keeping her silent for a few days would be no hardship. He wondered if she did more for his old friend Malcolm mac Aed—or Malcolm MacHeth as he was more popularly known—than carry his messages from prison.

An image of Halla, Malcolm's lady, swam before his eyes. For a prisoner, Malcolm really was a lucky bastard. To have a pretty, willing woman visiting him in captivity and a beautiful, wise, and loyal one to come home to. Eventually. Well, the Lady of Ross was beyond Fergus's reach, but Mairead, clearly, was not.

Pretending his young hawk had dropped something over the trees—when in fact the stupid bird was probably halfway home to Galloway—Fergus rode off to investigate. Although he made a lot of noise clumping about, Mairead didn't immediately appear. He had to search for her, find her tracks. And they led straight through to the other side of the wood, back in the direction of Edinburgh.

MAIREAD WAS NOBODY'S fool, except perhaps Malcolm MacHeth's. Giving Fergus the slip provided her with the time she needed to ride back to Edinburgh, summon her discreet messenger, and send him north to Ross.

That done, she cleansed and anointed her body, put on her best gown, and repaired to Fergus's rooms in the city. She'd only just settled herself in his best chair and, making use of the expensive writing materials she found on the table, begun to write a dull letter to her husband, when the dark, wiry figure of Fergus came striding in, scowling, no doubt with irritation at being made a fool of. However, his expression when he caught sight of her was almost worth it.

"What-what—what the…" he spluttered.

"Where have you been?" Mairead demanded, throwing down her pen, which spattered ink over the vellum. Oh well, it would still do. "I've been waiting here for hours."

"That's funny. I was scouring the wood for hours."

She narrowed her eyes. "Do I look like a woodsman's daughter to you?"

His gaze swept over her person, betraying only too clearly

what he'd like to do with it. "No," he said hoarsely. "God, no."

"I thought not," she purred, standing up to let him embrace her exotically scented person before she pulled free and spun around to seize her cloak and the half-finished letter. "On the other hand, you are too late. My husband misses me. I've been summoned home."

It spoke volumes for Fergus's frustration that it was late in the evening before he even thought to inquire who had left Edinburgh that afternoon while he'd been raking through the woods. And by then, he hadn't a hope of catching them.

TO COUNTERACT THE rumors that were already seeping in from Galloway, King Malcolm left Fergus in Edinburgh while he and the Earl of Strathearn traveled in private to Roxburgh.

King Malcolm had met the prisoner in Roxburgh castle once before, when he'd first become king and had gone through curiosity to see what sort of a monster he held that was so frightening even his grandfather King David hadn't had the courage to kill him. Or so young King Malcolm had told himself. In reality, he'd been well aware there were other reasons no one would execute that other Malcolm, the son of Aed, reasons to do with tradition and honor as well as pragmatism.

The prisoner represented a royal kindred that had been wronged by the king's own. They were cousins, distant but undeniable. Malcolm MacHeth could only be killed in battle, for those reasons. And because a martyr with heirs to his cause was a focus for the swirling discontent in the country, from slighted or greedy nobles to hungry bondsmen and serfs who'd suffered from raids or taxation.

The chamber housing Malcolm MacHeth was not uncomfortable. He had a tiny window, high up in the wall, that allowed in fresh air and light. He had a fireplace for warmth in winter, a bed to sleep in, a bench to sit on, and books to read. He was allowed to exercise in the big inner courtyard, to ride and practice jousting, archery, and swordplay. He had respectable clothes, books, writing materials, and an old harp to strum. He was even allowed an occasional female visitor, although none from his family, who would have been instantly seized.

As soon as the guard opened his cell door, Malcolm rose from the bench on which he'd been reading. He would have been warned to expect the king. A beam of sunlight shone from the high window onto the bench, falling partially still on the tall, saturnine prisoner. The other half of his face remained in shadow, and the king wondered if that was deliberate, to hide his true thoughts or to confuse his visitors.

Malcolm MacHeth bowed to the king but did not kneel. He had a certain stature, a presence that the young king envied because it wasn't haughty or arrogant, just…confident. Which was odd in a man who'd been incarcerated since the age of twenty-two. But then, he'd been in arms against King David since the age of thirteen.

Although now over forty years old, no grey marred the dark head of Malcolm mac Aed, one-time Earl of Ross. There was no submission in his somehow insolent stance. And if there was weariness or even hopelessness in his heart—God knew there should have been after all this time—it was well hidden behind the steady, intelligent dark eyes. If the king hadn't known better, he'd have imagined the prisoner was mocking him for coming here, for betraying there was something important in the wind.

Suddenly, the king felt uneasy. He should have left this to others, not turned up here like a child at a fair, avid to see the great attraction and the effect on him of the king's mighty presence. It was Malcolm MacHeth's presence that seemed likely to dominate this encounter if the king wasn't very careful.

The King of Scots straightened to his full, slightly gangly height and looked straight into his enemy's dark eyes. There was an edge of hardness there that he hadn't noticed before, a spark of something very like danger that made the king glad, suddenly, that he hadn't come alone. This was the man who'd turned the kingdom upside down, who'd fought and killed ruthlessly from a tender age to take Scotland's crown. *His* crown.

Malcolm lifted his chin to give himself courage. "Good day to you, sir," he said in English, grand and yet amiable. "I see that you are well."

"As are you, sir, by appearance," Malcolm MacHeth replied politely. "I'm honored to receive you in my humble dwelling."

"Actually, you are," the king said, scowling, though he recovered his grand manner almost at once. "But what am I thinking? You must forgive my discourtesy. I have brought you another visitor."

The prisoner's eyebrows rose, but he did not move as the guard pushed Donald MacHeth into the room.

Unarmed but unbound and with few hurts apart from those healing after his fight with Fergus of Galloway's men, Donald stood stock-still beside the king, his gaze fixed on his father. His Adam's apple wobbled as he swallowed. Tall, dark, lean, with those liquid dark eyes, he was unmistakably a MacHeth. Malcolm's eldest son and heir.

And his father didn't know him.

For the first time, the king felt ashamed, almost guilty. But he'd gone too far to back down at this stage. "I see introductions are required. Malcolm, son of Aed, meet Donald, son of...yourself."

Malcolm's lips parted in shock. Although this was what the king had wanted to provoke in his unflappable prisoner, for some reason, the success didn't make him happy.

Without permission, Donald took a stumbling step forward and fell to his knees—as he hadn't before the king.

"Father," Donald whispered, bowing his head. "Forgive me."

Malcolm stared, unmoving. Then, as if he couldn't help it, his hand reached down, touching the bowed head of the son he hadn't laid eyes on in over twenty years. "Forgive *you*? For what?"

Donald's voice was hoarse, difficult, almost as if he were being strangled. "Being taken, being here. That *you* are still here."

"Well, I can't blame you for either of the latter," Malcolm said with a hint of the humor that must have been his saving grace through his long isolation from the world. "I don't know why you're here, but I can't yet be sorry." He grasped his son's hair, tilting up his head. A smile flickered across his face. Donald's breath caught.

The king couldn't doubt the charged emotion between the two. He'd imagined somehow that there would be more anger, more gnashing of teeth than this silent, curiously helpless staring. He wondered what thoughts filled Donald's head, as he finally beheld his legendary parent, and something almost like jealousy pulled at him. He could never have been king without the death of his own father, whom he missed suddenly with the force of an armored punch in the chest.

"I see your mother in you," Malcolm said softly to his son.

"I see my brother in you," Donald said. "I never expected that."

"Where is your brother?"

"In Ross." In response to Malcolm's tug, he stumbled to his feet. His father held him by the shoulders in a grip that must have hurt. The man's knuckles were white.

"And your sister? And your mother?"

"Also."

As if forcing himself, Malcolm relaxed his grip without releasing it. Over Donald's shoulder, he addressed the king. "Why have you brought my son here?"

The king smiled. "To take your place. I'm sending you home."

No one moved. The silence rang in the king's ears. Slowly, Malcolm MacHeth's hands fell away from his son's shoulders and back to his own sides. In his eyes, that spark of danger flared and burned.

"Why?" Malcolm asked, the very quietness of his voice a

threat.

The king shrugged elaborately to cover his nervousness. "Everyone seems to want it. I'm told it's unfair to keep you so long, that there's no fight left in you after two decades. That if I let you go, your sons and your brother-in-law will stop attacking my people and my land. On the other hand, I can't have you raising rebellion again as soon as you flex your free muscles. One of your sons is still free to cause havoc. You must exert your fatherly authority and keep him in line."

Malcolm MacHeth smiled. "Must I?"

"Yes," the king retorted, resorting to an attitude of bluster. "Because I will have your other son here in your old chamber, hostage to your obedience *and* Adam MacHeth's."

Oddly, it was Donald who turned on the king with scorn. "Clearly you have never met my brother Adam."

"It makes no difference," Malcolm MacHeth said abruptly, seating himself once more on the bench. His firm mouth was set in a harsh line. "I will not leave my son here."

Donald blinked rapidly. "No," he said hoarsely. "You *must* go. For everyone's sake. For Ross."

Malcolm shook his head. "I will not compel you to a youth wasted in prison. Mine is over, and I'm used to this…half-life."

The king scowled with growing irritation. "By your leave, sir, it is not up to you! If necessary, I will simply have you thrown out of the gates!"

"Then I'll sit there, outside the castle gates," Malcolm Ma-cHeth said stubbornly. "But I will not go home."

This was not going at all the way the king or Fergus had planned. For the first time since he'd ascended the throne, the king found himself bereft of words. But help came from an unexpected quarter.

Donald threw himself onto the bench beside his father. "No, no, this is right," he said excitedly. "This is the way it's meant to be! Adam *saw* this, sir. That Fergus would bring about your release. Admittedly, we didn't expect it *this* way, but that doesn't matter. The gates are open for you, and you must go home for everyone's sake." His voice lowered, and he murmured something beneath his breath.

The king, however, had excellent hearing, and to him, it sounded like "It will be all right, I swear. Adam will come for me."

Poor deluded idiot had lived too long in the wilds of Ross. Everyone knew Roxburgh Castle was impregnable. And if no one, not even the notorious Adam, had been able to rescue Malcolm MacHeth, why on earth would he be able to release the son?

Malcolm MacHeth himself seemed to be of a similar mind. He gazed at Donald a moment longer before he said, "No. Keep both of us if you have to, but I will not leave here without my son."

Ungrateful *bastard*. The king knew an urge to run both of them through. Or just to walk away, leaving the door open and hope they'd be gone by morning. Instead, he stalked out and slammed the door closed. He hoped the noise would give Malcolm MacHeth second thoughts.

"Now what in the name of all the fiends of hell do I do?" the king raged to Ferchar of Strathearn, who'd acted as his guardian during these years of his minority.

"Send to Malcolm's wife," the earl advised.

The king blinked at him. "And force her to choose between her husband and her son? She hasn't laid eyes on the husband for over twenty years! Why would she choose him?"

The earl gave a wry smile. "Because absence makes the heart grow fonder? No, she is by all accounts a wise lady. And the husband has much more chance of negotiating the release of the son than the other way around. Or so she will imagine."

"WHO'S THIS?" ADAM MacHeth asked without a great deal of interest as a rather baffled and bedraggled man was hauled before him.

Adam was preparing to ride out with Henry, the Norman, to show him the land that had been set aside for him. In truth, it would pay little enough, especially in the early years, but it was a way of binding the Norman to him. The others gave their loyalty because of who he was. Henry, once his enemy, needed feudal allegiance, and Adam didn't mind obliging.

"He's a messenger," Cailean mac Gilleon said in English, pushing the frightened stranger forward. "From the king. He was met soon after he crossed into Ross and...*escorted* here."

Adam blinked and gave the man some more of his distracted attention. "What can the king have to say to me?"

Cailean kicked the messenger, who glared and said resentfully, "Nothing, unless you're Sir William de Lanson."

Lanson. So, Adam's ruse was working. The king still didn't know that his knight, Sir William de Lanson, was dead, and so for now, he would send no other army against the MacHeths. And yet, for some reason, the sound of his name stirred Adam to unease.

Cailean raised his fist to the messenger in an obviously threatening manner, but Adam, who'd just spotted his wife, Cairistiona, entering the hall with her arms full of wild roses, stayed him with one finger. There were many ways to elicit information, and they didn't all involve blood. "For quickness, would the Lady of Tirebeck do? Lanson's wife?"

Cairistiona—or Christian in English—frowned slightly as she caught the words. Changing direction, she came toward them and deposited her flowers on the table.

"What is it?" she asked the messenger.

Adam's heart warmed all over again. It seemed she knew what he wanted, picked up on a situation immediately, and acted upon it, even when she disliked, as Adam knew she did, being reminded that Lanson had been so recently her husband. That he had died at the hand of the man who had then promptly married her himself.

"You are the Lady de Lanson?" the messenger asked, although he must have known her by the now-famous linen mask she wore over one side of her face.

"Obviously," Cairistiona said haughtily. "I am Christian of Tirebeck. Tell me the king's will."

"Perhaps in privacy," the messenger said, casting an uneasy glance around her clearly Gaelic entourage.

"I'm losing patience," Cairistiona interrupted while Henry usefully brought his Norman presence to the messenger's attention by leaning on the table directly in front of him.

The messenger shrugged and took a deep breath. "His Grace greets Sir William and advises he should be ready as soon as the MacHeths march south."

Deliberately, Adam didn't look anywhere except at the messenger. "Is that it?"

The messenger nodded, his gaze flickering between Adam, Cairistiona, and Henry. "Find him refreshment and a place to sleep," Adam said to Cailean, then switched to Gaelic. "And don't let him leave."

Judging by the messenger's sudden resumption of struggling, he understood that, too.

"If he gives you any trouble," Adam advised, "kill him."

The messenger stopped struggling, and Cailean hauled him away again.

"What," Henry said thoughtfully, "should Sir William be ready to do? When the MacHeths march south?"

Adam shrugged with quick impatience. "Attack us where it matters. Take our halls and our womenfolk and kill as many men as are left behind to protect them. The more interesting question is *why* we should march south."

"You do so quite a lot," Cairistiona said dryly. "In fact, you have only just come back."

"Exactly," Adam said. "And yet the messenger didn't say,

'when the MacHeths *next* go south or raid south.' He said, 'march south,' as if this would be more than an opportunistic raid."

He became aware only gradually of Cairistiona's uneasy regard. This was difficult for her. She'd been brought up to regard the crowned king of Scots as the one true king, and her loyalty was too deep and true to be easily swayed. He couldn't be sorry for that, although he could and did wish to have first hold on that loyalty. In time, perhaps.

She said, "Maybe now would be a good time to send the messenger back to the king with an offer to negotiate peace."

"Maybe," he said to please her. Most of his mind was occupied with the reasons for the king's first ever message to his isolated knight in Ross. Something was happening. He just didn't yet know what. He could only wait. "Come," he said abruptly to Henry. "If we wait any longer, we won't have time today."

He took Cairistiona's hand and kissed it, and was relieved to see her brow clear as her fingers clung for a moment to his lips. "Take care," she said.

He didn't think she was referring to a ride through his own country. Like him, she sensed something was happening, or about to happen. His fingertips seemed to tingle with it as he left the hall and mounted the gray horse already waiting for him.

"Send after me," he said to Findlaech, "if any more messengers are found. Theirs or ours."

CHAPTER TWO

PEOPLE CAME AND went from Tirebeck all the time, carrying messages to and from Adam. If Adam wasn't around, most were passed on to Findlaech or whichever of the men were there. It was unusual for anyone to disturb him with a mere message before he had risen. But the morning after the king's messenger had arrived, a knock on the bedchamber door froze Christian's lips on her husband's shoulder. His finger, teasing her breast, paused too, but he didn't otherwise move away from her, merely raised his eyes from his finger to her face with a promising smile that caught at her breath.

"Adam," came Findlaech's voice through the door. "There's a message from the Lady Mairead. You need to hear it."

The exciting warmth died in Adam's eyes. Without a word, his hand fell away from her. So did his arms, and he rose at once from the bed, reaching for his shirt.

"Who is Lady Mairead?" Christian asked lightly.

"The Lady of Kingowan. You might have met her in Perth. Her husband is a great courtier of the king's."

Christian remembered Mairead very well. A beautiful, friendly flame around which the bright courtiers fluttered and, she suspected, came to grief. Worse, she'd been one of the few people who admitted to actually having met one of the MacHeths. "Ah. *That* Mairead. I thought she must be your mistress."

"She was," Adam said unexpectedly. "For a little. She used to be married to one of Somerled's captains, who'd died in battle. She left the Isles to marry Brian of Kingowan. And bring us what information she could." Adam shoved his feet into his boots. "She also carries messages to and from my father."

Christian blinked. "How…?"

"In disguise," Adam said, rising to his feet.

Christian dressed more slowly. She was aware she'd have scrambled after him to hear this news, only that would no longer be dignified now that she'd learned Adam had been Mairead's lover. He'd told her so openly and without shame. There was no need for demeaning jealousy. But still, she would not show unseemly interest.

Instead, she concentrated on the warmth gathering in her heart because he never kept things from her now, not past loves—she hoped it was past—and not even such secrets as his family's means of communicating with Malcolm MacHeth in the impregnable castle at Roxburgh.

Adam was not gone long. She was still brushing her hair when he erupted back into the bedchamber and seized up his heavy weapons belt. His dark eyes were grim and bleak, his mouth set in a thin line. Not quite his battle face, but getting there.

She set down the brush. "What is it?"

When his gaze met hers, her heart almost stopped beating. She'd never seen fear in his face before.

"Donald is taken," he said. "He went to Galloway anyway, despite agreeing that we would invite Fergus to Kintyre with my uncle instead. And Fergus took him prisoner and handed him over to the king. They wanted me, too, but apparently, Donald is enough for their purpose."

"Which is?" she managed.

"To bring our men south to face the royal army, so that Lanson can take Ross. And my father will command us to lay down our arms, in case they kill Donald."

She went to him, held his thick, muscled arms, and laid her cheek against his chest. There was nothing she could say. After a moment, his arms closed around her, and his hand stroked her hair as if in wonder. But no part of him relaxed.

"I must go to my mother," he said after a moment.

"I'll come with you," she said, and he didn't forbid it.

CHRISTIAN SUSPECTED THAT the lady of Ross had never broken down before anyone, including her children, in twenty years. As a result, when she sank suddenly down in the chair she'd risen from to hear Adam's news, her mouth open in a silent cry of grief, no one knew what to do.

Her breath came in gulps as if she couldn't control it, and one hand reached to her veil, clawing it off to reveal a halo of bright, golden fair hair. Tears coursed unnoticed down her cheeks. Adam gazed at her in shock. He'd known this would devastate her, just not how obviously.

Christian dropped to her knees, taking both of Halla's hands and holding them tightly. If ever she'd doubted the depths of emotion the lady harbored beneath her cool exterior, she knew better now. She couldn't recall ever seeing anyone in such pain, all the more shocking for being so unexpected.

"You'll come through this, too," Christian whispered. "And we'll find a way to get him back."

Halla closed her eyes as if struggling back to herself. Her fingers clung to Christian's, hard and then, slowly relaxed. She opened her eyes, ignoring the tears.

"How?" she demanded bitterly, although the unendurable despair no longer seemed so obvious in her ice-blue eyes. "By sending Adam, too, into the lion's den and losing all three of them?"

"It's not the end," Adam said in his abrupt way. "I dreamed

this, too. Chains around Donald... I just don't know what it means."

"It means Fergus of Galloway has betrayed us," Halla said in a hard voice. "I never thought he would do that, not to *him*." She dragged the back of her hand across her mouth as though to silence herself.

"Well, at least now I don't have to marry Fergus's pig of a son," Gormflaith, Adam's sister, said, in a rallying sort of a way. Although her mother ignored her, it brought a faint, reluctant smile to Adam's lips.

The lady stood, drawing Christian to her feet. "It's late," she said with clear effort, "and we should rest. If Donald is truly taken, we can expect some kind of demand from the king. We need to be at our best to decide what to do." She leaned forward, pressing her cold, smooth cheek briefly to Christian's. "Take care of him," she breathed.

Christian's throat closed. "I'll try."

When the lady had gone, Adam walked across the hall to the hearth, where the remains of a fire still glowed. He crouched and began methodically adding more wood from the box beside it. Then he sat back on his heels and gazed into the flames.

"He'll see what to do next," Gormflaith said confidently. "All will be well."

"Of course," Christian agreed. She glanced at the other girl. "Do you mean you—the MacHeths—base *all* your decisions on Adam's dreams?"

"Only the big ones," Gormflaith said with a quick, humorous glance. She was tall, like her mother, though she shared her brothers' darkness of hair, which she rarely troubled to cover except on formal occasions. "It was Adam who saw that our father would not die in prison, that we could and should rise up against the King of Scots."

How many people had died since then on both sides? And now his brother was imprisoned, too. "Do you think he regrets it now?" Christian asked, low.

"No," Gormflaith said. "There is no point. He can't undo it, so he'll just look for a way through it. As we all must." She walked across to Adam and touched his hair. He spared her a glance, even pushed his head into her hand like a large, shaggy dog before he went back to staring into the flames.

Gormflaith walked on to the chamber Christian had once shared with her and quietly closed the door. Christian went and sat by Adam's side, resting her head on his shoulder. He didn't move away. If anything, he leaned into her.

"Do you see anything?" she asked.

"Not yet."

Christian gazed into the flames with him until she had to blink and turn away. Instead, she watched him staring.

"What do you really see, Adam?" she blurted.

His eyebrows twitched. "Nothing. Yet."

She gave his arm a little shake. "I don't mean now, I mean *ever*. Have you truly seen that your father will be king?"

He blinked and slowly turned to face her. His lips parted and closed again. He swallowed. "My father will never be king. None of us, none of our issue ever will be."

Christian stared at him. "Have you always known that?"

He nodded.

"Adam, do *they* know?" she asked, waving one hand toward the front of the hall to indicate his family. "Does Halla?"

Adam shook his head. "They need to justify what my father has done, and they need more than a reason to fight for his freedom. After twenty years, they need a *cause*, or they might give up."

She touched his cheek. "Don't *you* need these things?"

Again, he shook his head. "The belief that he could and even should be king is my father's protection as well as our best weapon. His right adds to their fear of us. And yet, because of his blood, no one will kill him save in combat."

It was not a courtesy, she knew, that would be extended to Donald. He was a true, expendable hostage, and therein lay

Adam's fear for his brother. And Halla's.

For a moment, Christian felt all the weight of Adam's burden, the knowledge he carried alone, and the responsibilities, right or wrong, that he'd given himself. "And if and when he ever does come home? What then?"

"Life," Adam said vaguely, his attention drifting back to the flames. "Happiness and honor aren't bound to kingship."

Christian pulled his face back to hers. "But what is *your* aim, Adam? I've never truly grasped that. What do *you* want out of all this scheming and fighting?"

"Peace," he said, drawing her head back down to his shoulder. And so, they sat in silence before the fire until the men began to drift into the hall to sleep. Then, she rose and tugged at his shoulder until he stood with her.

He couldn't make the visions come any more than he could stop them. He knew that better than she did and never, ever relied on them. Like everyone else, he had to wait and think and plan with the knowledge he had.

IN THE CHAMBER that had been his father's prison for longer than Gormflaith had been alive, Donald MacHeth lay in the darkness and listened to his father breathing on the mattress against the opposite wall. Part of him couldn't quite believe he was breathing the same air as his almost legendary parent. Though hardly the place he'd have chosen for this reunion, he couldn't be sorry.

He wondered if his father had the same thoughts. Certainly, he hadn't seemed angry at Donald's capture, only with the idea of being forced to leave Donald in prison in his place. But he wasn't a talkative man. If he ever had been, lack of company had broken him of the habit. Still, what he did say tended to be amusing, whether light or sardonic, giving Donald little clue as to what went on behind the calm face and unquiet eyes. Eyes like Adam's, only saner.

Into the silence, Donald said, "When we were boys, Adam and I used to lie in the dark and describe you to each other, to see if we still remembered you."

There was a pause, long enough for Donald to wonder if his father was asleep after all.

"Did you?" his father asked.

"I don't know. I was three years old when you were taken. I thought we remembered, but now, seeing you in person, I think our version of you was a mixture of other people's descriptions and our own imaginations." He half laughed into the pillow. "All the same, Adam used to draw you in lead on the pages of our mother's books."

"I can't imagine that went down well with your mother." There was a smile in his voice that Donald found rather beguiling.

"Actually, she never complained. She seemed to recognize it as you."

"And I didn't even know you when they brought you in here. Even now, I can barely find the small child in the man you've become. You grew up without me. You all did. I never even had a verbal description from anyone who'd ever met you." His voice was deliberately light, without resentment, and yet Donald could have sworn there was pain there. Even more quietly, he added, "Until Mairead came." Again, his voice changed to one of amusement. "I gather your brother is something of a ladies' man."

At that, Donald grinned in the darkness. "Not really, though he seems to fascinate them. He doesn't notice subtle admiration, and then he seems slightly surprised when he receives more obvious attention."

"Like Mairead's?"

"I don't know. He met her with Somerled last year. I wasn't there. But I've never seen him pursue anyone except Cairistiona, and even then—" He broke off. "Did you know he is married?"

"Married?" There was a movement on the mattress, as if his father had propped himself up in an effort to see him. For the first time, he didn't sound pleased. "To whom?"

"Cairistiona, daughter of Rhuadri."

"De Lanson's wife... I am behind with the news."

"Adam claims she's descended from King Malcolm III," Donald said, trying not to give in to his inevitable anxiety. He needed this stranger's approval for himself and those he loved best. "He felt one of us should marry her to unite the royal lines. Fergus tried to steal her for his son, so he's probably right."

"What did Adam do with the husband?"

"Killed him."

Donald could have sworn his father nodded as if this was quite right and proper. "Then there is no longer a king's cuckoo in our nest?" his father said wryly.

"We defeated the cuckoos but kept it quiet to stave off the king's army until Somerled can give us his support again. Or until Fergus could get you released. Treacherous bastard."

His father shifted position in the darkness. "There's no point in hating Fergus. He does what he has to, as we do. And I am released if I choose to go. The rest, I will not forget."

They lapsed into silence for a little. Then quietly, almost reluctantly, his father said, "Does Adam really prophesy?"

Donald nodded, forgetting his father couldn't see. "It's why we began the rising, because he saw you would come home alive. He sees lots of things, often at very inconvenient moments—including at his own wedding."

"And yet Mairead says the men follow him?"

"He doesn't sit in the corner gibbering," Donald said, all the old defensiveness rising to the surface. "In fact, though they all hear rumors and most suspect his gift, he never talks about it. He leads and he fights and is often quite brilliant. For the rest, I cover for him. Findlaech mac Gillechrist looks out for him. His insights more than make up for the difficulties."

There was another silence, a movement as if the one-time

Earl of Ross had lain down again. "Maybe he's the Aed of the old prophecies. Adam and Aed don't sound so different."

"Well, they said Aed would expel the foreigners," Donald said humorously. "Though Adam seems more inclined to absorb those we didn't kill."

"I wish I could see him," his father blurted, betraying emotion for the first time since the king had left them alone. "I wish I could ride between you and him up to my old hall at Brecka and find your mother and sister waiting to welcome us."

"He's seen that, too," Donald said. "It *will* happen. You have to go home. Now. Without me."

"No," Malcolm mac Aed said with the same stubbornness that had got him here in the first place. "*Not* without you."

THEY HAD JUST decided that Cairistiona would return to Tirebeck while Adam would wait with Halla until formal word came from the king, when the shout went up of approaching men.

This was to be no secret, verbal-only message. A man wearing the king's livery was accompanied by two armored soldiers bearing the king's pennant. Naturally, they had an escort of the men of Ross, who'd met them as soon as they crossed into MacHeth country.

On hearing it, Adam began to stride down the hall with the clear intention of wresting from them whatever message they carried.

But Halla, once more thinking like the Lady of Ross, stayed him. "Adam. We will not behave as brigands. We will receive them here."

"And *then* kill them," Findlaech muttered quite audibly.

The lady ignored him. She tolerated much from Findlaech, not just because he was a loyal and fierce fighter, but because he was the nearest thing to a father her sons had known growing up, and he'd taught them well. Even Adam.

Adam's hands clenched at Halla's command, but at least he turned and came back to where she sat in her throne-like chair behind the dais table. On one side of her sat Gormflaith and Cairistiona, behind her, two of her women. The chair on her other side was empty, but Adam was clearly too restless to sit in it. He paced behind them, raising the hairs on Halla's neck because she couldn't see what he was thinking or feeling. Or dreaming.

The house guards, with Findlaech and a few other men who'd accompanied them from Tirebeck, stood menacingly around the hall, bristling with weapons.

The men of Ross brought the king's people into the hall. All three had been disarmed, although it wasn't clear exactly when. Someone prodded the messenger forward, and all three hastily strode the length of the hall toward their reception—presumably a daunting one, since the king's men all looked petrified. The messenger didn't even need to be prodded to his knees. He all but fell, gazing hard at the floor while he held out a rolled parchment in front of him.

"My lady. His Grace, the King of Scots sends you greetings and begs you to read this."

Halla doubted it had been phrased quite like that. "Commands" would have been more normal than "begs."

Sweyn, the burly captain of her house guard, took the parchment from the man and brought it to Halla. She was glad to see her fingers steady as she broke the seal and spread the roll out on the table before her. She stared at it for a long time in total silence.

Tension surrounded the hall, like a single thread pulled taut enough to break with one finger pressed upon it. Halla imagined cutting the thread with one word and watching a massacre unfold. She suspected the king's men had similar apprehensions. She was aware of Adam, standing perfectly still behind her, no doubt glaring at them with what Cairistiona called his battle face.

No wonder they looked frightened. If only they knew, that particular expression only meant that he was hiding what he wished no one to see. That it was he who was frightened.

At first, the words on the parchment made no sense. So, she read them again. Something new to bear. There was always something new. And yet… Her heart began to beat faster again, with something more than fear. Something, surely, could be won from this, if only she could see what.

Halla raised her eyes from the parchment to the three kneeling men. "You will be given refreshment and rest before you return with our reply."

"What?" Gormflaith demanded between closed lips before the men had got very far down the hall. "What does it say?"

Halla rose without replying, leading the way to the more private area near the bedchambers and waiting for her family, Findlaech, and Sweyn to sit. Only then, did she all but throw the message to Adam.

"The king holds Donald at Roxburgh," she said in a rush. "He wants to release Malcolm and keep Donald as hostage for his good behavior."

"So, Fergus kept his word," Adam said, spreading the letter open on his large knees. "I should have known this would be how—"

"It won't be how," Halla interrupted. "Malcolm won't go. He's refusing to leave without Donald."

Adam's breath caught. He met her gaze, and something flashed between them. It was almost laughter, although in Halla's case, it was very close to tears. Wretched, stubborn, perverse, *honorable* Malcolm MacHeth.

"So, the king will keep them both?" Gormflaith said anxiously. "Is there some demand for Adam and Somerled to lay down arms?"

Halla tapped the unrolled parchment on Adam's lap. "Not exactly. The King of Scots invites me to write to my husband, impressing upon him our need of him to uphold and maintain peace in Ross and the whole of Scotland."

Adam glanced up from the letter. "In other words, to persuade him to leave Donald in prison and come home for the sake of peace."

"If the royal army comes this autumn, can we hold them off?" Halla asked.

Adam shrugged. "We can pick them off, annoy them, try to persuade Somerled to draw them away with some distraction in the west before they cause too much damage. But the truth is, we need my father or we have no cause."

"Then you would leave Donald there?" Halla demanded, glaring up at him with surprised indignation. No one should be obliged to choose between husband and son, father and brother. No choice could ever be right.

Adam shook his head violently. "We'll take the battle to the king once more. With every man we have, we'll march on Perth or wherever he happens to be. Somerled *must* attack the west coast now. Between us, we'll sow the fear of God across—"

"It's what they expect," Cairistiona interrupted.

Halla blinked at her in surprise.

Even Adam's eyes came back into focus on his wife. "What?"

Christian said, "The messenger who came for Sir William told him to be ready when you march south, remember? This is what the message meant. They *know* you'll come in response to this. They'll be ready for you."

Adam gazed at her, expressions flitting across his face.

Halla's breath caught. "Cairistiona is right." Without yet fully understanding, the first seeds of a new plan began to germinate and grow. "So," she said slowly, "we must *do* the expected…to cover the *unexpected*. Sweyn, I need a man to send to Somerled. And another to Lady Mairead. We need to move quickly before they have time to think about this."

"Move where?" Gormflaith demanded. "What are you doing, Mother?"

"I'm going to write your father," Halla said, far more calmly than she felt. "To tell him he *must* be released at all costs."

Her gaze focused on her daughter-in-law. This would need Cairistiona to make it work. No one else would be safe with the King of Scots. No one else's word could possibly count.

"You were the Lady de Lanson," Halla said. "You were *forcibly* married to my son but have always remained loyal to the King of Scots. I'm afraid it's time you reported all this to His Grace, in person."

AS HALLA FORMED her plan into words, it sounded more ridiculous than audacious. And yet neither Adam nor Findlaech shouted it down. Although Adam was clearly trying to think of an alternative that didn't involve Cairistiona going to the king. But for the aftermath, for the sake of peace, the seeds only Cairistiona could sow were very necessary. It struck Halla that her son was still unsure of his wife. He might have trusted her not to betray him, but he didn't trust her to come back. It would have been laughable if Halla hadn't felt his pain as if it were her own.

That Adam loved Cairistiona was beyond doubt. And yet, he still seemed blind to the true extent of Cairistiona's devotion to *him*. A devotion Halla understood only too well. Perhaps the coming adventure would open his eyes to reality.

As they talked and planned and argued, the weight of decades seemed to fall away from Halla's shoulders. Because at last, she was *doing* something, not just waiting. All her rigid self-discipline, the myth she had deliberately built of the Lady of Ross, was pushed aside, releasing at last the wild young girl who had first come to Ross to marry Malcolm MacHeth, the young earl.

She'd been fourteen years old when her father had bundled her into a ship with Somerled and told her she would be a great lady on the mainland of Scotland. She'd railed and fought and kicked at her brother until he'd ordered his men to take it in turns holding her still. She'd jumped over the side twice and had to be rescued by islesmen who were fast growing tired of her. And she'd wept silently after they'd landed and walked inland, because she could no longer see the sea. Even the mighty Loch Ness hadn't made up for that. It smelled wrong.

By the time they'd reached Ross, she'd cheered up to merely sullen. But no one could resign her to her fate until she met Malcolm MacHeth.

CHAPTER THREE

A T EIGHTEEN YEARS old, Malcolm, son of Aed, Earl of Ross, was already the veteran of one failed rebellion and was still in the midst of another, which had already taken the life of his older brother, Angus, the Earl of Moray. And yet Halla's brother, Somerled, with ambitions to make himself lord of all the Isles, was clearly backing the victory of the remaining son of Aed, giving her, Halla, in marriage as proof.

To say that Halla resented being a political pawn would have been an understatement. Like many a young bride, she was afraid—only Halla would never admit to that.

Although she wouldn't speak to Somerled, she ran wild with his islesmen, joining their archery contests, running them ragged when they were trying to protect her. To the vocal outrage of her women, she'd bundled her skirts into the trunk the men carried through the glens for her, and wore the rough wool and leather tunics of a soldier, which made walking, running, and climbing much easier.

Not that her aim had ever been to speed the journey to its end. In fact, she did her best to slow everyone down as she extracted what she knew would be her last days of fun. Even then, Halla had been a realist. She knew she would marry the young earl, but she didn't have to like it.

And so, when the men rested at the foot of the waterfall that afternoon, she wandered away, climbing the wooded hills they'd just passed through until she could no longer see her escort. Which meant they couldn't see her. They intended to press forward and make camp in a few hours, and tomorrow, they expected to meet with the men of Ross. Halla planned to make sure there was no further progress today.

Following the sounds of the waterfall, she jumped over a burn and climbed higher. As she climbed, she realized she could hear distant voices over the rushing of the waterfall and paused. These rocks must look down on her own escort.

If Somerled saw her up here, it might be fun to play hide-and-seek with whomever he sent to fetch her. Or it might be over too quickly. She glanced upward, and there on a ledge, she saw a man gazing downward. He seemed very still but from here, he was too well covered to make out his age or station. He could have been a farmer, a woodsman, a Ross spy. But more importantly, he hadn't seen her.

Following her curiosity, she crept back the way she'd come for a few yards, then climbed, in order to come at him from above. Only when she could see him clearly did she draw the bow from her shoulder and thread it with an arrow, taking careful aim.

He crouched on the rocky ledge, looking down on Somerled and the men below. A quick glance showed her they were moving, preparing to leave, and looking for her, probably. Well, discovering the spy was a new variation on the adventure.

She returned her gaze to the watcher but could tell very little about him except that his hair was very black. He wore no hat or cloak, but a sword and a bow both hung across his back together with a small bundle wrapped in a blanket. He wore a belt she imagined was thick with daggers.

"Who are you?" she demanded, abruptly enough to startle him.

Only, he didn't start. He turned his head, and she saw that he was young. He eased his position, resting his back against the rock and lazily drawing one knee up to rest his elbow on. Now she could see that he did indeed carry two daggers and a purse at his belt. He was handsome, too. Devastatingly so, if one looked too long. Raven-black hair swept back from a high forehead, dark, deep-set eyes, strangely emphasized by the thick, arching brows. Refined, even features. He might have been eighteen or nineteen years old, no more. Annoyingly, he didn't look frightened.

"That's a big bow," he observed admiringly, "for such a small girl."

"It's a big arrow, too."

He surveyed the weapon critically. "You hold it well. How is your aim?"

"Let's find out," she invited. "Where would you like me to hit you?"

"I've never been target practice before."

"Maybe you've never been caught spying on islesmen before. Did your earl send you?"

"In a manner of speaking. Did your lord send you?"

She curled her lip. "In a manner of speaking," she mocked. "To Ross, at least."

"They're looking for you," he said casually, nodding downward in the general direction of the islesmen. "Perhaps we should make common cause and flee through the hills."

She pretended to consider. "I'd rather shoot you."

His lip quirked. In other circumstances, she might have found him fun. He made no effort to reach any of his own weapons. "Why?" he asked.

"I've had a bad day. A bad few days."

"I can see why you might want to round that off with a bit of murder."

"Executing a spy," she corrected. "Though you might not die."

"Thank you for the faint hope. In return, I offer you the information that the islesmen have been looking for you for some time now."

"So, I should shoot you quickly?"

"You're very bloodthirsty for a girl."

"You have no idea," she said grimly.

His gaze flickered beyond her, as if he'd seen movement. But Halla was not stupid enough to fall for such an obvious ruse. The distance between them was not great. If she was daft enough to turn and check behind her, he would probably lunge and overpower her before she could loose the arrow. With all those weapons, he had to be a fighting man.

He brought his gaze back to her. "He's behind you, you know.

She smiled at his naivety. "Who is?"

"Somerled."

That did jolt her. Not because she believed him, but because he called her brother by name. Without title. A new suspicion dawned, more satisfying and exciting than frightening. In fact, she wanted to laugh.

Until, behind her, Somerled said furiously, "In God's name, Halla, what are you doing?"

She jumped, and the arrow loosed, whizzing through the air. Somerled's enraged shout filled her ears as the arrow struck her spy. Interestingly, her victim didn't cry out at all, although she imagined she saw blood spread at his shoulder where the arrow stuck out. Her brother snatched the bow from her with one hand, yanking her back with the other.

"You stupid little fool! You've just shot Malcolm mac Aed, the Earl of Ross!"

IT COULD HAVE been a lot worse, Somerled acknowledged grimly. The arrow had struck little more than a glancing blow that had nicked the skin, held in place more by the earl's clothing than by his flesh. Malcolm had pulled it out himself and seemed more inclined to laugh than to demand Halla's punishment. Possibly because it was embarrassing to have been shot by a girl, especially one's betrothed. Or because he and Somerled appeared to be friends.

Somerled himself had bound the wound while Halla stood by, hanging her head and deliberately not looking at the injury she'd caused, or the naked, muscled shoulder beneath Somerled's makeshift bandage. Keeping uncharacteristically silent, she allowed herself to be hauled back down the hill to her women, who clucked over her, scolding.

Ironically, her afternoon's work did indeed mean that they traveled no farther that day. Instead, they made camp and built a fire, and her betrothed joined them there, which was hardly what she'd set out to achieve.

Apparently little the worse for her arrow, he ate and drank with the men until the sun went down. In fact, she saw resentfully, he appeared to be a great favorite with the islesmen, telling them stories in Gaelic and in Norse that made them howl with glee. He himself seemed quick to laugh and easy to please. Perhaps he thought his charm rather than military prowess entitled him to be King of Scots.

Of course, it was his bloodline that gave him the right. He was the grandson of King Lulach and, by all the old traditions, quite entitled to challenge for the throne. Which would make Halla Queen of Scots. Despite her childish tantrums, she understood perfectly well why Somerled and their father wanted her to marry Malcolm. In a few years, perhaps, she would agree with them, and be glad to be queen and the mother of future kings. Right now, she wanted only to be left alone to play and learn without being delivered to a stranger who didn't even live by the sea.

For some reason, it made it worse that the stranger himself was personable, that Somerled and the men liked him. That he made no fuss about her shooting him by accident, not even to joke about her, as Somerled did. "You think you were lucky she wasn't actually aiming at you? She'd have been less likely to hit you if she'd tried!"

Which wasn't even true.

The women tried to wrestle her back into a gown and comb her hair, presumably to show the earl how presentable she could be if she tried. But Halla refused. She felt, somehow, it would be the final indignity.

But at least she wasn't obliged to converse with him while they ate. She made sure she and her two women sat on the other side of the fire. Mostly, he didn't even look at her, although she did once meet his gaze through the flames while the islesmen were busy teasing Somerled. A faint smile lurked on his lips, but as if he'd just left it there for show while he thought. Although his musings were well hidden, the clash of his eyes disturbed her somehow.

After she'd eaten, she stayed by the fire only long enough to prove that she wasn't remotely intimidated by anyone's presence before she rose abruptly to her feet.

"Good night, Somerled," she interrupted the talk on the far side of the fire. "My lord."

Her women scrambled up with her, clearly disappointed not to have longer to ogle the young earl. Somerled merely nodded, not yet having drunk enough to forgive her for accidentally shooting his ally. More surprisingly, the earl stood courteously and, to her annoyance, actually walked over to her.

"Good night," he said civilly. "Allow me to walk with you to your tent."

She couldn't stop him, not without a fuss. And in any case, she might as well make her apology now and get it over with.

They walked the few paces in silence. Then Halla stopped and glanced at him. He wore a rather fine cloak now, fastened with a silver-and-enamel brooch showing the red lion of Scotland and the single word Ross around the top edge. Arrogant and defiant. She would have liked his style in other circumstances.

"I ask your pardon," she muttered.

"For what?"

The women passed them, discreetly going inside the tent.

"For letting the arrow go," Halla said in a rush. "I didn't believe that Somerled was behind me. I thought it was a ruse until he spoke."

"Startling you into releasing the arrow," he said gravely. "I understand."

She nodded. "Thank you." She would have turned away and followed her women then, except his voice stayed her.

"On the contrary, it is *I* who thank *you*."

"For what?" she asked, surprised.

"For not aiming at my heart."

An involuntary frown tugged down her brow. "What do you mean? I didn't aim at all."

Unexpectedly, he held out his hand. She hesitated, then, deciding it would be churlish to refuse in the circumstances, she reluctantly gave him hers. His fingers closed around it, long, strong fingers, warm on her cool flesh.

"Come, Halla," he said with a gentleness she suddenly didn't trust. "If we are to be married, we must at least be honest with each other. I've been around weapons all my life, as have you. I know when someone's taking aim, and when they distract me with false moves, like starts of surprise. You already knew who I was. You shot me deliberately."

Suddenly, she couldn't breathe. Even Somerled hadn't seen that, and her brother was nobody's fool. Malcolm was guessing. He had to be. She just couldn't seem to deny it.

He leaned forward as if to hear the words she didn't speak. "And hit me precisely where you meant to."

She lifted her chin. "Why would I do such a thing?"

"To hurt me and my pride without hurting our alliance."

His perception actually frightened her. From instinct, she tried to tug her hand free, to escape him, but he held on to it with ease.

"I told you, I understand. My pride isn't hurt. I *like* that you're clever." He smiled with rather dazzling effect. "Ross and the Isles is an excellent partnership. But I'm beginning to think the alliance between you and me could be truly formidable." Under her bemused gaze, he raised her hand to his lips and kissed it. The faintest gleam in his eyes gave her an instant's warning. "When you grow up."

She snatched back her hand in fury, but he'd already released it and was walking away, back to the fire. At least he didn't laugh.

IT HAD BECOME a shared secret that bound them, and, later a private joke. More than two decades after the event, Halla knew how to make Malcolm heed her instructions.

She sat down at the hall table, listening only vaguely to the discussions of the others.

"And if the king does not believe in your loyalty?" Adam said to Cairistiona.

"He will," Cairistiona replied, "if Alys is with me and tells the same tale."

Alys? Oh yes, one of Cairistiona's women, the one who had been mistress to her husband, the Norman, William de Lanson. The one who wished now to leave her service and take her chances elsewhere.

"Alys hates you," Adam said flatly.

"No, she hates *you*," Cairistiona corrected. "You killed William. When I denounce you for it, believe me, she will love me. Almost. In any case, because of her loyalties, she will be the most credible witness to the truth of what I say to the king."

This was for Adam and Cairistiona to sort out. Halla, surrounded by suddenly vivid memories that sharpened Malcolm's image in her mind almost unbearably, had her own tasks.

She picked up her pen, dipped it, and ran her hand over the smooth sheet of vellum before her, then began to write.

To my dear husband, Malcolm, son of Aed, all love and greet-ings.

It is surely the most difficult decision either of us has made, but I truly believe you must accept the liberty granted to you by the King of Scots. For the sake of your family, your country, and your people, it is important that you come home. I know you will believe me, who has always been as true as that first arrow between us.

Something splashed on the vellum, fortunately avoiding the ink. Hastily, she wiped the back of her hand over her stupidly wet eyes and continued to write.

CHAPTER FOUR

IN CONSTERNATION, MALCOLM MacHeth gazed at his wife's letter.

If it hadn't been for the mention of the arrow, he would have been sure someone had forced her to write it. Certainly, she'd known the king's men would read it and that he would be aware of that, too. Reference to the arrow, a story known only to the two of them, was her secret validation...of unpalatable and unforgivable advice.

Although he hadn't laid eyes on Halla for twenty-two years, he'd always believed somehow that the understanding between them was still there. It had been in the few letters Mairead had smuggled into him, making Halla suddenly vivid and strong in his life once more, and in the news he received second- and third-hand from his gaolers.

Halla had ruled in Ross in his name ever since the king's men had taken him. She had never gone back to the Isles, but brought up his children in their home, which had never been captured and never turned over to the King of Scots.

The king had deprived him of his title of earl but had never ruled in Ross. Although the royal soldiers had left triumphantly with their captive, Halla had remained *de facto* Lady of Ross. And in time, she had supported his sons to carry on the cause, in alliance with her brother Somerled. She had always understood what he needed and what was right.

So, why in God's name would she sacrifice her son just to get *him* back? He'd never been a good husband to her. He'd pursued his own dreams relentlessly and left her to pick up the pieces. She should have been able to expect better. And no one could ever have said that Halla's love was blind. Why would she give up Donald for him?

She wouldn't.

His breath caught.

"What?" Donald asked, coming to read over his shoulder. "What does my mother say?"

"That I should come home."

"She trusts Adam."

That might have been it, part of it. *I know you will believe me, who has always been as true as that first arrow between us.*

That arrow had flown true, but no one except Halla and himself had ever known it. It had been her trick, and he alone who had understood.

Excitement surged. For an instant, he saw that angry, beautiful, young girl in his mind as vividly as if she stood in front of him, proudly stretching her bow and aiming straight at his heart.

"It's a trick," he whispered.

Donald frowned. "How do you know? Are you guessing?"

"Trust me, your mother is plotting." Laughter, the sheer joy he'd once felt in his youth, swept over him like a tide. "Let the world beware! And let *us* be ready."

HAVING RIDDEN SOUTH with all speed, Christian discovered the king at Glasgow, holding court at the bishop's residence. Everyone she encountered was uneasy because warships had been seen from the Firth of Clyde and, in fact, from all along the west coast. They bore the banners of Somerled of the Isles, but rumors abounded that they'd been joined by a thousand Irishmen and even men from Norway. Presumably, the king was there to allay fears, or perhaps to command any necessary defense.

Escorted by Henry and the few other Norman soldiers who were all that was left of William's once-proud force, Christian entered the town on horseback. By her side rode Alys, whom she'd brought south with her, just as the girl wished.

Glasgow was a growing, bustling little town on the majestic River Clyde. Although centered around the stone cathedral, the king's presence had filled it with noblemen and their servants and an influx of tradesmen eager to improve their lot from the royal visit. People stared at Christian as her party made its way along the river toward the bishop's house where Henry had already ascertained the king to be. Everyone was always curious about her mask.

Christian looked straight ahead of her, ignoring all her old dislike of being gawped at. After all, more important things now concerned her, but even those couldn't drown out some of the whispers she heard from passersby.

"That's...that's the Lady de Lanson. I saw her in Perth..."

Interesting. If she'd never worn the mask, he'd never have remembered her.

Another voice murmured, "What's she doing back here? Shouldn't Lanson be pursuing the MacHeths?"

"Perhaps he's been defeated. Perhaps she's come to the king for help."

"Or to report victory over the MacHeths before Malcolm is released. Insane to release him with their army already approaching, and Somerled's ships practically in the Clyde."

"They're not as close as that."

"I heard the MacHeths are not fighting. They've just come south to conduct Malcolm home."

"Ha! Don't be so gullible. Wait, though, the other woman, is that not Lanson's mistress? There is an odd friendship for you!"

Christian, aware of Alys's sliding glance in her direction, continued to gaze straight ahead.

"Lady de Lanson," came a shout directly beside her. Ahead, Henry pulled in his horse and glared. It was a nobleman on foot, youngish, stocky, and fit. "Let me take you to the king!"

"I have my escort, thank you."

The man came closer, and she halted. Henry placed his horse right beside her. The nobleman bowed respectfully, and it came to her that she'd seen him before.

He said smoothly, "I can't hope to be remembered, but we met in Perth. I am Ferchar, Earl of Strathearn, and I know the king will be eager to speak with you."

"I am eager to speak with His Grace," Christian said. "I bring vital news."

"Then follow me," the earl said, and suddenly two royal soldiers were clearing the way for them to pass unhindered to the bishop's house. At least Christian didn't have to hear any more conversation about herself.

And the earl's cooperation did make things so much easier. His people took care of her horse and Alys's, leaving Henry and the other soldiers free to kick their heels until she returned, while Christian and Alys were led inside and in response to a series of clipped orders, soon found themselves being led along a narrow corridor, no longer by the Earl of Strathearn, but by some lower minion who might have been a secretary.

Noble men and women passed in the opposite direction. Christian gazed straight ahead, plodding rather grimly onward as her heart beat faster. Then, perhaps because she felt the power of a fixed gaze, she made the mistake of glancing at the woman who walked toward them. A simple but elegant gold robe draped over a dark brown underdress, an embroidered net veil revealing the gorgeous red-gold hair beneath. And hazel-green eyes staring at her in shock.

Mairead, the Lady of Kingowan.

Mairead, who knew everything. That William was dead, that Christian was married now to Adam MacHeth. How much of Christian's role in this plan had Halla committed to writing? Did

Mairead even know she was a friend?

The woman's eyes flashed with contempt as she passed. She might as well have uttered the word aloud. *Traitor.*

Christian and Alys were taken to a small antechamber where they were left alone between two closed doors.

Christian sat on the window bench seat and took one of the two purses from her girdle. "Your dowry," she said wryly, throwing it to Alys, who caught it without difficulty. "You may accompany me to meet the king. After that, our contract, association, or whatever you wish to call it, is at an end."

Alys tucked the purse away inside her cloak, no doubt in some hidden pocket she'd sewn there. "I like you better like this," she remarked.

Christian considered the woman who had contributed to so much of her past misery. "I don't care," she discovered.

Alys's face flushed slightly, almost as though hurt that Christian didn't reciprocate her softening. Dispassionately, Christian wondered if she'd have forgiven Alys if the other woman hadn't tried to seduce Adam, too. Although he hadn't succumbed, not even a little, that mattered. Adam mattered. He was the real reason she was here.

The inner door opened, and the young king himself stepped into the room, accompanied by the Earl of Strathearn and another man she didn't recognize.

Christian rose and sank into a deep curtsey. So did Alys, who, closer to the king as she was, might have expected to be the first recipient of the royal attention. And certainly, the young king's gaze swept over her. There might have been an instant's hesitation before his eyes raced on and found Christian. They lit up like lamps and, ignoring Alys altogether, he strode to Christian.

Alys didn't have a mask.

The thought shook Christian with inappropriate laughter she had to swallow back down.

"Please, rise and sit, lady," the king invited.

"Thank you. May I present my attendant to you? Alys de Fauvoir. I believe she was fortunate enough to meet you once before."

The king accepted Alys's curtsy with civility and a faint frown as he tried to remember. When he did, it was obvious because his skin actually colored. "Of course," he said hurriedly with another glance at Christian. "Your friends are welcome, too."

Alys's face was a picture. Even at court, where she had been such a success before, she was forced to stand now in Christian's disfigured shadow.

The king swept himself into the chair close to the window seat where Christian had been sitting and barely waited until she resumed her seat before he said, "I am anxious to hear your news. How does Sir William? Did my message reach him?"

Christian licked her dry lips, using the brief seconds it took Ferchar of Strathearn to take his seat next to the king, to order her reply.

"Your message did not reach him, Your Grace," she said sadly. "Though I did receive it. Sire, events in Ross have moved on apace, so let me tell you at once that Sir William is dead."

The king's jaw dropped. "Dead?"

Did he imagine William invincible? It wasn't so rare a thing to die in Ross, not for the king's men sent to subdue it.

"In battle with the MacHeths," Christian said. "Who then overran Tirebeck, taking back all of the estate, including me."

The Earl of Strathearn scowled. "What do you mean?"

"I mean Adam MacHeth took me as his wife in order to keep Tirebeck from his enemies. And also, because he discovered I share an ancestor with Your Grace."

The king's eyes widened. "Indeed? How is that?"

"Your Grace," the Earl of Strathearn said heavily. "There will be time for such discussion later. May we keep to the point? Lady, what is now the situation in Ross? If you received our message, did you act upon it?"

"I couldn't," Christian said. She glanced at the earl. "The men you found me with in the street are all that is left. We lost several back in March before we even reached Tirebeck; a few more were picked off in subsequent skirmishes, and the rest died in the last battle, leaving nowhere near enough to take advantage of Adam's absence. Which is why I came south with all haste to warn Your Grace that Adam MacHeth has a huge force with him."

"We know," the earl said wryly.

Christian leaned forward. "It's bluster," she said, low.

Alys, from her isolated stool, lifted her head and gazed at Christian.

"Bluster?" the king repeated.

"He won't fight," Christian said simply. "Not this time. Unless the royal army divides, he knows he can't win. He just wants to make sure his father is released, and when he is, that he makes it safely to Ross. In effect, he's come to escort his father home. And to show Your Grace the risks of reneging."

"Meaning he'd fight anyway," the earl suggested, "whatever the cost, if we changed our minds and kept Malcolm MacHeth?"

"Oh yes," Christian said.

"Then this has nothing to do with the son, Donald?" the king asked. "*He* seemed certain his brother would come for him, which is surely ridiculous..."

"Not entirely, Your Grace," Christian said heavily. "In a way, it has everything to do with Donald. Adam is hoping the double threat of his army heading for Fife and the Lord of the Isles' approaching ships on the west will compel you to release Donald, too."

The king and the earl exchanged glances. "Will he fight if we keep Donald?"

Christian shook her head. "Not this time. Not until his father is safe."

"After that, it will all begin again," the king said ruefully.

The earl leaned forward in his chair. "How do you know this? How sure are you of Adam MacHeth's intentions?"

"They speak in front of me all the time. Their plans are quite fixed."

Unexpectedly, the earl swung around to Alys. "And you, mistress? In your lady's service, did you hear the same things?"

It was quite clever, and why she'd brought Alys, who had no reason to love Christian and every reason to avenge her dead lover. If the possibility existed that Christian might lie for the MacHeths, for whatever reasons, Alys was most unlikely to do so.

Alys lifted her head. "Oh yes. They don't perceive the lady's loyalty to Sir William—neither did I until now, not clearly. Nor do they understand our unbreakable loyalty to Your Grace."

Christian inclined her head. It was doubtful Alys saw the irony in her gesture.

"This is most useful information," the king said, "and we thank you for it." He hesitated, gazing at Christian with a half-troubled, half-eager expression in his eyes. "What will you do now?"

She dropped her gaze to her lap, trying to hold on to the part she needed to play, that of a loyal young widow who'd suffered the indignity of a forced marriage with her husband's killer, whose life was in ruins that she had to try now to rebuild.

Through the drumming of her heart, she raised her eyes once more to the king. "I would, if you will allow me, help Your Grace keep the peace. I know these people, and through them, I have come to know Malcolm MacHeth without ever laying eyes upon him. I believe your best hope of binding him is to make him promises, make him what appear to be concessions in return for his peace. He may then agree with dignity, and I will return to Ross with him as your eyes and ears."

The king's eyes widened. He exchanged thoughtful glances with the Earl of Strathearn, who finally said, "What promises would you have us make?"

Promises that would appear to satisfy Malcolm MacHeth's anxieties over his son, and so lull the king's and Strathearn's inevitable suspicions, giving Malcolm and Donald time to get far away.

"Tell him that if he keeps the peace for a year, you'll release his son," Christian said boldly. "And that at the end of that year, you will also return his earldom to him—that is an easy concession since his family effectively holds it anyway, but it makes you magnanimous and further binds him to you for that year. Which will surely be long enough for him to appreciate all the benefits of freedom."

MAIREAD COULDN'T POSTPONE her departure much longer. But Christian's presence here threw her. Had she come to plead for the MacHeths or to betray them? The short message from the Lady of Ross had made no mention of Christian, merely given instructions for Mairead's own part. She had trusted in the lady to arrange the rest and had seen it in the sudden threats from Somerled and Adam. But Christian's arrival here could well be an obstacle none of them had planned for.

Surely Adam, a surprisingly good judge of character, would have told her nothing that could endanger Malcolm's release?

She hung on, gossiping, flirting with anyone she could find, desperate for Christian to emerge from her audience with the king. The trouble was, in a house this size, there weren't too many places to lie in wait, so it all had to be public.

Rumors, of course, were rife.

The Lady de Lanson had been kicked out by her husband and now had no land. Only, if he'd kicked her out, wouldn't it have been in favor of the woman she'd brought with her?

No, she'd brought messages to the king from her husband who'd taken Ross and was about to fall on Adam MacHeth's rear.

No, the MacHeths must have kicked the Lansons out of Ross. Lanson was either dead or licking his wounds or had run back to England or Normandy. But the lady had Lanson's men with her.

Lanson had a plan to defeat the MacHeths once Malcolm MacHeth was released…

And so it went on until Mairead was almost ready to scream. Finally, she glimpsed the figure of Christian's pretty attendant, whom everyone knew to be Lanson's mistress. Mairead wasn't the only one who moved toward her in the hope of encountering either the Lady de Lanson in her wake, or news of her.

And the girl, who called herself Alys de Fauvoir, hid nothing. As soon as someone inquired for news, she said tragically, "Sir William de Lanson is dead. Adam MacHeth murdered him."

Her bitterness and her grief were probably genuine, Mairead thought, watching her closely if surreptitiously from her own place against a nearby wooden pillar, although the girl overlaid it with an air of exaggerated drama for the sake of the attention she took as her due.

"Is that why the lady is here?" someone asked. "To seek redress from the king?"

"To seek vengeance for Sir William," Alys said. "And for herself. Adam MacHeth slew her husband and forced her into marriage with himself. As soon as the MacHeths rode to threaten the south, we escaped to the king to warn him. The lady has a great deal of useful information for His Grace."

Everyone, naturally clamored for details, which Alys was coy about revealing. She was clever, Mairead saw with some amusement. She knew she could keep everyone's attention for far longer if she drew this out, even if she had no more information to give.

When Alys paused for breath, Mairead seized the moment. "Tell me one thing, Mistress Alys. Why did she bring you?"

Alys turned to her wide-eyed. "I am her attendant."

Mairead didn't laugh, but she did smile. Alys blushed slightly and tilted her pretty chin. "I am leaving the lady's service, but I stand her friend."

And Lanson's. Christian was playing some deep game here, but Mairead had no idea what it was. Nor did she have time to wait any longer to get answers from the lady herself. Her husband was sending her home to Kingowan, although she'd go via Roxburgh. Hardly on her way, but necessary.

Her stomach churned with rare anxiety as she left the court with the blessing of both king and husband. At least she was going to see Malcolm again, and meet Donald for the first time, which would be fun if he was anything at all like his brother. But what really tugged at her heart was that this would be the last time she'd ever see Malcolm mac Aed.

MAIREAD ABANDONED HER escort just east of Glasgow, with instructions to meet her in the town of Dundee a week hence. In the meantime, Mairead rode southeast for Roxburgh.

From an early age, Mairead had been an adventurous girl, sneaking off alone behind her family's back to get into trouble with those of a lower station in life. As a result, she was good not just at finding excellent hiding places but at rediscovering them when necessary.

In the woods near the castle of Roxburgh, Mairead retrieved her whore's garments from their hole behind two large rocks and some huge gnarled oak tree roots and hastily changed, before taking out the square of polished bronze she used as a mirror. Gazing into it for guidance, she stained her lips bright red and added kohl liberally around her eyes, and then color to her cheekbones.

Then she stuffed her own clothes into the hole and replaced the stones before walking up to the castle—which was a harder journey than usual because she wore some vulgar red-dyed shoes with built-up heels that made her even taller than she was. It had caused her some qualms to deliberately scuff such beautiful works of craftsmanship, but they were far too expensive for a mere whore to wear unless they were castoffs.

She was expected at the castle and had no difficulty in gaining admittance through the south entrance. The soldiers were even more playful than usual, making their search of her body particularly thorough.

"What's the point, lads?" she demanded. "He's going free in the morning. Why would I help him escape tonight?"

"Perk of the job," one soldier grinned, running his hand between her legs.

"Here, have you grown?" another demanded, looking up into her face.

Mairead stretched her painted mouth into a smile and lifted her cheap frilled skirts enough to reveal the magnificent red shoes.

The soldiers growled with gratifying lust.

"You'll be missing your client after tonight," one observed with a gleam in his eyes that implied he'd be happy to take his prisoner's place on her schedule.

"I heard he has a son to replace him," she said cheekily before letting her mouth droop in a pitiful kind of way. After all, she needed an excuse to be crying when she left in the morning. "But I'll miss him all the same. A sweet, strong man, and refined, too. I wouldn't meet his like in the normal way of things."

"Speak nicely to him," the soldier advised. "Better still, keep these shoes on all night, and maybe he'll take you with him."

She let her eyes light up with hope. "Oh, do you think so?"

"Well, he asks for you. Never asked for any other whores by name. I think he likes you."

"Really?" she said breathlessly.

"Really. And if he says no, you can always ensnare the son. He's just as handsome."

"Wouldn't be the same, though," she said with a sigh. "Wish me luck, gentlemen!"

Her friendly soldier conducted her to the prison tower, where he invited her to think of him if she was ever in need. She nudged him in equally friendly spirit. "They don't pay you enough, soldier. Come back when you're captain of the guard."

He grinned and unlocked the prisoner's door. She tripped in, and the door slammed behind her.

Two men occupied the room now, each sitting on the cots against opposite walls. Malcolm MacHeth got up from his and came at once to meet her, tall and dark and strong. As always, he kissed her hand in a smacking sort of a way in case the guard still lingered outside. Her heart thundered with a longing that would never now be fulfilled.

Malcolm mac Aed was everything she'd ever wanted in a man. Handsome enough to turn an impressionable girl's knees to jelly, with just that edge of danger that thrilled her blood. On top of which, he was clever, witty, able to laugh at himself and the world, and learned enough to talk about most subjects under the sun without ever once being boring. But in truth, she liked his quiet as much as his speech. It took only his presence to move her.

Once, she'd put his effect on her down to the almost legendary status of the man. Now, she knew better.

"Allow me to present my son, Donald," he murmured.

The son, an even more handsome but somehow less dramatic version of Adam, came across from his bed and also kissed her hand. "Lady, I'm as indebted to you as the rest of my family. Your bravery leaves the rest of us standing still."

"I never heard the sons of Malcolm stood still for very long," Mairead said lightly.

"What's happening?" Malcolm demanded. "I had a letter from my wife, delivered by the constable himself, urging me to consent to my own release, leaving Donald here. She mentioned things known only to us, so she *meant* it. She wasn't simply giving my gaolers something to read."

"No, she means it," Mairead said, waving her hand to urge both men to sit. "We have a plan. Adam has brought the men of Ross to the edge of Fife. Somerled has sent part of his fleet close enough to the west coast to worry the king, and our friends exaggerate the numbers to spread rumors and dread. But we're doing nothing that isn't expected of us in the circumstances. So, they truly *won't* expect what we *are* going to do." She frowned. "Unless Christian betrays us."

"Christian?" Donald repeated. "Cairistiona won't betray us. I'd swear she loves Adam. Why would you even think that?"

"Because I just saw her in Glasgow two days ago, cozy as you like with King Malcolm. The lady never mentioned her to me." Mairead shrugged. "Then again, she didn't tell me what Adam and Somerled were doing either. I suppose she has to be careful what she commits to writing for the sake of all of us, should something go wrong. She would protect Adam's wife as much as she could."

Donald looked at his father, then back to Mairead with doubt. "Why? Why would Cairistiona go to the king now?"

"It seems she took the opportunity of Adam's departure to depart herself," Mairead said.

Donald frowned and sat down heavily. "She never made a secret of her loyalty to the King of Scots. But there was definitely something between her and Adam. She covered for him when the dreams swamped him at their wedding. She looked after him. She *must* love him."

"Donald mac Malcolm, you are an innocent," Mairead said with a hint of tartness. "Do you not know that most betrayals take place *because* rather than in spite of love? If Christian loves him, does he love her? And with Adam, how in God's name would she know?"

"Did you know how he felt about you?"

"He liked to bed me," Mairead said brazenly, "and he liked to talk with me. I made him laugh. Beyond that, I really have no idea."

"It doesn't matter," Malcolm said abruptly. "We can do nothing about Christian now. We'll have to proceed and be ready to alter our plans if necessary. Mairead, what *is* the plan?"

CHAPTER FIVE

B Y DAWN, WHEN the guards came to let Mairead out, Donald was already dressed in her clothes and instructed to the best of his poor ability to walk and move like a woman. His head was covered by a red veil and a capacious shawl into which he wept copiously, even before the guard opened the door.

"Come on, love, cheer up," the soldier urged. "You should be happy for him!"

Donald sniffed and glanced back over his shoulder at his father. Malcolm, sitting on the bed half-dressed, smiled once and reached for his boots. From the other bed came gentle snores.

Donald sobbed and rushed from the room, clutching the shawl to his eyes.

Mairead was right. The soldiers barely looked at him on the way out. They'd no real reason to check on the departure of the whore who'd arrived with permission the night before. They were more concerned with the protection of the king, who'd ridden into the castle last night to make Malcolm MacHeth's release formal. In the light of those major events, the threat from Adam MacHeth to the northeast and Somerled of the Isles to the west all made quite trivial the departure of said Malcolm's whore.

And so, Donald simply walked—well, stumbled, half running and constantly weeping—out of the castle, across the bridge to the south, and on toward the town which had sprung up beyond the castle walls. It was only just beginning to get light, and although the castle was awake and bustling, the road was quiet. No one was around to see him turn away from the town and into the forest.

This, now, was the difficult and the dangerous part. For Mairead had had no idea who, if anyone, would meet him here, or if, once out, he had to make shift for himself, which would be damned difficult in this garb. He needed to beg or steal some other clothes. And a sword. At the very least.

Still, it was sweet to smell the fresh, damp air of freedom after his weeks of incarceration. How much sweeter would it be to his father after *twenty-two years*? Even now, Donald's mind boggled at that length of time, almost the whole of his life. But he was warmed by knowledge of his father—quiet, erudite, funny at times, and not at all like the wild warrior he'd expected. Twenty years of captivity had done that to him. But they hadn't made him boring.

And Mairead... Mairead, whom he'd suspected of being in love with his brother, seemed instead to be more than half in love with his father. It went against Donald's sense of honor to leave her in prison while he walked away, and yet he couldn't see any other way that would work. His father wouldn't leave if Donald didn't, and so he'd gone, more aware than ever of what he personally owed to Mairead.

At one point during the night, when Malcolm had snatched some sleep, Donald had asked her bluntly why she risked her life for his family.

She'd shrugged. "Because it sounded exciting when Somerled suggested it. I'm not the stuff meek wives are made of. And I confess I had a little *tendre* for Adam. I was happy to help him."

"Do you still have a *tendre* for Adam?"

He heard the smile in her voice as she said, "There are many kinds of tenderness and love. Of course, I love Adam. But I grew up."

And yet there she'd lain beside his father, not even touching him; but it was the place she'd chosen. Donald wasn't sure how he felt about that. His father hadn't seen his wife in more than twenty years. If ever a man was entitled to infidelity—and most believed they were—surely it was this one.

"Did you ever play your disreputable part to the full?" he asked curiously.

"You mean am I your father's whore in reality?"

"I was going to say lover."

"The answer to both is no. For your mother's sake, you might like to know that I was willing, but he wouldn't touch me."

The sound of soft thudding hooves on the forest floor broke into Donald's reverie. They were close, so God knew how long it had taken him to register their presence. If he wasn't careful, he'd end up back in the castle, having spoiled his father's chance of freedom, too.

Donald threw himself into a clump of trees and waited to see who rode along the track. From where he hid, he could see the dip in the forest floor that Mairead had directed him to, the place he was to meet unnamed friends of Ross who would guide him through the next stage of his mother's plan. But blind trust was foolhardy in the circumstances. He needed to know exactly who came for him before he revealed himself.

Two horses…no, three. They slowed to a walk, and he saw a soldier and a woman on horseback. The woman led another horse by the reins, presumably to leave the soldier free to use his many weapons at will. The soldier wore de Lanson's colors. And the woman, when she turned her head, was Cairistiona, his sister-in-law.

Cairistiona who'd gone to the king, who Mairead believed was betraying them.

"Donald?" she said, low.

Donald listened intently. He could hear no other horses, not even a breaking twig. He straightened his shoulders and stepped out of the trees.

"Oh, Donald," Cairistiona said shakily. "Cover yourself, or

Henry will be undone."

Henry dismounted, grinning, pulling the roll off his saddle-bag.

"Are you well?" Cairistiona asked, anxiety creeping through the slightly desperate humor. "Is your father?"

Donald nodded, still scanning the trees for signs of soldiers. Henry deposited some clothes at his feet and added a helmet and a sword. Finally, Donald breathed again.

"Mairead?" Cairistiona asked.

"With my father."

"Good. Then you're one of my Norman guards. Your job is to escort your father safely home to Ross."

WHEN DONALD'S SOBS and footsteps had faded down the stairs, Mairead sat up in the bed, and Malcolm passed her handfuls of clothing and books from his trunk—the sum of the things he'd amassed in prison. It wasn't much, but it was enough to shape under the blanket the figure of a sleeping man. Mairead even placed Donald's rumpled hat where pillow and blanket joined.

"Nice touch," Malcolm said gravely. "You know, you and Donald are not so dissimilar in build as one might imagine."

"I'm sure Adam took that into consideration when he con-cocted his plans."

"I'm looking forward to meeting this meticulous son."

"As you will very soon, if Donald has managed to get away." *If Christian hasn't betrayed us.*

Malcolm sat down on his bed. Mairead sat inside the empty chest, and they both watched the narrow slit window high above them lighten with the coming day. A sense of calm broke over Mairead. Malcolm would, God willing, return to the Lady of Ross. But she, Mairead would always have these moments, and all the others she'd spent alone with him. He would remember her.

When the first footstep sounded on the stairs, Mairead lay down in the chest and Malcolm set his hand on the lid. He paused for an instant, his dense brown eyes softening as Adam's sometimes did. He reached down and touched her cheek.

"Bless you, Mairead," he murmured and closed the lid.

In the darkness, a tear trickled down one side of her face, but she smiled, listening to the opening of the cell door, and the brief exchange with the guard.

"No, I will carry it," Malcolm said proudly, and she felt herself hoisted high before settling on his shoulder. It was a long way to carry such a weight. He couldn't have done it so easily with Donald in the chest.

She felt him pause, presumably gazing toward Donald's bed as they'd discussed.

He said softly, "Farewell, Donald. I promise you, you *will* be freed, too."

"Shall I wake him, my lord?" the guard asked.

Interesting he called him that, although the earldom had been taken from Malcolm over twenty years ago. Mairead just prayed the guard wasn't helpfully shaking "Donald" and discovering he was made of clothes, a couple of books, and a hat.

"No," Malcolm said, beginning to walk again. "We said our true farewells last night."

The guard's footsteps followed him. All was well.

Fresh air seeped through the chest as Malcolm arrived in the courtyard. His breathing was heavy now, but he walked several paces before lowering the chest to the ground. He didn't even bump her. She probably wouldn't have noticed, her heart was drumming so forcefully. This was it. This was as far as they'd get if Donald had been discovered.

Almost there, almost there.

"Malcolm mac Aed," said the familiar voice of the young king, forceful and dignified. He was becoming, Mairead allowed, a good king. "For the sake of peace in this kingdom, we grant you your freedom. On certain conditions for which you must now give us your word."

And if he didn't, Mairead thought suddenly, then they'd be discovered. As would Donald's escape. Malcolm had to agree to whatever the king demanded. And Mairead rather thought Adam had planned it that way. She just hoped he hadn't misjudged the parent he hadn't met in twenty-two years.

⟫⟫⟫⟪⟪⟪

CHRISTIAN HAD SEEN at once that Donald didn't really trust her. She could return that mistrust since he was the one who had broken his agreement with Adam and gone to Galloway, thus setting off this whole mess.

Of course, Donald only knew whatever part of the plan Adam had managed to impart to Mairead via their messenger. And Christian had been right in Glasgow. Mairead *had* been suspicious of her and had passed her doubts on to Donald. Who, however, soon began to laugh softly to himself as he stripped off Mairead's alarmingly revealing clothes and donned those that Henry had brought.

"So now I greet my father on his official release?" Donald asked with clear amusement.

"Yes, you do," Christian said happily. "Providing no one has discovered you've released yourself in the meantime. So, keep your helmet on and blend in with the others. And you need to hurry because we have an appointment with the king."

Donald threw himself onto the spare horse with enthusiasm.

"You make a fine French knight," Henry said wryly.

"Ha," Donald retorted. "Maybe you will too one day."

Side by side they rode behind Christian out of the woods and around to the northeast entrance to the castle, from where they'd left for their early morning ride. Because of the king's presence, there was already much coming and going across the drawbridge, and no one noticed that Christian had left with one soldier and returned with two.

In the courtyard, they were joined by the rest of the men, already mounted, apart from Henry, who stood respectfully behind Christian so that the fact they now had an extra mounted man wouldn't be so obvious. But providing no one had yet discovered Donald's escape, no one would be paying them much attention. That would all be on the prisoner of Roxburgh himself, and the king who emerged with his entourage, to stand in the center of the courtyard.

The king looked impressive, somehow no longer the boy Christian had first met. He wore a rich blue tunic, and a bright scarlet cloak hung from one shoulder by a jeweled gold brooch. His hat boasted a magnificent white plume that swayed in the breeze.

And then, only moments later, the door of the south tower creaked open, a soldier stepped through, and then the prisoner himself emerged.

In spite of herself, Christian found her gaze fixed on the legendary Malcolm MacHeth. He was tall and dark, like his sons, and lean, though not, it seemed, from prison deprivation, for he carried his own chest on his shoulder, and Christian knew its contents. No one could have guessed its weight from the way he bore it. He walked toward the king with measured, steady steps and set the chest on the ground at his feet before he straightened and fearlessly met the king's gaze.

The courtyard had shrunk with his presence. He was just one man, a defeated rebel, a prisoner, in the presence of a king and his entourage; and yet it was undoubtedly Malcolm MacHeth who dominated the scene.

Suddenly, without even hearing him speak, Christian understood why so much of the country had followed him into battle so often, how he'd gained and retained the obsessive loyalty of his people, to say nothing of a woman like Halla. No wonder generations had been too frightened to let him go and yet could never bring themselves to kill him. It was about more than his royal blood and half-forgotten traditions.

Christian didn't think anyone expected him to kneel, and he didn't. But he did bow.

The king, emphasizing his superiority didn't bow back. "Malcolm mac Aed, for the sake of peace in this kingdom, we grant you your freedom. On certain conditions for which you must now give us your word."

Christian held her breath. This was the moment Malcolm's intransigent pride could ruin everything. But surely it wouldn't. Even the weather seemed to be smiling upon the spectacle in the castle bailey, spreading cool morning sunlight over both major players below.

The breeze blew a strand of still-black hair across Malcolm MacHeth's forehead. He ignored it, gazing slowly around the surrounding walls of the great castle before returning to the king.

"After twenty-two years of these walls," he said mildly, "I will be very glad to see beyond them."

"I will be glad for you," the king said. "And I thank you for changing your mind about leaving your son behind. He is, you understand, a hostage to your acceptance of our peace."

Malcolm MacHeth's gaze flickered beyond the king to the Earl of Strathearn and farther, to Christian and her mounted escort. Could he pick out Donald among them, or was he too taken up with the moment? Impossible to tell.

"I understand," he said.

"Then I will introduce to you your daughter-in-law, the lady Christian, who will accompany you to Ross. On the way, I expect you to collect your other son and his army and keep the peace of the realm."

Malcolm's mouth twitched in distaste. He didn't want to promise anything, but this was such a little thing, and the Lady of Ross had advised him to accept it all. If only he would take her advice…

His gaze remained on Christian. In many, very different ways, it was as difficult to withstand as Adam's. Neither could she tell anything from his veiled, secretive eyes. He had no reason to trust her. He must at least have heard all of Mairead's suspicions.

He said, "I can and do give my word to that."

"Will you further keep the peace of the realm forever?"

Christian closed her eyes. She'd asked them to offer the king's concessions first, to ensure Malcolm would make the necessary promises. Only now, Malcolm's peace was demanded before any concessions were offered. The man was too proud. *Please remember Mairead is in that chest at your feet, that your son is still well within range of recapture. You must know that, even if you don't see him right behind me.*

Malcolm MacHeth said, "I will do my very best to keep the peace under all reasonable circumstances."

Christian breathed again. She thought Malcolm must have caught her tiny motion, for a smile flickered across his lips and vanished, so like Adam's fugitive smile that her heart lifted. Malcolm MacHeth could not be such a bad man.

The king said, "Then in return, I will undertake to release your son Donald after one year of peace, at which time you and I will sign a formal agreement, and I will reinvest you with your old title of Earl of Ross."

Yes. They'd taken her advice after all.

But Malcolm MacHeth was still an unknown quantity in the plan. His gaze flew to the king, then after a moment to Christian, who gazed back, trying to will his agreement. Again, the smile flickered before he returned his attention to the king.

"A year is not so unreasonable for a young man. If you promise him the same conditions with which I was treated."

The king inclined his head.

"Then we are in accord," Malcolm MacHeth said with such obvious reluctance that Christian was sure the king would bridle.

However, something more must have passed between the boy king and the rebel who shared his name, for a slightly crooked smile curved the king's lips.

"You will have to kneel to me, then," he said with a complete lapse from formality.

"I know," Malcolm MacHeth said.

"Then go in freedom," the Earl of Strathearn said hastily.

Christian stepped forward, offering her hand to her father-in-law, who took it in his. Still, his eyes revealed nothing of his thoughts.

"I appear to have the sweetest of escorts," he observed.

She could barely speak. "Henry," she managed, and Henry led forward a horse.

Malcolm dropped her hand and picked up his chest.

"We have a couple of packhorses," Henry said, and while they arranged the bestowal of the chest, Christian went to the king and curtseyed low.

"It's working," the king murmured, raising her.

"I know," she murmured back. "Your Grace struck just the right notes. This must be what the world sees, all the world *ever* sees, so your authority remains paramount. I am Your Grace's servant in Ross."

The king looked slightly puzzled, although she prayed he would remember her words later. They would all, God willing, see the sense in them. The king could not be allowed to look foolish after his apparently masterful agreement with Malcolm MacHeth.

Christian was conducted by Henry to her own horse. Malcolm MacHeth was already mounted. Henry led the way, with Malcolm MacHeth and Christian falling into the middle line behind them. She didn't even look to see where Donald had placed himself.

In formation, they rode sedately over the drawbridge from Roxburgh Castle.

All the castle servants and soldiers had come out to wave them off, and townspeople lined the road ahead, gazing with avid curiosity at the celebrated prisoner who'd lived so close to them, unseen for more than twenty years. Spontaneous cheers began to erupt and rang in Christian's ears as they set the horses' noses north and broke into a gallop.

CHAPTER SIX

MALCOLM MACHETH COULDN'T speak for the massive constriction in his throat. He was afraid he would weep. The horse under him thundered along the road, carrying him away from Roxburgh, away from captivity. Sun and wind battered his face and body.

Just like that, after more than two decades, he was free. Even more stunning, he rode side by side with his son. The small child he'd left in Ross had become a tall, strong man, and Malcolm's heart almost burst with pride, with joy, with sheer euphoria.

But he still couldn't speak.

When they could no longer see the castle, they slowed to a walk and then halted in tacit agreement, and the soldiers unstrapped Malcolm's chest from the packhorse. Malcolm dismounted and strode forward to open it.

"Mairead?" he said anxiously into the chest. "Are you well?"

"Ecstatic," came Mairead's acid voice. "Every bone in my body is shattered. Could you not have traveled at a sedate walk?"

"We couldn't stop in sight of the castle, and we were afraid you'd run out of air." Malcolm bent, hand outstretched, and Mairead, tall and slender in Donald's clothing, rose up and stepped out of the chest, stretching her neck and then each limb one at a time.

Then she gazed around her companions until she found

Christian, his daughter-in-law who had not betrayed them. So far. But then, she was Rhuadri of Tirebeck's child, which perhaps explained the mask she wore over one side of her rather beautiful face. There had been an accident, he remembered, involving Rhuadri's child. And now she was Adam's lady. An enigma.

"I thought I heard your voice," Mairead said neutrally. "How safe are we?"

"We should be fine if we keep going," Christian replied. "We have the king's safe conduct through Lothian, Fife, and Angus, all the way north to Moray. We'll meet Adam and the bulk of the men in Fife."

"Then he knows you're here?"

"Of course, he knows," Christian said calmly. "He doesn't like it, but it was his lady mother's idea that I insinuate myself and my men as his father's escort. If I couldn't do it, your journey and Donald's would have been rather more…perilous. I'm sorry if my presence caused you disquiet. I think the lady was worried about too much information falling into the wrong hands if her messenger was captured. Or any of yours. If it makes you feel better, you worried me, too."

Mairead and Donald were gazing at her with rather peculiar fascination. Malcolm knew how they felt, but now he wanted to laugh instead of weep because, of course, Halla was behind this whole escapade. All she'd needed were the pieces in place.

"Well, new daughter," Malcolm said to Christian. "It seems you managed very well."

"So far," Christian allowed with a rather charming, self-deprecating smile. "Please, let's move on. The farther away we are from Roxburgh when they discover Donald's escape, the happier I'll be."

"HE'S *WHAT?*" THE king exclaimed, staring at the messenger who'd just arrived at one of Fergus of Galloway's houses where the king was spending the night on his way to inspect the west coast defenses and the position of Somerled's ships.

He'd already had good news, that the ships seemed to have melted into the mist and vanished, so he wasn't prepared when the messenger from Roxburgh brought such impossible news.

"Gone, Your Grace," the messenger repeated nervously. "The cell was empty. The figure under the blankets that the guards had taken for Donald mac Malcolm was found to be Malcolm MacHeth's clothing."

"How the devil did they do that?" the king wondered, distracted and not a little impressed.

Fergus began to laugh.

"It doesn't matter, does it?" Ferchar of Strathearn said bitterly. "We've lost every hold we had on Malcolm MacHeth. His son threatens Fife with a huge army that can cause incalculable damage before we can get to it. We're reduced to *praying* Malcolm MacHeth keeps his word to us. God's teeth, we can't even admit we've lost Donald, or Your Grace will look ridiculous."

The king felt his eyes widen. *"This must be what the world sees,"* Christian de Lanson had said to him. *"All the world ever sees, so your authority remains paramount. I am Your Grace's servant in Ross."*

"I have a servant in Ross," the king said ruefully. "Perhaps all is not lost."

MALCOLM MACHETH WOKE after his first night of freedom. Since it had been raining, he'd slept under a canvas tent with Donald, but at some point, he'd obviously stuck his head outside, for gentle rain pattered on his face.

He opened his eyes. It was still dark, the camp quiet. He lay half-in, half-out of the tent. The top of his blanket was soaked, so he'd obviously been like that for some time. He didn't mind. He welcomed all the discomforts of freedom.

When he was young, he'd generally camped without tents, just finding what shelter he could when the weather turned bad. He'd quite often woken to rain on his face like this. Such as when he'd first met Halla in the hills of Ross…

He'd been so young and foolish then that he hadn't regarded marriage as such a big thing. It was an alliance, a means to an end, to cementing his friendship with Somerled of the Isles. It was only as he and his men set off to meet the islesmen that he'd begun to wonder what the sister herself was like. After all, he would be fathering children upon her. And so, he'd left the men and raced ahead to watch the islesmen in secret.

He'd seen the boy wandering away and watched the women panicking. He'd assumed the boy to be some younger sibling of Somerled's. It hadn't entered his head until she'd spoken behind him that she wasn't a boy at all. But she'd certainly gained his attention.

Beneath the grime and the baggy boy's clothes, he could see she was pretty enough, and when she'd actually shot him, he was thoroughly intrigued. It became an obsession to understand how she saw their marriage, and everything else, too. Very quickly, Halla grew into moments of his busy life that he looked forward to, oddly exciting, fun moments because he was never sure where they would go.

It had helped that the morning he first awoke in her camp, rumpled and soaking from the night's rain, her women had pushed her from the tent, washed and scrubbed, in a bright blue gown, with her hair combed into a shining golden mass like a halo. She no longer looked remotely like the child he'd called her. In fact, his bold, clever urchin was a breathtaking beauty, but by her slightly embarrassed manner, he assumed no one had ever told her so.

"Good morning," he greeted her cheerfully, trying not to stare. "I hope you can run and climb in that gown."

"Of course," she said scornfully.

And she had done.

Although it hadn't exactly been a courtship—there had been neither the privacy nor the time—Malcolm had wanted to make her comfortable with him. And in that, he'd succeeded. Just as well, for as soon as they reached his chief hall at Brecka, they were married.

It hadn't been the most glittering wedding ceremony in the world. Because of his quarrel with the King of Scots, most of the great nobles had stayed away, and those of a more independent spirit who did attend—his cousins of Moray, Somerled of the Isles, Fergus of Galloway—had left their ladies and their heirs at home.

But the chief men and women of Ross had come in force, and their children had run about the hall in high excitement. Halla had spent a lot of time watching the children, her expression unreadable, perhaps regretting that her role as bride prevented her from playing with them; she wasn't so very much older.

And for the first time, as they'd stood before the priest and her shaking hand had been formally given to him, he'd realized her fear. Behind the beautiful woman still lay the defiant child.

He'd been eighteen years old, the ruler of an earldom, and pretty much used to having any women who took his fancy. Even then, he'd been aware that having Halla would be different, and he'd wanted her all the more because of it. It hadn't been easy taming the hungry beast of his lust, but he'd defeated it by whisking Halla outside the hall, away from everyone, as soon as the ceremony was over.

Her quick breathing was all that gave her away.

He said, "We are friends, are we not? Friends who occasionally shoot each other."

She laughed as she was meant to, and he took her hand and kissed it. It felt hot under his lips. And she still trembled.

"When you're used to me," he said gently, "then I will be your husband. Until then, we'll let the friendship grow. Do you agree?"

Her face flushed at his words. Her eyes searched his face before they fell. "I agree," she said hoarsely. Her hand tugged to be free, and she vanished back into the hall.

ALL THOSE YEARS later, the memory stirred Malcolm to desire. At eighteen, it wasn't so easy to control one's rampaging lusts. Nor after two decades of captivity. Especially when he understood now what he hadn't then, that part of Halla had wanted to be made his wife in every sense from that very first day. There had been disappointment mingled with her relief.

And now he was going back to her. It would be like those first days all over again. In twenty years, they must both have changed beyond all recognition, outwardly and inwardly. All through his imprisonment, he'd hugged his love for her close to himself. His love for the girl she'd been. He didn't even know if he loved her still. He loved a shadowy memory, an ideal. And God knew what she felt for the man who'd turned her life upside down; had, in effect, wasted her life and left her alone.

No rumors overheard or extracted from his guards had ever besmirched the name of the Lady of Ross. No embarrassing glances or blurted words had ever slipped from Mairead or Donald to accuse her of the slightest infidelity. And yet his wife was only human. And passionate. And damnably beautiful…

"Time to rise and go," Donald's voice said from inside the tent. "Today, we cross into Fife and meet up with Adam."

Derisive laughter pushed out Malcolm's breath. Right now, it wasn't actually unpleasant to feel like a falling leaf, blown this way and that by the wind without him being able to control its speed or direction. The trouble was, that man so blown and led didn't feel like *him*. Like Malcolm MacHeth.

MALCOLM NO LONGER noticed the biting wind. Through the all but horizontal rain, a swirling mist had resolved into a massive horde of wild men, a huge villainous army, guaranteed to put the fear of God—or at least of the MacHeths—into the southern Scots. Certainly, none of the locals seemed to have stayed to watch.

A scattering of horsemen rode among the host, and it was to those Malcolm's gaze clung, searching for anything that would identify *him*, his other stranger son.

Beside him, Christian and Donald came to a halt, too. Their Norman escort spread out on either side, bows drawn, although there was nothing so few could possibly do if it came to a fight with such a huge force.

"Run for your lives." Donald grinned with barely suppressed excitement. "The MacHeths are coming!"

Malcolm's breath heaved. He didn't know if it was pride or grief, or even what or who it encompassed. White Christ, but he was a mess.

Or perhaps he was just stunned by the sheer size of the horde which had come to bring him home. He couldn't even blink in case the dam of his emotion burst.

At last, he made out a figure on horseback, pushing forward to the front—a tall man in a dark red cloak riding a big gray horse. Adam. This must be Adam, his seer son who'd begun the rebellion all over again in his name. At least, Donald said he was a seer, which might have been wishful thinking. Mairead had been more ambiguous. Others again called him mad.

"Don't shoot," the Norman Henry said dryly to his bowmen, who were already lowering their weapons. He understood they were the remains of Lanson's army, acquired by Adam when he'd married Christian, but the details of how they'd come to be trusted were unclear. It couldn't have been easy for them to just watch such an advance of fighting men who'd so recently been their enemy.

The man who had to be his son rode harder across the flat

plain, his men streaming after him. He looked wild and unkempt. And he was clearly Donald's brother. The wind—surely it must have been the wind—swept Malcolm's breath away. The horseman veered to the left, as if he were riding straight at Christian.

For an instant, Malcolm feared he would actually crash into her at full tilt, but at the last moment, he pulled on the reins. The horse half reared, whinnying in complaint. Before its front hooves hit the ground once more, Adam was out of the saddle, and as the other riders slowed to a halt, his gaze, oddly wild and unfocused, clashed with Christian's.

Oh yes, he could easily be insane. And yet his task in all this could not have been easy, as Malcolm well knew—to sit and wait and keep such a huge force of idle men in order while others did his bidding in the lion's den.

Adam's eyes met his wife's for only an instant, for it seemed his real attention was elsewhere. He strode past the head of Christian's horse and slowed. Without looking at her, but as if he couldn't help it, he reached for her hand on the reins. She covered it with hers at once, and a half smile flickered on the madman's lips.

And then he broke away, once more the unstoppable force, striding toward Malcolm, as though, without even having looked, he knew where to find him.

From his own saddle, Donald reached down to grip his brother's shoulder on his way past. "'*My brother will come for me,*' I told the King of Scots," he drawled into the wind. "I never imagined you'd send two women."

"Two remarkable women," Adam said without pausing. Not, then, totally insane.

"I'll give you that," Donald allowed. "Gladly."

Adam halted at last at the head of Malcolm's horse, and slowly, almost reluctantly, brought his strange, unquiet gaze to his father.

The men on foot were catching up by then, but one could

still have heard a pin hit the ground amongst that group of normally boisterous, noisy soldiers. Or so it seemed to Malcolm until he realized rain clattered against steel helmets and shields, and the wind gusted and growled around them while he stared at his son.

It came to him quite suddenly that he didn't care if Adam was mad or strange or not. Who loved him or not. He was his son, his blood.

Malcolm's breast heaved as he stared at his son. Involuntarily, his hand lifted from the reins, reaching, and Adam seized it in silence, pressing his lips to his father's knuckles. Almost in wonder, Malcolm touched the bent head with his free hand, stroking, clutching the wet hair in his fingers.

And still, no one seemed to breathe, until Adam flung back his head, his smile dazzling.

"*That* is how I saw it," he said, and under his father's still-fascinated gaze, he turned his head and raised his voice. "Malcolm mac Aed is returned! The Earl of Ross is coming home!"

And the cheer broke and soared so loudly, they might have heard it from Edinburgh to Perth. The men surged forward, surrounding Malcolm, acclaiming him, as if he were some legend reborn that many had never expected to see again.

The Malcolm they'd taken to prison over twenty years ago would have rejoiced in this display. Now, he'd no idea what to do with it.

Of course, it wasn't all for him; it was because at last the MacHeths were reunited. Or nearly so. In Ross, Halla and Gormflaith must have been waiting with desperation to know if the plan had succeeded.

His gut twisted with longing and something else he had no name for. Shaking it off, he found himself beside Mairead.

"It seems this cause is won," he said. "Thanks to you. What will you do now?"

"Go to Kingowan and search for another," Mairead said lightly.

She wore women's clothes again, but for the first time since he'd known her, she looked tired. The droop of her shoulders seemed just a little hopeless.

Was that his fault, too? "I hope you find it," he said gently.

Mairead smiled, straightening her shoulders, but whatever amusing retort she was about to make remained unspoken as Adam suddenly materialized between them, his hand on Christian's bridle, although his head turned toward Mairead.

"My thanks," he said, "to the cleverest baggage in Scotland."

Mairead laughed. It almost sounded like relief, as if Adam had given her the path she needed. "If I didn't love you, Adam mac Malcolm, I'd kill you."

It caused Malcolm a twinge. Not quite jealousy, because it was clearly an old joke between them rather than a declaration to rile Adam's wife. But he envied them the banter, an art he'd never lost in prison and yet which eluded him in his first days of freedom. It almost felt as if he'd left his true self in those clothes they'd bundled up in the bed to look like Donald.

Mairead's gaze flickered to Christian, and she nodded in what looked like farewell before she pulled on the reins to turn her horse.

At last, Adam looked up at Christian.

His eyes searched her face, almost devouring her. Then, uncaring of who saw, he bent his head and laid his cheek on her thigh. As she stroked his soaked hair and his dripping face, they might have been quite alone. Rain glistened on Adam's eyelashes.

"Shall we go home?" he said huskily.

"Yes, my love," Christian answered. "Let us go home."

Which was when Malcolm knew for certain that he couldn't.

CHAPTER SEVEN

HALLA HAD SPENT over twenty years waiting. Why should the last couple of weeks have been so hard?

Perhaps because she had less to do, with nearly all the men being away with Adam. Of her children, only Gormflaith remained at Brecka, and all she could speak about was her father and the plan to bring both him and Donald home. And it seemed Halla had ruled his country too well. There was little more to do than the everyday demands to ensure the proper running of farms, markets, dairies, and tribute; little thought was required to care for the people as she always had, to administer the justice that had become second nature.

Wherever she went, journeying between her halls around Ross, even visiting Bishop Symeon in Rosemarkie, everyone knew that the earl was returning, and their excitement infected whatever calm she had achieved. She just had to live with the constant knot in her stomach, the constant fear that Donald would be left behind, that the plan would go awry and she'd lose both of them. Perhaps even Cairistiona would be imprisoned, and Adam would never forgive her.

Or everything might work. In a couple of weeks, in one week, a few days, tomorrow, they might all be home. Malcolm MacHeth might be home.

Sometimes, the thought made her heart drum like a young

girl's about to receive her first kiss, drowning even her fear for Donald. And so, she returned to Brecka in a state of veiled panic, knowing in her heart it would be the first place they would come. It was where she had first been brought as a bride, the place she now regarded as home.

A headache had begun to plague her on the journey, and now the patter of the rain on the hall roof seemed somehow ominous. Dismissing her women, she sank into the throne-like chair on the dais and closed her eyes. Finally, in the hope of soothing away both headache and groundless fears, she sent for Muiredach, her harpist.

A few minutes later, she heard his quick, distinctive footfalls on the hall floor, and opened her eyes.

Muiredach was a rare being in Ross—a man of birth and education who was neither soldier nor priest. Rumor said he was a king's son come from Ireland as a child slave in some raid or other. Muiredach himself never said so. If he'd ever been a slave, he was a free man by the time he'd walked into her hall ten years ago, a wandering harpist, offering to play at her Easter feast. He'd been here ever since, for she had never heard anyone play the harp as he did. He made it sing and weep and laugh. He made it do everything she ever asked and more. He told stories, too, of great heroes, Scots, Irish, and Norse, always with variations to suit his company.

"Will you play for me, Muiredach?" she asked. "My head is throbbing and needs to be soothed with soft, gentle music."

Muiredach bowed and walked at once to his large harp. He was a graceful man, tall and handsome. It was still a wonder to Halla that no woman had yet ensnared him into marriage. Into her bed, perhaps, for he was a charming man, but nothing of even a semi-permanent nature seemed to bind him to anyone but her. If she was honest, she liked that about him. He'd become necessary to her, a cross between a companion and a priest, his unspoken devotion a balm to her own secret loneliness.

As always, he found the music she needed, playing to suit her mood. She should never, she reminded herself, take Muiredach for granted. Leaning her head against the chair's high back, she closed her eyes once more and let the music in, comforting the tangle of fears and crude, coursing desire that had plagued her since the others had left to bring Malcolm and Donald home.

Most terrible of all was the fear that she would no longer love her husband. What man had he become in prison? Could her exuberant, quick-witted, handsome young husband, who fought like ten devils, even in play fights and training, have grown into a whining, dull, middle-aged man, fat, perhaps, or sick through neglect? Mairead had always reported him as fit and well, but Mairead had never known him before.

Mairead. Mairead, whom she'd never met, had brought something of him back to her in recent months, at no little personal risk. There had always been gratitude and guilt over that. And jealousy.

None of which she ever had or ever would reveal to another living soul. With yet more guilt, Halla recognized that Mairead, too, could be imprisoned or killed for her part in this. The entire plan depended on her.

She opened her eyes and turned to Muiredach. Although his fingers glided across the strings, making their magic, his deep blue gaze rested on her face. This attention no longer bothered her. He always watched her for changes of mood and expression, his guide to what and how to play.

"Have you ever met the Lady Mairead of Kingowan?" she asked him on impulse. After all, he did have odd, mysterious absences, usually, if not always, sanctioned by her in advance.

He shook his head while his fingers played on. "No, I never have."

"She must be a very brave young woman. I wonder, sometimes, if she does it for love of my son or my husband."

"Does it matter?" Muiredach asked.

She shook her head. "No, not to me. Although it might matter to her."

"Perhaps she does it because she believes the cause is just," Muiredach suggested. The music intensified under his clever hands, without increasing in volume. "Why do you fight on? Why did Malcolm mac Aed want to be king in the first place? Was being a great earl not enough for him?"

Halla smiled. "No, that was the curse of his family. Whatever they had was not enough. Certainly, Ross was never big enough for Malcolm. Even Scotland wasn't. To become King of Scots was merely a stepping stone to the larger world, which he could then meet on something like equal terms. He was full of ambitions and ideals and even the imagination to resolve the two."

She paused, her smile of memory dying. "Of course, there was also the smaller matter of avenging his grandfather King Lulach, who had not been killed in a fair fight, whatever was said to the contrary to excuse the act. And the persecution of his mother and his uncle by King Malcolm Canmore. And although he rarely spoke of it, because it hurt him too much, there was the death of his elder brother Angus at Stracathro. He needed Angus's death to count for something."

Her eyes refocused on Muiredach to find his own unreadable.

"He is a restless spirit," he observed.

"He was," Halla agreed. God knew what he'd become now. His letters, short and formally affectionate, with just a hint of the old humor, had given little real clue. All she had was the distant memory of those few short years together. Marriage, love, war, adventure, motherhood, and tragedy, all squashed into a little less than four years.

But now, the long, long wait was almost over. As Muiredach's strings quietened, she imagined the distant thunder of drumming hooves and running men, bringing him home. She could reach for it now, with utter longing, because talking of him had brought back more than Malcolm's turbulence. She'd remembered his patience and his companionship. However long the parting, however deep the changes, enough of him must remain to build a new life together. And, right or wrong, she realized she was trusting *him*—not Adam or Cairistiona or Mairead, but Malcolm himself—to bring Donald home.

The hall door sprang open, and Gormflaith ran in, white-faced with excitement.

"They're coming."

MAIREAD OF KINGOWAN had left the MacHeths in Fife.

"Come with us," Malcolm had urged as if he'd understood. "There is no need for you to go back, except on your own terms. Unless you wish to."

She didn't really. Leading her double existence had provided all the meaning in her court life, in her married life. Part of her wanted to keep going north with the MacHeths, into Ross, just to be with him, and to meet the famous, seldom seen lady who held Malcolm MacHeth's heart. But she didn't think she could bear that.

No, she would go back to Kingowan, hopefully, while her husband was still with the king. Sooner or later, she would return to court, and there, perhaps, she could still work on the Ma-cHeths' behalf. And on Somerled's.

And so, she'd parted from him without looking back, refusing all escort, and had ridden alone to Dundee where, as planned, she waited for her own trusted people, her maid, Grizel, and her men-at-arms, and made the final leg of her journey in perfect propriety and in the style expected of her rank.

She saw at once the banner that blew from the battlements at the top of the house.

"Brian is home," she murmured as unease twisted her stomach.

John, her most trusted man, urged his horse closer to hers. "My best advice? Turn back. Go to one of your own houses and send a messenger. At least until you know what he's doing. Or thinking."

But that was an admission of guilt. And Mairead was nothing if not reckless. The MacHeth adventure was over. It was time for another.

"Nonsense," she said briskly, kicking her heels into her horse. "I am his wife."

Which was, of course, the problem. She rode through the gates, where she was immediately surrounded by soldiers, and her men disarmed.

"Told you," John said without moving his lips as Brian of Kingowan himself walked down the steps from the main house.

"Clever clogs," she said beneath her breath, stripping off her gloves. "Help me down."

He obeyed at once while Kingowan and his own men advanced.

"Take my ring," Mairead breathed. "To Adam MacHeth at Tirebeck."

By the time she slithered to the ground, the ring was tugged from her finger, and she turned to face her husband.

"Where have you been?" he asked without preamble.

"Greetings to you, too, husband," Mairead drawled. "Where have *you* been?"

"No more games, Mairead," Brian snapped. "The truth now."

"You have obviously decided on the truth already, otherwise, my men would not be treated as criminals. What difference would it make what I say?"

"The difference between house arrest and being locked in the north tower," Brian said grimly.

Mairead let her eyes widen. "You would really put yourself in such a ridiculous position?"

A flush darkened his already florid face.

Mairead took advantage. "Let there be no public accusations, husband. Give my men—who are your men—their arms back. They have no idea where I've been either. They only met me in Dundee as I commanded them. You and I should conduct our quarrels in private."

"To hide your shame, lady?" he said between his teeth.

"And yours," she said sweetly. "There aren't many who thrive under the banner of a cuckold."

She had him, and they both knew it. Unfortunately, he had never learned to govern his temper. His hand shot out from pure instinct, she was sure. His closed fist drove at her face, and her head seemed to explode into blackness.

⇛⇚

MAIREAD WOKE WITH her head in Grizel's lap. Her neck and her head both ached abominably, and when she tried to speak, pain shot through her jaw. Still, somehow the words got out.

"He struck me!"

"He did, lady," Grizel said shakily, placing a cold cloth over her face. "You have a terrible bruise, and it is quite swollen, but John says it is not broken."

At least she was in her own bedchamber.

"The door is locked," Grizel said, reading her mind.

"John was right," Mairead mused. "We should have turned back. Where *is* John? Did my husband hurt him or the others?"

Grizel shook her head. "John's gone," she whispered. "I saw him slip away before nightfall."

Mairead sighed with relief, then struggled to sit up. She felt dizzy still and held on to Grizel. "What is he accusing me of? Adultery? Treason?"

"Just disobedience," Grizel said anxiously. "So far. But he asked me about you...and other men."

"What did you say?"

"That I'd never seen nor suspected any man save himself in your bedchamber. Nor known you to visit any man."

It was as well she never took Grizel with her when she did so. When she'd visited Malcolm in Roxburgh, Grizel and the men-at-arms always left with her publicly and were abandoned somewhere discreet until she was ready to rejoin her husband or the king's court.

"He knows, though, doesn't he?" Mairead said. The question was rhetorical.

"He knows there must be some purpose to your disobedience," Grizel admitted with a nervous blink. "I could not tell him what."

"I think I might like to go back to the Isles," Mairead said dreamily.

Grizel's jaw dropped. "And leave your lord?"

Mairead looked at her. "I have not always been honest with my lord, and for that, though I've done him no ill, I always felt I owed him something. It was why I came back against my own and John's better judgment."

"And now?" Grizel asked with foreboding.

"He struck me," Mairead said again. No doubt it was his right as seen by most men and most women, too. Even by the law. But Mairead had always seen things differently.

"It makes no difference," Grizel said, sighing heavily. "We are locked in here."

⇢⇢⇤⇤

As if she had reverted to childhood, Gormflaith held tight onto Halla's hand as they walked out of the hall and into the yard, which was already lined with house guards and servants. The whole household had turned out to welcome the earl home. Halla had no doubt that their path had been followed and cheered for miles.

The big gates stood open, ready to receive as many of the host as could fit within the stockade. Arrangements could easily be made for the rest.

From the hiss in Gormflaith's breath, Halla realized she was squeezing her hand and deliberately eased her grip. Neither of them said anything, nor did either of them let go. In normal circumstances, Halla would not have allowed such a visible sign of dependence, of weakness.

Adam and Donald rode through the gates first, slowing to a trot.

"Thank God," Halla whispered. "Thank God."

A huge cheer went up from the Brecka people. Anxiously, Halla scanned her sons for signs of injury, but tall and straight, neither showed any of the signs she'd learned to look for. No tightness of lips, or fixed smiles, no stiffness or covering each other's weaknesses from the men. If Fergus or the king had hurt Donald, then he'd healed.

As riders surged in behind, Halla couldn't bring herself to look. She was vaguely aware of Cairistiona, of her Norman bodyguards, of Findlaech, and other well-known and trusted officers. No one else leapt out. No tall, dark figure who rode with such strength and grace he seemed to be part of the horse. But of course, he could be grey now, and ill or lame…

Forcing herself, she walked forward on shaking legs, just as she'd done at their wedding. But it was Donald who fell into her view, Donald whom she hugged convulsively.

"You are well?" she whispered. "Unharmed?"

"Just angry with myself."

She drew back, searching his face. "Well, there, it worked out for the best, didn't it?" Her eyes slid over Adam, who was kissing her hand to avoid looking at her and then at last upward and deliberately over the mounted men.

No. Oh no.

Her throat constricted. Her ears began to sing. "Where is he?" *Not dead. Not dead after all this…*

Donald cleared his throat. "My father says he will be home very soon."

"Then he came with you? He is free?" Halla said, uncomprehending.

"He came with us into Ross," Donald said awkwardly. "He begs your forgiveness, but I think he needs…he needs time."

A sudden gust of wind whipped her veil back from her face. Perhaps it was the same wind that had snatched her breath. There was nowhere to hide, not here. A lifetime of dignity could not cover this hurt. He hadn't just kicked her. He'd crushed her.

She felt herself sway, forced herself to steadiness even before Gormflaith's hand took hers once more, and Adam and Donald moved to catch her. But she couldn't bear that. Before they even touched her, some sense of preservation was already turning her away from them all. Still alone.

"Time?" she repeated with indifference. "After twenty-two years, how much more time does he want? Bring the men inside, Findlaech. All are welcome."

Chapter Eight

ALTHOUGH THE FEAST at Brecka was huge and merry, for Christian, it fell just a little flat. Muiredach the harpist surpassed himself with music, accompanying the exaggerated tales and gales of laughter that followed. Donald, delighted to be reunited with his son, Adam, named after his brother, barely seemed to notice the huge absence while he dandled the smiling child on his knee. But Gormflaith did. Seated at her mother's side, she asked her brothers almost constant questions about their father.

Halla asked nothing. The perfect hostess as always, serene and hospitable, she appeared to treat the homecoming like any other Christian had witnessed. She didn't even appear to be listening to her sons' replies to Gormflaith. As if she didn't care.

Beside Christian, Adam ate with the mindless thoroughness that told her he was lost in thought. Or dreams. She covered his hand with hers. "What are you thinking?"

His eyes focused on her. "That he should have come home to his own feast."

"Be reasonable, Adam," Donald said at once on his other side. He passed the baby back to his mother, one of the housemaids, with a grin. Though they did not appear to be together any longer, they retained an amity based on love of little Adam. "He's been in captivity, in almost total isolation for over twenty years.

He can't be expected to jump straight back into the bosom of his family and his duties as if he only left them yesterday. This is hard for him."

"Do you not think it is hard for her, too?"

Donald followed his gaze along the table to their mother, who was smiling at some jest of Findlaech's. "She's fine."

"She's not," Adam said simply.

Donald opened his mouth to ask more, but, like Christian, he clearly saw that Adam's eyes had lost focus as they so often did. Visions passed before him so often and without warning that he could have been excused for being as insane as many thought him. That he had learned somehow to navigate between them, to use the visions to enhance his already impressive clarity of thought, was a personal triumph few could appreciate. Donald was one of the few.

He waited until Adam's gaze dropped to his food, and he began to eat again.

"What?" Donald said urgently. "What did you see?"

"I don't need to see to understand that he's spoiling every reason he had for coming home."

IT WAS AS well for Muiredach that he retained all the skills of a strolling player. In the last ten years serving the Lady of Ross, he had grown used to following his own heart where his music was concerned. But mournful melodies and angry chords would not do for her triumphal feast. His heart ached for his strong, beautiful lady who had borne so much alone, only to have her excitement slapped down again, not by her enemies, but by her own husband whom she had caused to be free.

Muiredach was not a violent man, but if Malcolm MacHeth had stood in front of him at that moment, he would have struck him, and to hell with the consequences—which would have been severe. He was well aware of the man's fighting prowess, at least according to legend, and Muiredach would only be allowed one punch, so he'd have to make it count.

He reined in the fantasy, carefully controlling his hands and bringing them back to the happy music required of him. It was hard.

For years now, he'd been aware that he loved the lady, hopelessly and unconditionally, with the kind of love that was all the sweeter for being doomed to remain forever unrequited or even noticed. It was a pain he lived with proudly because it improved his art, but it had always been eased to bearable levels by the belief that the lady's own absent love was a man truly worthy of her. The legendary Malcolm MacHeth, a great warrior, entitled to be a great king, wronged by his most powerful enemies.

It hurt Muiredach physically, in his gut, to think of her bound to a shallow man, not by mere ties of matrimonial duty, but by those of love. His heart broke for her pain.

Before too much ale had flowed and the hall grew too rambunctious, the lady wisely retired with her daughter and daughter-in-law, who were all soundly toasted by the men.

Muiredach used the opportunity to stop playing. Rising, he pushed the harp away and went to find himself some more ale. As he strolled among them, many of the men were drinking other, private, toasts to Mairead, the lady who had occupied Halla's mind and conversation earlier. Muiredach knew she was the MacHeths' woman who'd carried messages to and from Malcolm MacHeth in Roxburgh. Now, he heard the tale of how she'd dressed as a whore to gain access to the prisoners' cell, swapped clothes with Donald MacHeth so that he could walk out heavily veiled while she hid in Malcolm's trunk and was carried out of the castle with him.

Muiredach loved a good story, and he was more than happy to drink a toast with the men to the health of such a brave and loyal lady. Again, he wondered at the devotion inspired in such noble women by a clearly inferior man like Malcolm MacHeth.

Why? How?

Answering a call of nature, he made his way down the length of the hall to the door. Outside, campfires had been built in the yard, well back from the main hall and the outbuildings, round which more of the Ross host were gathered. They'd been served the same feast as those inside and were already in a much later stage of inebriation. With consideration of their position, Muiredach walked farther around the hall than he normally would to relieve himself.

Others had much the same idea. As he walked back toward the light of the campfires, a man came toward him. Adam MacHeth. Muiredach nodded, unsurprised to receive no response. Adam was strange, living largely, Muiredach suspected, in his own world of dreams. And yet the men not only followed him but treated him like some kind of god, much as they regarded his father, Malcolm.

"Muiredach?"

He glanced back in surprise to find Adam a foot away from him, half turned toward him. The light from the nearest fire flickered over his shadowed face.

"My lord?" Muiredach returned politely.

"Don't let her leave alone," Adam said and walked away.

MALCOLM MACHETH SPENT the night of his feast alone under the stars. He'd thought he was just aimlessly wandering until he'd found himself at the foot of that same waterfall where he'd first seen Halla. He let his horse drink from the nearby stream and then, since the surroundings seemed deserted, he stripped off his clothes and waded into the river, letting the currents pull him where they would, swimming only when he was in danger of being dashed against the rocks. It felt like the rest of his life since that letter had come from Halla and he'd lost control of his own destiny.

It didn't make him unhappy. How could it? He was free and so was Donald.

So why wasn't he at home in the bosom of his family? With Halla, for whom he'd longed all these years.

He scrubbed at his skin with his fingers, wondering if he was washing off Roxburgh or trying to find the man he'd been, the man Halla might recognize. But he was more than that now. He was the man who had to care for his family. Who had no idea where to begin.

Dragging himself from the river, he dried himself on his shirt and struggled back into the rest of his clothes. As he pulled his boots on, it struck him suddenly that Halla might feel as he did and come here, too.

He let his foot fall back to the ground. That was why he'd come here. Without even thinking about it, he'd understood that this was the place he needed to be, to meet with Halla in private before they faced the world together. And suddenly, he was sure that she would come.

With new purpose, he leapt to his feet and went into the trees to collect wood and brush for a fire. He caught a rabbit and cooked it with a sense of anticipation more intense than any he could remember. Halla. Sweet, passionate, loving Halla.

He'd been right all those years ago. She had been more than worth the wait. Although he couldn't remember now how long he actually had waited for her, it had felt like an eternity. For one thing, it hadn't just seemed wrong to slake his lust on other women, he'd discovered he didn't actually want anyone else.

It had been her curiosity that had undone him in the end. They'd been traveling north to Tain together and made camp under a clear sky. For warmth, he'd wrapped them both together in the same blankets, resolved still to be good but loving the tempting feel of her soft body in his arms. He'd forbidden his own hands from exploring, but not hers. Her fingers had been inquisitive and increasingly sensual, and he'd kissed her in the same way as a warning to stop, but then, quite suddenly, it was he who couldn't.

And so, with a care and patience previously unknown to him, and which he struggled to maintain until the end, he'd finally taken her as his wife, giving her pleasure and receiving it with more intensity than he'd ever known.

That had been another beginning, another step in their often turbulent relationship. Remembering, Malcolm was forced to adjust his position where he sat before the fire. Loving Halla had been sweet and addictive and joyful, for she'd never been afraid of giving.

She had to come here, now. She would.

And what would she find, he wondered, as the light began to fade. A broken man who'd let her down.

But of course, she wasn't coming. She was waiting for him at Brecka. And he'd probably hurt her by coming here. He shouldn't have done it. It had seemed quite sane and necessary, until now, when he forced himself to see it through her eyes.

One more night. One more night to fix myself, to remember myself. And then I'll go home.

HALLA DID HER duty, as she always had. Only the emotions seething behind her serene facade had changed. And the words repeating endlessly in her head: *Damn him. Damn him.*

The morning after Donald's return, the host began to disperse, back to their own homes. Between them, Donald and Adam sorted out any drunken fights and other bad behavior that might have disturbed her. Halla barely noticed. She just wanted them all to be gone. But annoyingly, even when the only men remaining were her sons' permanent followings, the boys themselves hung around the hall.

"You should go home," she said abruptly to Cairistiona when they walked back from the village church together.

"I think Adam is hoping to see his father again first."

"If his father comes, I will send him to Tirebeck," Halla said wryly. At this moment, it was by far the pleasantest of the places she wished to send him. "Seriously, Cairistiona. Take him home. Don't let him waste his life waiting."

Cairistiona searched her face for a moment, then nodded and walked on in silence, leaving Halla to her own thoughts, which veered off in wayward directions.

"Tell me about your first husband," Halla said abruptly. "De Lanson."

There was a pause. It was hard for Cairistiona. Because she loved Adam. And Adam had killed de Lanson.

"What do you want to know?" Cairistiona asked.

"Was he ever charming? Did you love him when you first knew him?"

Cairistiona's gaze flew to hers, then quickly away. "No. I suppose I wanted him to love me, but that's not the same thing, is it? It was more a need to be useful, in return, I think, for some kind of security or peace."

"Security and peace," Halla repeated. She smiled. "Some hope. You won't find those things with Adam either."

"I never expected them," Cairistiona admitted. "And yet I *do* have them, momentarily at least."

It was never Halla's way to interfere. But if she didn't yet love Cairistiona, she'd grown to like and admire her, and she recognized where Adam's happiness lay. A happiness he so deserved.

She said, "You do know that you have his love as well? You always have."

Cairistiona flushed, nodding wordlessly. A moment later, she glanced at Halla with a slightly anxious curiosity. Deliberately, Halla kept her face smooth and tranquil.

The next morning, Adam and Cairistiona left for Tirebeck, taking Findlaech and their men with them. Halla persuaded Donald he should go north and sort out some disputed land near the border with Sutherland. She even allowed Gormflaith to go with him, and sent one of her women to serve her. And when they'd gone, she bade Astrid, who had journeyed with her from the Isles all those years ago, to pack a few things for both of them.

They left Brecka Hall with only two men from the house guard. After all, travel within Ross was perfectly safe for the lady. She didn't tell Sweyn or Astrid that they wouldn't be staying in Ross.

The gates were opened, and Halla rode through. She suspected Malcolm had felt much like this as he'd ridden out of Roxburgh.

Another rider moved in front of her, facing her, and just for an instant, Halla felt threatened. Her hands tightened on the reins.

"Muiredach," she said, hoping she hid her relief. A bedroll, and two bundles, one of which was distinctly harp-shaped, hung from his saddle. "Where are you going?"

"With you," he said.

"I did not command you."

"Adam mac Malcolm commanded me."

Without a word, Halla rode forward, hiding the tears that stung her throat. She and Malcolm had at least made wonderful children.

It might have been for that reason she did not forbid Muiredach to come. Or it might have been she was secretly glad of the company.

IT WAS HALLA'S plan to travel down the coast into Moray, where no one would know the Lady of Ross, and from there hire a ship to sail to the Isles. It would be a long journey, going around the northern coast of Caithness, but she was in no hurry, and her route was flexible. She might even call in at Orkney. It could be time to remind Earl Harald of her daughter's existence.

However, they hadn't yet left Ross before they encountered some of Adam's men with a prisoner—or at least a stranger, a southern Scot by his dress and speech, whom they felt compelled to escort. Adam had trained his watchers well.

"Lady," one of them said, coming to a halt with surprised recognition. They all bowed to her, including their prisoner, who was admittedly given little choice in the matter.

Halla inclined her head in response. "Who have you there?" she inquired in Gaelic.

"He says his name is John, and he has a message for Adam mac Malcolm."

"My name *is* John," the man interrupted bullishly in the same language, "and I *do* have a message for Adam mac Malcolm."

She would have sent them on to Tirebeck, only something about the urgency of the stranger caught and held her attention. No longer young, he still had the body and manner of a soldier, and he was clearly determined to get to Adam. He was no spy, or, she was sure, king's messenger.

"Who sent you?" she asked curiously.

"I will tell that to Adam mac Malcolm."

One of the Ross men cuffed him on the back of the head. "Answer! This is the Lady of Ross herself, Adam's mother."

John flushed, jerking another, unforced bow in her direction. "Forgive me, I didn't know."

"How could you?" Halla agreed. She wasn't exactly traveling in the style of a great lady, although Muiredach's presence surely added to her consequence. "And so, your message is from…?"

"The Lady Mairead of Kingowan," John said at once.

Halla schooled her face to impassivity. At least she sent to Adam and not his father. Even though it no longer mattered.

"She is in trouble," John said urgently. "When we got to Kingowan, we found the lord had arrived before us. He suspects something, and since she can't say where she's been, he's locked her up."

Halla kept her gaze on his face. "Will she be able to convince him of her innocence?" Halla inquired.

"Maybe," John said. "But I doubt it. More to the point, the lady herself doubts it, or she wouldn't have sent me."

It would, Halla reflected, be the perfect trap. Having lost two MacHeths in one magnanimous act, the king could be aiming to claw in another.

"How do we know you are who you say you are?" she asked.

"Adam mac Malcolm knows me. And besides, the lady gave me her ring for him."

"Show me," Halla said and waited patiently while the man raked inside his clothes and then opened his fist to show a small circle of gold set with jet and emerald stones. Reaching out, Halla took it from him. He let her, watching anxiously as she inspected it. She glanced back to his face. "And Adam will know this ring?"

"He gave it to her, lady. Before I even knew her. Before the Lord of Kingowan did."

On the whole, Halla was inclined to believe him. Moreover, Mairead should not suffer for all the aid she had given the MacHeths. And yet she could not allow Adam to walk into even the possibility of a trap. Neither of her sons should leave the safety of Ross until they understood if the king was keeping the secret of Donald's escape.

She closed her fingers around the ring, then passed it to Muiredach beside her. "Keep this safe."

John took a step nearer and was immediately hauled back by his captors. "Lady—"

"I will see what I can do for your lady," she interrupted, then turned to the men of Ross. "Take our guest to Brecka."

"Not Tirebeck," one of them said carefully.

"Brecka," she repeated. "And remember he is our guest."

She passed on, sure that her orders would be obeyed. They always were.

Muiredach rode beside her, clearly uneasy. At last, he said, "You can't mean to keep this from Adam mac Malcolm."

"That's exactly what I mean to do," she said calmly.

"But he will know eventually anyway," Muiredach argued.

"True. But by then, I hope to have solved the problem."

"How?" he asked, a fascinated glint in his rather striking blue eyes.

"By freeing the lady one way or another."

At this, his breath caught. He must have tightened his hands on the reins, too, for his horse snorted and tossed its head. "Dear God, you don't mean to go there yourself, do you?"

"You are not obliged to come," she said mildly. "I don't even recall inviting you this far."

"That's not what I mean, and you know it," Muiredach exclaimed. She'd never seen him so agitated before. It brought a rather thrilling vitality to his normally sleepy if perceptive eyes. "Kingowan is in the heart of the king's undisputed territory."

"Don't be so grudging. I have not left Ross in more than twenty years."

"There's good reason for that!"

"There was," she agreed. "I could not risk capture and allow myself to be used against Malcolm mac Aed or my sons. Now Malcolm and my sons are free and safe in Ross."

"And your capture would still compel them to anything. You know that."

"I know no one has laid eyes on me in twenty years. No one would possibly imagine the Lady of Rosstravelingg south with no maids, just a single packhorse, two men-at-arms, and one lady-in-waiting."

"And a personal musician," Muiredach pointed out.

"That does give me a little extra cachet," she allowed. "We shall consider it on the way."

"Lady, please," he said earnestly. "Why undo all the good you have just done in securing the release of your husband and son? Why hand them yourself on a platter?"

"I have no intention of sitting on anyone's platter. On the other hand, neither have I any intention of letting Mairead suffer for what she has done for us."

"And if she isn't suffering? If this is a lie, a trap?"

"Then we'll discover it and take ship for the Isles as originally planned."

It was, of course, the first time Muiredach had heard of any Isles plan, and it at least had the effect of stilling his tongue.

"It's an adventure, Muiredach," she said. "And it's so long since I've had one of those." Not since she and Malcolm had played hide-and-seek with the king's army and sent them home with nothing. Not since the royal troops came back and won the last battle. "I shan't allow any of us to be taken. But if Mairead is anyone's prisoner, I will free her."

"How?" Muiredach demanded helplessly.

"I shan't know until I get there," Halla said. She even smiled into the wind, because her spirits had suddenly risen. This was better, much better, than sailing the long way around to the Isles.

It reminded her forcefully of another time she'd broken away from her people and done the unexpected. Although new love and boredom had played their parts then, too. By the time Malcolm had made her his wife in every sense, she'd been hopelessly in love with him, and the wondrous physical joy he'd taught her had only dragged her deeper. Yet, bewildered still by the speed of these changes in her life and emotions, she'd been unprecedentedly docile and stayed hidden in Brecka most of the time, with her new house guards while Malcolm led his men across Ross, pushing out the king's troops in battle and conducting lightening-swift raids into the royal territories to keep him busy.

She'd lived only for the stories borne back to her and his whirlwind visits home for a day or so of wild passion and laughter that cocooned her in happiness. Until he left again.

She'd woken up quite suddenly while gazing into the hall fire one morning.

I am the Lady of Ross.

For a few moments, she couldn't breathe. She wasn't a child or a maid or a favored pet dog to be kept safe and given orders, to be confined in a box and given the odd sweetmeat on her master's return. She was Halla of the Isles. She was the Lady of Ross, and no one could say her nay.

She turned to the woman beside her. "Astrid, pack some things for a few nights and send me the captain of the guard. We're going on a journey."

The whole household had been uneasy, of course, because they'd known it wasn't Malcolm's wish. However, since they'd seen at once she was quite capable of going alone, they'd all obeyed her, and they'd set out to find Malcolm.

Even then, she hadn't been stupid. She'd known not to draw the attention of the enemy and lead them to her or her husband. Her guards were well trained, and she'd used that, learning from them as she went. Her spirits had soared along with her excitement as they'd drawn closer to where he'd last engaged the enemy. He and his men had gone to one of his own halls in the Strathvaich glen, no doubt preparing for another attack from the Black Water, which flowed south through the valley.

She'd thought at first it was mist that filled the valley. The pungent smell of smoke was so unexpected that, foolishly, it took her several minutes to recognize it. But her soldiers did. They'd halted, surrounding her and sending scouts ahead before they advanced slowly down the slope.

The hall was burned to the ground. And there were bodies. While she sat white-faced upon her horse, her men raked through the still-smoking ashes and charred remains until Torcul, her captain, walked slowly back to her with a piece of singed fabric in his hands. Attached to it, almost unharmed, was Malcolm's brooch of silver and enamel, depicting the Lion of Scotland and the word Ross in clear black letters around the edge.

"No," she'd whispered. "I won't believe it."

"Lady—" Whatever Torcul might have said was lost in the shout from the hill above. Approaching enemy soldiers.

"Why could you not stay put?" Astrid raged.

Halla ignored her. Even then, she'd understood Astrid's anxiety was not for herself but for Halla. Torcul swore between his teeth, then issued swift commands to his men.

"We're trapped down here," he said in frustration.

"Can we fight them?" Halla asked, her voice hard and cold.

"Not with you here. We need to get down the river to—"

"If he's dead, I'm nothing," Halla interrupted. She knew the tears were there, buried beneath a pyre of fury and pure hatred for the men who'd taken her husband, her lover. "Kill them."

And so, with fierce joy, Torcul had gathered his men in front of her and Astrid, and they'd battered their swords and daggers on their shields and yelled for the king's men to come and die for killing their beloved lord.

The day taught Halla many things, among them the dangers of making decisions to fight while full of rage and grief. Despite the ferocity of her men who carried vengeance in their hearts, she knew almost at once, as she watched the king's men pour down the hill, that they were seriously outnumbered and could not win.

Torcul knew it, too, but still he fought. He would have done so anyway, without her orders. It was only her presence that had held him back. But he was losing. And Halla knew that hand in hand with her grief, she would have to carry the guilt of her guardsmen's deaths. If she lived.

At least she had her bow and arrows and gave herself the minor satisfaction of picking off several of the king's men before she understood it would never be enough to make a difference. Their best chance was to lure the king's men into the boggier ground on the river banks. Since the enemy was more heavily armored, it *might* give Torcul some slight advantage.

"Fall back, Torcul!" she screamed. "To the river!"

Only, when she really looked at the river, it seemed to be alive, shimmering and wriggling like some monster sweeping toward her. Legends she hadn't thought she believed in swept through her mind, along with doubts of her own sanity, before she realized that the river had not become some wild, undulating monster. It merely carried boats full of soldiers, furiously rowing, while others ran along the river bank at their side.

"Oh, dear God," she whispered. "What have I done?"

There was no hope now. Astrid, Torcul, all the men would die. The king's men had no reason to grant mercy in this fight. And if she died, the child she might be carrying would die, too.

She crossed her arm over her belly in a uselessly protective gesture. *Forgive me...*

In the leading boat, someone stood up, shouting orders. Halla, unable to make out the words, saw that Torcul and his men were at least falling back, but toward her rather than the river, where he must have seen the boats landing. He must have seen, as she did, the man who leapt ashore first. Ironically, heartbreakingly, he looked very like Malcolm himself.

With sword and axe in either hand and his mouth open in a roar, this man fell on the king's troops like some kind of vengeful god, his followers streaming in behind him and spreading out, pushing the king's men back and into Torcul's arms.

Halla's mind, apparently as paralyzed as her body, took several stunned moments to realize that the boatmen were neither enemies nor gods, but Malcolm's fighters, that their leader didn't just look like her husband, he *was* her husband. And the king's men, trapped between Torcul and Malcolm, were cut down like grain in the fields.

She had never seen him in battle before. Even with her heart in her mouth, she couldn't look away. The grace and quickness of his swordplay was still there, somewhere, but there was no showing off here. Grace took very much a third place to grim brutality and a terrifying economy of movement, balancing maximum carnage with the preservation of energy.

Beside her, Astrid was laughing and clutching Halla's arm. "He's alive! He's alive!"

And Halla, tears of joy and horror streaming down her face, could think only, *I caused this. I caused this.*

When a horn sounded the retreat and the king's men extricated themselves to fight another day, only a portion of

Malcolm's men pursued them. Malcolm himself, covered in blood, his eyes red and almost alien with battle lust, had pushed his way through to her. She hadn't even known he'd seen her until then, but it seemed he'd always known exactly where to find her.

The men fell back, allowing him access. Her heart jumped into her throat as he strode toward her, his gory sword and axe still gripped in either hand, and came to a halt a foot from her.

"I thought you were dead," she whispered. "I thought you were dead. Forgive me?"

His fingers opened, and the weapons fell to the ground. A strange noise issued from his throat. Then he lunged forward and seized her by both shoulders in a bruising grip. "White Christ, Halla, are you trying to *scare* me to death?"

Emotion surged out of her, and suddenly, she could still play.

"Scare *you?*" she retorted. "You're the one who pretended to be dead."

"I did," he admitted. The frightening violence was dying from his eyes, but only slowly. "I burned the hall myself to draw the king's men into this valley. It was meant to be a trap. The brooch was to convince them of my death so that they'd lower their guard and be slaughtered more easily."

"Well, it looked fairly easy to me," she said, lying through her teeth. But it was too much, and she clutched his tunic in a genuine agony of remorse. "I'm so sorry, Malcolm. I didn't mean to spoil your plan, to cause—"

"Carnage?" he suggested. He grinned suddenly, dragging her against his chest, his bloody cheek pressed to hers. "Cheer up, you didn't actually spoil anything, just brought it forward a little. They still came, and we still defeated them, and you even brought us a few extra men. Only next time, don't terrify me by standing within yards of the battle."

He turned his head, kissing her roughly so that it was some time before she could say excitedly, "Next time? Then you don't mind? I may stay with you?"

"You'd better," he said, swinging around with one arm holding her hard to his side. "I need to know where you are and keep a husbandly eye on you!"

AND SO, SHE had stayed. She'd crept through forests and glens, hidden in caves and huts with him. She'd discussed plans with him and then kept out of the way while he fought, so that his mind would not be distracted by fear for her. She stayed with him while they ejected several royal forces from Ross and raided into Moray and Angus, only to double back and defend Ross again. She would spend some nights in the luxury of friendly halls, others under the stars, wrapped with him in one blanket while they made love under clear skies or rain. When times were good, and in winter, and when it was time for her to give birth, they retreated to Brecka.

Even after Donald's birth, she'd traveled with him, taking the baby with her. Once she had Adam, too, less than a year later, it became more difficult, and she stayed more at home, but the reunions, whether there or elsewhere in Ross, had been frequent and passionate.

These had been years of excitement and danger, companionship and camaraderie, and sheer, joyful *fun*. When they'd been young and imagined they had forever to live and love and change the world to the way they wanted it.

Now, Halla wondered if she'd always known they were doomed, if she'd always realized it was a war Malcolm could never win. The king's forces were greater. It had only ever been a matter of organizing enough of them to find and trap Malcolm, and eventually, inevitably, they had.

Left alone with two children and another in her belly, Halla had known real anger for the first time, anger with the king, with Malcolm, with herself. It had taken time to understand the waste of such energies, and to channel them instead into caring for her people and raising her children to be strong and loyal and good, and to believe in their father.

If the old gods still existed anywhere, they must have been laughing their heads off.

HALLA'S IMPROMPTU RESCUE party camped for the night close to the Moray border. Muiredach was happy enough to sleep under the stars, especially when he had the felicity of joining the soldiers in guarding the entrance to the lady's tent. She seemed so little bothered about being seen leaving Ross that Muiredach suspected she knew exactly where Adam's sentries watched. In any case, they were looking for threats coming inward, not for small, respectable parties going in the other direction.

One of the house guards sat by the fire on watch. His fellow lay down and slept loudly at Muiredach's side. Muiredach, still wakeful, gazed up at the stars and the wispy clouds drifting over them. He wondered how Adam had known his mother would leave. Either he knew her very well, or he had the foresight attributed to him. In which case, did he not know about the Lady Mairead, too?

Reaching down to the purse on his belt, he took out the ring which John had said was a gift to her from Adam, then turned over to let the light of the fire glint on it. If the ring had been meant for Adam's eyes, then even if it was a trap, it probably really did belong to Mairead. The men claimed she did everything for the love of Adam. Which was sad for her when Adam's love appeared to be with his wife. And yet still she'd risked her life and walked back into the lion's den for one kind of love or another. Despite Muiredach's fear for the lady, his heart warmed with admiration for her willing tool.

CHAPTER NINE

GORMFLAITH HADN'T GONE very far with Donald and the men before it struck her.

"This is the first time," she told her brother, "that Mother has ever urged me to go anywhere with you or Adam. The only occasions I've gone with you before are when I begged."

"Well, at least you were spared that indignity today."

It was true, and part of her was joyfully looking forward to new people and different sights. But still… The forest closed in around her, quiet, isolating, as if those thick, immovable trees were preventing her from ever seeing her mother again. Foolish fancy.

"She was getting rid of us all," Gormflaith said bluntly.

"Don't take it personally. Everyone needs time to themselves, and she can't have liked our father not coming home with us."

"Yes, but what's she going to do with that time, Donald?"

"None of our business," he said simply.

Gormflaith looked at him. "She feels things much more deeply than you know. You don't see what she's like when you're gone, when she's afraid of the men coming home without you or Adam. And she won't take comfort from anyone. She can't. When you were taken—"

"I understand, Gormflaith," he said impatiently, although she knew he didn't really. He had, inevitably, a man's blinkered view of his world. "But what do you imagine she's going to do? Hurl herself from the hall roof? Even if she did, she'd only break a bone or two."

Gormflaith scowled at him. "I don't know, but I shouldn't have left her. I have to go back."

Donald groaned with frustration. "You can't go riding about on your own! Mother would annihilate both of us, apart from anything else."

"Give me one man, then. It's hardly far, and he'll easily catch up with you again."

Donald threw up his hands in a mocking gesture of surrender.

SHE DIDN'T KNOW how she felt about her mother having left Brecka, but since she'd taken Astrid and two of the men with her, Gormflaith decided she had less reason to worry than if she'd found her mother moping alone in the hall. The lady had told Sweyn she was visiting in a southerly direction, and the captain's lack of concern helped influence her own.

She slept an untroubled sleep that night, and in the morning set about her own and her mother's duties in the hall and to the people. She had all the straw swept out of the hall floor and changed for her mother's return. And then, leaving the hall doors and windows wide to air the hall in the sunshine, she went to fetch her cloak in order to visit a young village woman who had just given birth.

Reemerging into the main hall, she found a stranger standing in the middle of the floor and stopped dead. Every instinct screamed danger. And none of the servants, none of the men were in sight.

The stranger was tall and dressed for riding in good but worn clothing. He turned at the sound of her footfall and stood very still, but the sun shone directly on her face, blinding her.

"Greetings," she said as pleasantly as she could.

"To you also," the man replied. He was undoubtedly a gentleman, although she didn't recognize the voice. Strangers were both unusual and, as a rule, unwelcome, especially if he was not alone. Where were his followers?

She stepped forward, out of the direct beam of the sun, and saw that he was a handsome man, although there was a dangerous hardness in his face. Most definitely, she had never seen him before. Every nerve in her body tensed for flight, though if it came to a fight, she had a sheathed household knife at her belt, recently sharpened. Deliberately, she prevented her gaze from darting around the hall in search of support. "How might I help you?"

The stranger didn't stir. "That rather depends on who you are."

Who the devil did he think *he* was? In her hall! She lifted her chin. "I'm Gormflaith, the lady's daughter," she said tartly. "Who are you?"

A smile flickered over his face, just touching his suddenly intense eyes, which never left her face.

"I'm Malcolm, the lady's husband," he said, and her heart seemed to jump into her throat. "Which makes me, I believe, your father."

Gormflaith couldn't breathe. She could only stare.

"You?" she whispered. Her legs seemed to be moving without permission, one after the other toward him. Blood sang in her ears so loudly, she wondered if she were dreaming. He hadn't come with the boys days ago when all was prepared for him. Why had he come now? If it was even him.

He stretched out his hand quickly, almost as if he couldn't help himself. She stared at that long, slender hand. If she touched it, she would know.

She wrenched her gaze back up to his face. She'd never seen such naked, boiling emotion. Longing was easy enough to recognize, as was the peculiarly intense joy, all shot through with doubt, even fear, and hope.

Even before she touched him, she knew.

Somehow, she was squeezing his hand between both of hers, pressing it to her lips as her tears dripped on his knuckles. His other hand reached to the back of her head, drawing her against his strong, hard chest in the gentlest embrace she'd ever imagined.

"Father," she got out on a sob. "Father."

"WHERE IS YOUR mother?" The words seemed to be torn from him, even if they sounded deliberately light.

Gormflaith drew back at last, drinking in every feature of his face. Even with the tears still threatening, she couldn't stop smiling.

"South. She should be back today or tomorrow. I was meant to be with Donald, but I was worried about her and came back."

"Worried?" he interrupted. "Why?"

Gormflaith held his gaze. "You didn't come."

His eyes fell, then returned to hers. "Is she angry with me? Hurt? Are you?"

"Not visibly," Gormflaith replied, driven to defend her mother from the stranger who was her father. She refused to discuss her own feelings, which were far too jumbled to sort out. "But you didn't come home. She moved heaven and earth for you. All my life, she's moved heaven and earth for you. And you couldn't even come to your own feast. She deserves better. *Visibly* better."

A rueful smile flickered over his face and was gone. "She always deserved better. I can acknowledge my ill behavior, to you and to her. I will even freely apologize for it as much as you like. But I can't explain it." His arm slid away from her, and he began to walk toward the big table on the dais. "I thought that when I got here, she would understand better than me. She usually did."

He hadn't expected her to have gone.

"She takes care of *all* the earldom," Gormflaith said, following him. "Not just the bits that feed us most." She caught up with him at the table, which was made of oak and polished to within an inch of its life. His hand slid over it, perhaps trying to remember if it was the same one he left.

"She doesn't know you, Father," Gormflaith blurted. "You don't know her."

Again, the half smile flickered and vanished. "It is back to first impressions," he agreed. "And I have begun badly. The last time, it was she who did. Did she ever tell you about our first meeting?"

Gormflaith shook her head, her eyes widening as he began to talk, vividly conjuring up the image of the girl in men's clothing who'd deliberately shot her betrothed. And yet Gormflaith had difficulty recognizing that defiant, turbulent girl in her stern, tranquil mother.

By the time he'd finished on Halla's confession, he was sitting in her mother's chair, his strong hands resting on the carved arms. There were many scars crisscrossing his right knuckles, a swordsman's scars like Adam's and Donald's, and they weren't all faint with age. Had he fought, or just trained, with his captors in Roxburgh?

"Who sits in that chair?" he asked, nodding to the other throne-like edifice beside him.

"Donald, usually. Or Adam. It is yours."

He nodded, but it hadn't really been what he was asking. The MacHeths ruled indisputably in Ross. But in twenty years, who could blame Halla if she had taken a lover to ease her burden? Had he?

This was not her business. It was his and her mother's.

He stirred. "Where are your brothers?"

"Donald's gone north to adjudicate some boundary dispute. Adam is in Tirebeck. You and I are the only family here. Oh, and little Adam!" she added, brightening. "Would you like to meet your grandson?"

"I insist upon it," her father said promptly, springing to his feet in a manner that allowed her a glimpse of the quick, reckless young man her mother must have loved to distraction.

Sweyn and several of the house guards stood straight and alert in the yard, two of them on either side of the hall door, where they must have always been, even while she'd imagined her father to be a threatening stranger. She could tell at once that he'd already made their acquaintance, for they deliberately stared straight ahead as he walked past beside her.

Eithine was discovered sweeping out the main guesthouse while her child sat in the sunshine, playing with a tiny puppy. As her father crouched to compete with the pup for the baby's attention, Gormflaith beckoned Eithine who, blushing and tongue-tied, could barely take her eyes off her legendary lord.

"A beautiful girl and a beautiful child," her father remarked as he and Gormflaith strolled together around the yards and houses that made up her home.

"Eithine's going to marry the blacksmith," Gormflaith told him.

"But Donald is not yet married. Nor are you."

And she was already older than her mother had been when Malcolm had been captured.

"Choices are limited," Gormflaith said wryly. "Which of the great houses of Scotland wishes to ally with the outlawed MacHeths?"

"You may look as far and as high as you wish," her father said.

"To Orkney?" she said quickly.

He blinked. "Harald Maddadson?"

She couldn't help smiling at his quick understanding.

"It would be a sound alliance," he allowed. "But why him?"

"I met him once," she said simply.

Although she quite expected scorn or at least ridicule, her father merely searched her face and nodded as if this was perfectly reasonable.

"I heard his wife had died," he said casually.

Gormflaith stopped in her tracks. "Really?" she said breathlessly.

He raised one eyebrow. "What an unfittingly gleeful expression."

"I know, but I never met her, and I can't help it. I never heard anything about her death."

"Lots of news comes to Roxburgh. Some of my guards liked to talk."

She suspected he'd charmed them as he was charming her. And yet it was so natural, she didn't mind. He'd missed his feast, and yet she found she was glad to have him to herself, just for a little.

MALCOLM HAD HAD no idea how he would feel in Brecka, but he hadn't expected to be comfortable. The lovely girl who was his daughter changed that. Friendly and naive, unworldly and yet wise, she was a wonderful surprise, distracting him from the changes of the decades, from the absence of Halla.

They ate together at the big oak table on the dais, with the men-at-arms and other members of the household in the main part of the hall. The atmosphere of slightly nervous awe had begun to melt into one of genuine warmth as Gormflaith encouraged their easy customs of conversation between the dais and the rest.

"Who plays the harp?" he asked as the instrument caught his eye once again. "Do you?"

"A little. Muiredach taught me." She frowned suddenly, turning to gaze around the hall as if searching for someone. "Where is Muiredach? Sweyn, where is Muiredach?"

"He rode out with the lady," Sweyn called back.

"Oh." She remained still, her knife poised just above the

chicken she was cutting.

For no obvious reason, Malcolm's heart began to beat faster. "Muiredach is the harpist? Does he often travel with your mother?"

"Sometimes," Gormflaith said. "If she's going far, or to a feast or a wedding. But there is nothing like that. And she only took Astrid and two of the men."

"And Muiredach." Something twisted inside him that felt laughably like jealousy. "Tell me about him. How long has he been with you?"

"About ten years. He traveled with his harp, a strolling musician, but he was so good that Mother offered him a place with us. Rumor says he is the son of an Irish king. Or a runaway slave. Or both. He never tells."

"Do you like him?" Malcolm asked.

She laid down the knife. "Why do you ask that?"

"Because I suspect you are a good judge of character."

"I am. I always knew Fergus of Galloway would betray us. But yes, I do like Muiredach. I just don't quite understand why my mother would take him on so short a trip."

Malcolm unfurled his clenching hands, forced himself to pick up his cup and drink. The wine was good. Halla still kept up standards. "How do you know," he asked as mildly as he could, "that the trip is short?"

"Because she took so little. And so few men."

"Astrid came with her from the Isles," Malcolm remembered.

Gormflaith stared at him. "No," she said forcefully. She wasn't denying Astrid's origins.

He knew how she felt. He didn't want to believe either that after twenty-two years, it was his homecoming that had driven her back across the sea to her own people.

The hall doors opened to admit three men, one of them wearing wrist guards and a breastplate. Sweyn, the captain of Halla's house guards, got to his feet.

"Who's this?" he demanded.

"Messenger from the Lady Mairead. The lady bade us bring him here."

Malcolm leaned forward, crooking his finger.

The man in armor strode forward, the men of Ross at his heels. "I seek Adam MacHeth."

Malcolm had no time for that. "Well, you'll have to make do with Malcolm MacHeth. When did the lady bid you come here?"

"Y-yesterday," stammered one of the Ross men as they all stared at Malcolm in wonder. He felt like a rare beast exhibited at a traveling fair.

"Where?" Malcolm demanded evenly.

"Near the coast, just by the River Peffery."

"Who was with her?"

"Two of her own guard, and her lady. And another lad, a servant maybe. I don't know him."

"Did he have a harp?" Gormflaith asked.

The man scratched his head. "There could have been a harp. Something was tied to his saddle. Why?"

Malcolm released him to stare at the supposed messenger instead. "Give me your message to my son."

The man drew in his breath as though debating, then blurted, "The Lady Mairead has been imprisoned by her husband."

"For what?" Malcolm snapped.

"Who knows? Suspicion of adultery or treason for all I know. But if she sent me to Adam mac Malcolm, she must fear it's serious. She wouldn't otherwise endanger him."

"No," Malcolm agreed. "She wouldn't." He refocused his gaze on the messenger, whom he was now tempted to believe. "You also told the Lady of Ross this?"

He nodded. "She took the ring I was meant to give Adam mac Malcolm to prove who sent me."

Malcolm threw himself back in his seat, new fear and pride and frustration threatening to swamp him. If she took the ring, she meant to go herself, use it to prove her identity to Mairead. And keep Adam out of it. That was why she'd sent the man here and not to Tirebeck. She was still his Halla.

Slowly, he became aware that everyone was staring at him. He waved his hand to the men before him. "Sit. Eat." And as they walked away, their shoulders relaxing with relief, he turned to Gormflaith. "It seems I must leave you again, to find your mother."

CHAPTER TEN

MAIREAD JUMPED TO her feet as the key scraped in the bedchamber lock. She'd been sitting in the window seat, ramming at the shutters with Grizel's laundry pole. They'd clearly been bolted or blocked from the outside. Which was annoying, because there was probably enough ivy growing up the walls to be able to climb down. If there wasn't, there was always the bedding for backup—if only she could get out of the window.

At the sound of the key, she threw the pole to Grizel, who tossed it back in the corner where she'd found it, and moved to stand beside her mistress. She shook like a leaf. Mairead was touched by the courage of her timid handmaiden.

She'd hoped for a man-at-arms, or even his captain, anyone she had a chance of manipulating. But it was Brian of Kingowan himself who stood revealed in the open doorway, his unctuous secretary, Cardon, at his back.

"Please, come in," Mairead invited. "Be comfortable, if you can."

She'd been locked in here for almost a week. Under guard, a maid came once a day and set a tray of barely edible food on the floor before scuttling out again. If she couldn't batter her way out the window, Mairead was contemplating leaping over the maid and using the guard's surprise to bolt for the stairs. Or even hitting him over the head with the tray. Her chances of getting out of the house weren't high, but they were better than going insane in one room without any daylight.

Brian of Kingowan inclined his head ironically. The door was locked behind him. Perhaps she should just hit him with the laundry pole. After all, without him to give orders to the contrary, she could soon bend the household to her own bidding.

Her husband, dressed in a long blue tunic heavily embroidered with purple, no doubt to emphasize his position and authority in the world, walked deliberately across the room and lowered himself into the window seat she'd just vacated.

Mairead waited in silence. She allowed herself to smother a yawn.

"You have not been honest with me," Brian said at last.

"When?" she challenged at once.

"You tell me you're going places you never reach. You travel at breakneck speed, and yet you take twice as long to get anywhere than you should. For example, why did it take you more than a week to get here from Glasgow?"

Because I went south first and spent a night in Roxburgh. And then waited in Dundee for my people to turn up. "I went to visit an old friend of my mother's who was dying."

"I trust she made a miraculous recovery," he mocked openly.

Mairead stared at him. "Sadly not. She died. Isobel of Quarter, if your spies wish to check. She was the last of her line."

Kingowan tutted with impatience. "Stop it. Who is your lover?"

"This is *your* story," Mairead said with a contemptuous toss of her head. "You tell me."

"Very well," he said, staring at her. "Fergus, the Lord of Galloway."

Mairead laughed with genuine amusement. "He wishes."

"Then explain why you both went missing at the same time from the king's hawking expedition from Edinburgh last week."

"Who said we did? I was bored and went back to our lodgings—where you found me, if you recall! I have no knowledge of

Fergus of Galloway's movements."

"And yet you visited him in his rooms."

Mairead gazed at him with a provoking smile. "Did he say that? The man's less trustworthy than a fox. You told me so yourself. Why should you suddenly start quoting me his lies as truth?"

It was an arrow shot in the dark, but she saw in his face that it had hit its mark. She just couldn't quite work out yet what reason she could give Fergus for telling such a "lie" to her husband.

"There is, however, a more serious accusation against you."

"More serious than bedding Fergus of Galloway?" she said flippantly. "Heaven forfend."

"Treason," Kingowan barked.

Damn. She kept her gaze steady on her husband. "Nonsense," she said calmly.

"Then you deny visiting Roxburgh regularly and secretly meeting Malcolm MacHeth in his prison?"

He shouldn't have given her the warning. Since he had, she was ready for the name and was even able to smile with amusement.

"Malcolm MacHeth? How in God's name am I meant to have done that? And why? Even the king has released him!"

But she was worried now, for this was clearly the true reason for her arrest. The question about Fergus was Brian looking for any motive for him to lie. Which at least gave her the source of his information.

More worryingly, she wondered if the king knew. If he was about to renege on his pardoning of Malcolm and accuse her of aiding in Donald's escape. The Lady of Ross's whole plan could be crumbling. But at least Malcolm and his sons must be safely home in Ross by now.

Oh, dear God, what if they're not? What if they've been taken?

"It has been alleged," her husband said carefully, "that you are in league with Somerled of the Isles and with the MacHeths, to overthrow His Grace the king."

Mairead laughed. "Oh, who has alleged such a piece of nonsense? Fergus again? Can't you see the man is trying to make trouble between us? And succeeding!"

"And why, pray, would he trouble?" Brian of Kingowan asked with heavy sarcasm.

"Probably because I refused his advances in Edinburgh," Mairead said dryly. "That is the real reason I left the hawking early. To avoid him."

Her husband's face was unreadable. It was Cardon, the secretary, who spoke. "If I may, what would the Lord of Galloway gain from such a petty revenge?"

Mairead shrugged. "Not so petty. He's been courting the King of Scots quite assiduously all year. The Lord of Kingowan's fall could only help him gain position."

"But the Lord of Kingowan wouldn't fall," Cardon said gently. "Only the Lady of Kingowan."

"If you believe that, you're an imbecile," Mairead said with a curl of her lip. "A husband is always tainted by a wife's treason. And the other way around. And even you must see that the Lord of Kingowan has already damaged his position by attacking and arresting his own wife. Even without any talk of treason, what king would trust a man who thus admitted to the weakness of cuckoldry and betrayal in his own home?" She turned away and walked to the bed, where she sat and modestly smoothed her skirts before raising her gaze to her husband's face. "You're doing Fergus's work for him."

Her husband rose without a word and swept from the room, leaving Cardon to scuttle after him.

"Close the door," Mairead said provokingly. "Make it easy for Fergus to rule all of Scotland."

The key scraped in the lock once more, and footsteps faded along the passage. Mairead stared at the door, deep in thought before she became aware of her maid's anxious gaze.

"He'll be back," she said with more confidence than she felt. "He won't keep us here much longer." Unless, that is, he had actual evidence of what she'd done in Roxburgh.

WHEN THE SLIVERS of daylight around the edges of the shutters turned to blackness, Mairead and Grizel prepared for bed.

Mairead was disappointed that her husband hadn't returned to release her. Even if she hadn't convinced him of her innocence, surely the smart thing to do was to *appear* to release her and brush the incident off as a marital quarrel that had got out of hand.

Mairead climbed between the sheets. "Blow out the lamp, Grizel," she said with a sigh, then froze in the act of punching her pillow.

The sweet strains of harp strings drifted past her ears. Mairead glanced at Grizel who, by the lamp, was gazing at her wide-eyed. A moment later, a male voice lifted, deep and true and curiously beautiful, joining the melody of the strings. He sang in Gaelic, not a song Mairead knew, but when she heard her own name, she sat up. The singer praised her famed beauty, claiming that the fierce Somerled himself had wept when forced to send her across the sea to be a bride to another.

Mairead, who doubted that Somerled had ever wept for a woman in his life, let alone one sworn to promote his interests in her new life, sprang out of bed with curiosity and padded across to the window. Kneeling on the seat, she leaned forward, her head against the shutter to peer through the tiny gap which was all her worrying with the laundry pole had managed to achieve.

"Who is it?" Grizel asked. "What's going on?"

"I don't know yet. I can't see anything. Wait." She changed position and peered in the other direction.

There wasn't a great deal of moonlight, but a darker shadow stood in the road, less than fifty yards from where Adam MacHeth had once demanded that Brian of Kingowan hand over the King of Scots. But it wasn't Adam's voice she heard. Nor did the shadow look to be John-shaped. Besides, the figure held a small harp to his shoulder. She could make out the movements as he plucked it and sang with the kind of voice that would melt a woman who didn't have quite so many other things on her mind.

"Who the devil are you?" she wondered, although secretly touched that someone cared enough to try to raise her spirits in this way.

Grizel knelt beside her, peering through a crack in the other shutter.

One of the guards called from the castle ramparts, rudely advising the harpist where to stick his instrument. If anything, the harp got louder, the voice even more plaintive. It was almost funny, especially since it seemed to enrage the sentries.

"Be off with you!" one yelled.

The harpist carried on, although the words of his song changed to a rapid catalog of sweetly sung insults. A moment later, an arrow whined through the air and landed just in front of him. The music and the voice cut abruptly. The harpist fell to the ground and for a moment was lost in the grass and brush at the side of the road.

"Oh no," Mairead said, distressed, but then she saw the figure scramble to its feet a couple of yards away and run like a hare—a curiously effeminate hare—into the darkness. The sentries laughed, calling lewd suggestions after him until someone else, perhaps their captain, shushed them. A few moments later, a door crashed below and several men ran from the house and across the road after the insolent harpist. They'd probably catch him.

"Pity," Mairead said, sinking down on the seat. "I liked him."

"You have support in the community," Grizel said warmly. "I hope the lord heard."

"It might be better for our troubadour if my husband *didn't* hear," Mairead said ruefully. "He hasn't forgiven me yet."

"Forgiven you what?" Grizel asked.

"Whatever it is he truly thinks I've done."

"You do go off on your own," Grizel pointed out. "Often. It isn't…fitting."

While the wind rustled the ivy on the stone wall, Mairead regarded her maid. Was she wrong about Grizel's devotion? Was this the way Brian and Fergus and the king meant to gain her confession?

"You do know the MacHeths, don't you?" Grizel whispered. "I saw Adam MacHeth kiss you the night he robbed us. You didn't mind."

"Who would?" Mairead said lightly. "Every woman should kiss Adam MacHeth at least once. Trust me, it's an experience. He does it very well."

The ivy leaves, or perhaps nearby trees, waved and rushed harder, blowing against the wall outside. Only there was no wind.

"How can you—" Grizel began passionately before Mairead seized her hand and squeezed, nodding at the window. Something definitely clumped against the wall. More like a boot than an ivy leaf. Then, as both women stared, it touched the shutters, too.

Mairead stood, dragging Grizel back with her. Silently, she pointed toward the corner where she'd thrown the laundry pole earlier, and as Grizel hurried across to fetch it, Mairead reached for the nearest heavy object, which happened to be the lamp they'd never got around to dousing.

They were safety measures because Mairead liked to be careful when she could. But in fact, whoever was releasing the shutters was likely to be a friend. Even if it was her husband's men, which was the likeliest scenario. It was just like him to have her released when he imagined she was asleep, and tomorrow he would pretend he'd never held her captive at all. And she would play the game as he wished. For now, at least.

But just in case he'd decided to have her murdered instead…

The shutters opened, one at a time, and someone catapulted himself headfirst through the window. The man fell onto the window seat, already trying to right himself as he bumped onto the floor.

In the glow of Mairead's lamp, an extraordinarily handsome man sat on the floor and gazed up at her. His eyes were a bright, clear blue, his face lean and almost ascetic, the fine bones of his forehead and jaw emphasized by the light and shadow surrounding him. No one she'd ever seen before. There was no way to tell if he was a friend or foe.

He gazed at her, unmoving, for several seconds before dragging his eyes free with what looked like considerable effort and taking in the figure of Grizel in her shift, laundry pole still held high and threatening.

He looked back at Mairead. "Greetings," he said mildly.

"Who in God's name are you?" Mairead asked, lowering neither guard nor lamp.

"Muiredach."

"Just Muiredach?"

"I don't imagine you're interested in a list of my ancestors. They'd mean nothing to you."

"Perhaps not, but I am interested in why you climbed in my bedchamber window."

"I thought it was the only way to see you. If I'm wrong, please forgive me."

Mairead leaned her head to one side. "And why, exactly, are you so eager to see me?"

For answer, he delved into the little purse at his belt and shook something out into his palm. Opening his fingers, he showed her a ring of jet and emerald.

Slowly, she raised her eyes to his face. "Where did you get this?" she asked evenly.

"From a soldier called John, who said you'd given it to him."

"For whom?"

"For Adam MacHeth." His gaze flickered over her as if he couldn't help looking. In all fairness, the lamplight probably showed more than was comfortable through the fine linen of her chemise. She refused to care.

"And what do you know of the fearsome MacHeths?" she mocked.

Her visitor only smiled, a lazy, rather charming smile. "More than you'd think. I taught three of them to play the harp."

She blinked. "That was you?" she blurted. "Playing outside? I thought you'd run away!"

"No, that was for the sentries' benefit, to give me peace to climb up unobserved while they chased a decoy. It was my accomplice who ran away."

"Who was your accomplice?" she asked, feeling as if the whole situation was finally out of her control.

"You wouldn't believe me if I told you. Are you in trouble, lady?"

"I certainly am now. I have a strange man in my bedchamber in dead of night, and I'm wearing no more than a chemise."

"It could be worse. I could be singing you love songs."

"You got that part over with earlier, as I recall."

"I wanted to attract your attention," he confessed. "So that I wouldn't startle you by climbing in your window."

"Only partial success," she murmured. "How did you know which window is mine?"

"Observation. Yours was the only one shuttered all day. Besides, it moved every so often, as if someone were battering at it."

"The wretched thing would not budge."

"It's been barred from the outside with a thick plank of wood. I nearly fell just lifting it."

She regarded him, trying to work out who and what he was. He had gone to a lot of trouble to get in here, and, more to the point, he'd given her a way out. He had the ring she'd sent to Adam.

"Where is John?" she asked abruptly.

"In Ross."

Finally, she lowered the lamp and clearly surprised him by sitting down on the floor opposite him. "Who sent you? It wasn't Adam MacHeth, was it?"

"No. But I have come to rescue you."

She rested her chin in her hand and smiled at him. "How?"

IT WAS A long time since Halla had enjoyed herself quite so much. She was glad that she'd always walked a good deal and kept herself fit, but since running hell for leather was far beneath the dignity of the Lady of Ross, there was both joy and acute pain in the exertion. Pounding through the grassy, muddy ground in Muiredach's spare clothes, doing her best to avoid obstacles and pitfalls in the darkness, she would have laughed aloud if only she could breathe.

By the time she reached the cover of the forest, her legs ached and trembled. She almost collapsed against the first tree in her path. For some time, she could hear only the thundering of her own heart and the sound of her panting, almost sobbing breath. And yet she grinned because it had been thrilling and fun.

Of course, now she had to worry about Muiredach. She'd heard no cries of discovery as he'd climbed up the castle wall like a cat, so she assumed he'd made it to Mairead's bedchamber. A day listening to local gossip had told them she was locked in there by her lord, although not why. Sympathy seemed to be with the bright, exotic lady who always smiled at them, rather than with her dour husband, although none seemed eager to go against him.

Gradually, as Halla's breath quietened, she became aware of other sounds, of creatures scuttling through the undergrowth, rustling leaves and snapping twigs and, surely, a human-voiced murmur.

Hell and damnation to them, they must have sent men after her. Was that not excessive zeal against an insolent musician? Unless they suspected more. Unless Mairead's imprisonment was the trap they'd always known it could be. In which case,

Muiredach could be taken even now.

There was nothing to be done except follow the plan and lead any pursuit well away from the small camp where Astrid and the men waited with her baggage and the horses. Halla crept through the trees to the path, where she deliberately stumbled, and then fled back toward the castle. In a little, when she judged the sounds that might have been pursuit were faint enough, she veered back in the direction she needed to be—as well as she could judge with moon and stars so well covered by clouds.

The trouble was, in the darkness and this unfamiliar area of the wood, she could no longer find the path to orient herself. She had to guess and hurry before the Kingowan men realized she'd changed direction once more. She wished they'd give up and go home. What if they returned just in time to see Muiredach shinning down the castle wall?

Following her instincts, and what she imagined was a patch of slightly paler darkness in the distance, she moved stealthily on. Her straining ears no longer picked up human footsteps or heavier rustling. She'd lost them.

Or so she thought until she paused, leaning against an old oak tree, realizing she'd been right also about the edge of the woodland. From nowhere, something pricked the back of her neck and someone whispered, "Don't move a muscle or you're dead."

Blood surged through her veins in a sickening lurch. Somehow, she suppressed the natural start of fear and merely obeyed, standing very still. It wouldn't take much movement, though, to reach the dagger at her belt.

Every nerve was aware of the movement behind her as the man drew closer without the blade at her neck ever wavering. Close enough to have left his chest unprotected, close enough to strike with her elbow and run.

Unless he pushed his sword into her neck first, which seemed more likely. He was tall, from the faint breath tickling the top of her hair before he bent and searched her. Inevitably, while she stood rigid, his hand found the folds and rolls of Muiredach's too-large clothing and then, more seriously, the belt at her waist and the dagger, which he removed. His hand lingered at her waist, searching.

She itched to slap it before he discovered her sex. But if that didn't lead to him stabbing her, it would, surely, fuel his suspicion that she had something to hide. His hand withdrew slowly. His wrist just brushed against her breast as he straightened, but she thought—she hoped—that she might just have maintained that secret.

For a long moment, he didn't move. Although his body didn't quite touch her, its warmth seeped into her skin. He smelled distinctively male and yet clean. No common soldier or peasant. A captain, perhaps, or even—God help her—the Lord of Kingowan himself.

After what seemed like an eternity, the sword point withdrew and she heard the sound of it being sheathed.

Sheer relief caught at her breath. She took one step away from him, then another and another, and knew that she might yet survive this intact.

"Don't you want your dagger back?"

She closed her eyes, for, of course, she did, for any number of reasons, chief of which seemed to be that it was Malcolm's. And yet every instinct told her to run.

She compromised by halting and nodding. She couldn't make up her mind if it would be better to turn and receive it or wait for him to bring it. But then, why should he? Drawing a deep, almost shuddering breath, she turned to face him.

CHAPTER ELEVEN

A S SOON AS he'd touched her, Malcolm had known she was no boy. The too-large, rolled-up clothes could have been cast-offs from a wealthier man, but no boy had an inward curving waist like that, let alone a soft plump breast. Or troubled to stuff too-long hair inside clothing. And no peasant ever smelled of that subtle blend of rose petals and heather.

The knowledge hit him like a battering ram. For several seconds, he couldn't move, because, after twenty-two years, he again inhaled the scent of his wife. He stood so close, he could feel her tension, her trembling, the very fear she would never give in to. He could take her in his arms right now. If only he hadn't been holding a sword to her neck.

Carefully, he lowered the weapon and sheathed it. And held on to the dagger he'd taken from her as she began to walk away. His eyes devoured her shape in the darkness, while his fingers stroked her dagger, its hilt and its sheath intricately carved. He knew it, too, because it was his. Her brother had given it to him. And he was letting her walk away.

"Don't you want your dagger back?"

She halted, nodding. Some hair had come loose from the neck of her tunic. Self-consciously, she shoved it back in as she turned to face him, her hand held out. It became a game, to see if he could make her speak, make her trust in a stranger.

He closed the distance between them once more. Even in the dark, he could tell she watched him warily, poised for flight. So, he halted a pace away and held out the dagger, hilt first.

Although she didn't snatch it, he could tell she wanted to. Instead, she closed her fingers around the hilt and drew it slowly from his fingers. She inclined her head by way of thanks, still avoiding speech. He was debating what question to ask her, to force her to answer before she again walked away, when he became aware of faint movement in the darkness beyond her.

Her nearness had dulled his instincts. He leapt forward, knocking her to one side even as he drew his sword once more and clashed with another on its vicious plunge downward. Malcolm wrenched the other sword upward, then twisted and crashed the hilt of his own sword into the side of the assailant's head.

He fell like a stone. Malcolm turned, his sword before him as he searched every direction. As he should have done in the first place.

"You seem to have annoyed a few people," he observed, finally re-sheathing his sword. In case his assailant came to quicker than he should, he kicked the man's sword a few feet away and crouched down to feel his clothing and see what he could of him in the dark. A soldier, judging by his array of weapons. One of the Lord of Kingowan's, presumably.

"But you are not one of them."

Malcolm smiled because she'd finally spoken to him. The soldier attacking her had done him a favor, allowing him to win a part, at least, of her trust.

"Certainly not," he agreed. "What did you do?"

There was a pause until he glanced up at her. Then she said, "My companion insulted them."

"And left you to their wrath? I would like to meet this companion." He rose to his feet, gazing down at her.

"It is not what you imagine," she said in a rush.

What he imagined was that Halla and her harpist had already

botched Mairead's rescue. But perhaps she was right. Certainly, he didn't fully understand.

"What did you imagine *I* was?"

"The Lord of Kingowan," she admitted. "What other gentleman would have reason to be lurking in the forest at this hour?"

"Did your companion insult him, too?" he asked wryly.

"Not directly. I couldn't quite understand why he would concern himself with such a minor annoyance."

Malcolm cast his gaze around the woodland, listening intently. "His men shouldn't have either," he murmured. "Come, let me escort you to safety."

"You are very good, but I shan't trouble you. I mean to rejoin my friends." At least she began to walk with him toward the edge of the woods, which was where he'd left his horse if his sense of direction hadn't failed him.

"I would advise against it," he said, and when she didn't respond, he added, "I would advise against the disguise as well. It only works in the distance, in the dark, and as long as you don't speak."

"That was the plan," she said ruefully.

"You intrigue me. What plan?"

"With respect, that is not your concern," she said hastily.

"Then you won't consider me one of your men?"

She peered up at him, and he wondered if she would, finally recognize him. He realized that part of him was piqued that she had not. "I do not know you, sir. And I would not trouble you further."

"Please trouble me," he said, only half in humor. "If I explained to you the extent of my insufferable boredom, you would indeed take pity on me."

"I would be doing you no favors, sir, to involve you in my foolish affairs of the heart."

She could have said nothing more guaranteed to silence him. She might have meant she loved her harpist. She might have been trying to mislead him or to say anything to make him leave her.

Whatever, he couldn't recall ever being so churned up with such painful jealousy.

He could think of nothing to say until, finally, they broke from the edges of the wood, when he said abruptly, "At least let me offer you my horse."

"No, sir," she said firmly, although she did turn toward him and offer him her hand, an oddly graceful gesture in her overlarge men's clothes. "But I do give you my heartfelt thanks. You have restored my faith in the goodness of strangers. Give me your word you will not follow me."

There were ways around such a promise. "I give you my word," he said gravely. He took her hand, small and soft and slender. It was the first time he'd touched her in over twenty years, and yet he remembered. His whole body remembered.

He bowed over her hand, then raised it to his lips. Her breath hitched, and he wondered if, at last, she, too, was remembering. But there was no recognition in her veiled eyes. Or none that he could make out in the darkness.

Now was the moment to reveal himself, to own his right and his need to look after her, to lead the rescue of Mairead. And yet...and yet this story was not yet played out. He'd lost the true moment for directness when he'd failed to go home with their sons.

"Farewell, lady," he murmured, releasing her hand with reluctance.

"Farewell, sir."

He walked away toward his horse, which still stood tethered to a pine tree. At least he didn't have to watch her walk away from him, although his ears strained to catch the direction of her footsteps. She was walking in the direction of the monastery.

He untied the horse, mounted, and walked the animal after her. He could no longer see her. But as he reached the road, he glimpsed her once more, only half-hidden in the nearest trees, with two soldier-shaped men and a woman.

She was safe with others who were used to protecting her.

He tugged the horse to the left, away from her, and rode on to the old priory of Restenneth. Or at least, where it had been.

He was glad to find it still there and still occupied. In fact, as he drew nearer, he saw that it had grown somewhat larger. It was, he remembered hearing, an Augustinian house now, under the authority of Jedburgh Abbey and endowed by the king himself, although the sleepy young monk who opened to his peremptory knock was not best pleased to be disturbed in the middle of the night. He admitted Malcolm grudgingly and conducted him through the hall to the cloisters. It was as they were crossing the courtyard to the guesthouse that they encountered the prior himself.

He was an elderly, gentle-looking monk with unexpectedly sharp blue eyes.

"Another one," the young monk said gloomily.

"Go to bed, Brother Andrew," the prior advised. "I shall take our guest to his quarters."

Although the prior's words clearly made the young monk ashamed, he obeyed the instruction without question.

"Forgive him," the prior said. "He is a different man in the daytime."

"There is nothing to forgive," Malcolm assured him. "I'm not at my best either when wakened up in the middle of the night."

"You are most understanding. And..." He lifted his sharp gaze to Malcolm's face. "And you appear to know the way."

"I stayed here before. More than twenty years ago now, when Aidan was prior. I'm glad to see the guest quarters still the same."

"Somewhat expanded," the prior said with a shade of pride, "Although you are welcome to stay in the old house." He opened the door to the guesthouse Malcolm only vaguely remembered.

Malcolm hesitated. "Forgive me. Is anyone else staying with you just now?"

"We have one other guest. But he, too, prefers privacy. He has quarters next to my own and will not disturb you."

Malcolm stepped inside and found a clean, bare room with a

bed, desk, and chair.

"Twenty years is a long time between visits," the prior observed.

"I've been away," Malcolm said vaguely.

"Far away?" the prior asked with open curiosity.

Malcolm let out a breath of laughter. "A different world."

But the prior clearly misunderstood, for his eyes sparkled with wonder and admiration. "The Holy Land," he breathed. "You've been on crusade."

"It's not something I wish to discuss," Malcolm said. After all, the loyalties of this man, of the entire house, were unknown to him. Aidan had been an ambiguous character with sympathy for romantic causes, including his own dying religion. But the priory stood in the heart of Angus, an earldom constantly loyal to the King of Scots. And one of its nearest neighbors was the equally loyal Lord of Kingowan.

"Of course, of course," the prior said with what he probably thought was understanding. "I'll leave you now. May I bring you food and ale, or will you last until after Nocturns?"

⊰⊱

"I can't," Grizel said simply, stepping back from the window. She knew her limitations, clearly, and recognized that climbing down the sheer wall of the castle clinging only to precariously rooted ivy was well beyond her.

"We could use the bed linen," Mairead said. "I can easily make her a sling to sit in."

"I rather think we're running out of time for that," Muiredach said. "The…my friend will only be able to distract the soldiers for so long. And your linen is so white, it will shine in the dark like a beacon."

Mairead regarded him thoughtfully. He had the lean, ascetic look of a devout monk, and yet his shoulders were broad. He must have scuttled up that wall like a spider, and yet he'd arrived in her chamber barely even out of breath.

"You are stronger than you look," she observed. "Could you carry Grizel on your back as you climb?"

"If the ivy will take our weight."

"No," Grizel said flatly. "Lady, you go. I will stay and hide your absence as long as I can."

Mairead hesitated. Her need to be free was a gnawing pain in her heart, made all the worse, somehow, by the abrupt arrival of the musician and the hope of escape he'd brought with him. More than that, something about him disposed her to trust him. She didn't have much choice in that.

"It might be the best solution," Muiredach said. "If she will be safe—"

"She won't be," Mairead interrupted. Without meaning to, she touched the bruise on her face, then hurriedly dropped her hand as she saw Muiredach's gaze following it. She lifted her chin. "She has no one to protect her but me. No one who counts, that is. When he discovers she's lied and covered for me, he'll kill her. If he truly believes she knew of a connection to Roxburgh, he'll torture her. She has to come."

There seemed little point in hiding such matters now. Grizel and Muiredach both knew her connection to Adam MacHeth and, no doubt, to Malcolm whom she devoutly hoped was safely home in Ross.

Oddly enough, Muiredach neither scowled at her nor berated her. Instead, he bestowed a surprised smile upon her, like a teacher just discovering he has an unexpectedly bright pupil. "Then we had better reconsider. I wish the—my friend were here to do the planning."

"I planned my way in and out of Roxburgh for nearly two years," Mairead said tartly, throwing the last remnants of caution to the wind. After all, the three of them were in this together now. "I'm sure we can manage without your mysterious friend." Her eyes widened suddenly as she stared at him. "Please tell me you haven't brought Malcolm MacHeth here!"

"I have never met Malcolm MacHeth."

Relieved, she turned from him, searching the room for inspiration. Until she saw the laundry pole. "Grizel! They'd let you out to do my laundry, would they not? You could even go outside to dry it."

"Perhaps," she agreed hopefully.

Mairead swung on Muiredach. "What if Grizel then escapes? Another distraction to keep the guards away from her and let me climb down the wall. Then we flee."

Muiredach considered. "Maybe," he said, doubtfully. "But we'd have to do it in the daytime, which means I'd have to bar the window again when I leave tonight, in case anyone notices. Then I'd have to climb up to release you, and we'd both have to get back down, all unseen in broad daylight. It would have to be a spectacular distraction."

He paused suddenly, staring at her, though she had the uncomfortable feeling it wasn't her he was really seeing.

"No," he said, shaking his head. "No. And yet…"

"You're making no sense," Mairead said a trifle tartly.

"Oh, I know." His eyes refocused on her. "Tell me about the castle."

For the next ten minutes, Mairead answered his questions about the castle layout. She even helped him draw a plan on a folded-up piece of parchment, with a sliver of lead he always carried.

Then he threw the lead on the floor, frowning. "It's all too blatant," he said in frustration. "They'll be in pursuit in no time, and sooner or later, I'm afraid they'll catch us. Is there no one close by whom you would trust to hide you? And us."

"There's the priory at Restenneth," Mairead said thoughtfully. "Prior Robert is a good man, and he has no great love for my husband since he spends everything trying to turn this house into a castle and nothing on endowing the priory, which is really quite poor."

"Can we trust him?"

"Entirely. Just warn him in advance." She laughed and removed Adam's ring from her finger yet again. "Give him this as a token of my plea," she advised. "He will recognize it."

He took it from her, lifting his direct gaze from the ring to her face.

"What?" she asked.

"Don't you mind giving away Adam mac Malcolm's token?"

She smiled. "You are a romantic, Muiredach the harper."

To her surprised pleasure, his fair skin actually flushed. "What do you expect in my profession?" He rose to his feet in one smooth, fluid movement. "We need to time this perfectly."

BY THE TIME Muiredach reappeared at their little camp, Halla was so pleased to see him that she didn't even mind that he was alone.

"Could you not see the Lady Mairead?" she demanded, leading him to the still-glowing fire. Astrid ladled the leftover stew into a cup and held it out to him.

He crouched down to take it. "Oh, I saw her, and she didn't seem to doubt her ability to climb down the way I went up. But she would not leave without her maid. She's afraid her husband would kill the girl if he thought she was in league with Mairead's...intrigues. She's probably right, judging by the ugly bruise I saw on Mairead's jaw."

Halla gave a quick frown of distaste. "Then it won't be as quick and easy as we hoped," she said restlessly. She supposed Mairead was being foolish about the servant, but against her will, she rather admired her for it. "I'm not sure how long we can skulk here without drawing attention to ourselves."

"Mairead said there is a priory to the west which would be safe for us. In fact, I'd suggest we all hide there for a few days once we get her out. Wait until they think she must be halfway across Moray or far out to sea before we move."

Halla could see the sense in that. "But we still need to extract her—and the maid—from the castle."

"We need a distraction for the guards and for the Lord of Kingowan himself."

"What could distract him from his wife's misdemeanors?" Halla asked dryly.

Muiredach grimaced and drank some of the still-steaming soup. "I wondered that. And then I thought…you."

"No," Astrid said in tones that brooked no argument.

"No," Muiredach agreed. "But if someone of the lady's demeanor claimed to have seen Adam mac Malcolm in the village, wouldn't they at least check?"

Halla gazed at him thoughtfully. "You know, it's possible you've been wasted as a mere musician all these years. Let us sleep on this, and tomorrow, we'll go to this priory of Mairead's."

CHAPTER TWELVE

As a young man, Malcolm had always found monasteries and churches to be peaceful places. But the monks' chapel was small and the priory closed in behind doors and walls that it seemed he could no longer bear. He'd chosen to come here for reasons of discretion and secrecy. A traveling nobleman retreating into a monastery for a few nights was nothing out of the ordinary. A nobleman camped alone under the stars with no following was a curiosity.

He left morning prayers before the service was even finished, saddled his own horse, and rode out alone. Keeping away from the road, he moved around the edges of the wood until he found the signs of a campsite. The fire had been kicked over. A tent had been pitched and struck. He found signs of about six horses of varying sizes, which accounted for all of Halla's party and a packhorse.

Unless they meant to abandon their baggage or ride two to a horse, they would need another mount for Mairead. But he was sure they hadn't released her already. There had been no sign of her among the people welcoming Halla last night.

Before he returned to the priory, he checked the place he'd struck down Brian of Kingowan's soldier. Both the man and his sword had gone.

It was time, he decided, to ask the prior about Mairead. See if she'd acquired a companion prisoner in the shape of Halla's tame harpist. As he rode back to Restenneth Priory, it struck him there weren't very many animals for such rich, farming land. A few cattle and sheep, a few scattered pigs and goats, but none in any quantity.

Then he remembered his sons had raided here by land and sea only a few months ago. The story went they'd carried off all the cattle in the area, but since the king had proved not to be in Kingowan, Adam had kindly left the lord with one cow and one bullock. Malcolm grinned to himself before he also remembered Mairead's precarious position. It really wouldn't be good for her to be connected with the MacHeths.

The monks and their lay brothers were hard at work in the fields and gardens as he rode through the priory gates. He dismounted in front of the stable and waited for the monk in the doorway to lead another horse out. It was the same monk, Brother Andrew, who'd let him in last night, only now he was smiling as he uttered a cheerful greeting. Malcolm led his horse inside and unstrapped the saddle. He was hanging it up when he heard the young monk's voice again, speaking respectfully to someone he called lord. So, not the prior but, presumably, the house's other shy guest.

Leaving the horse in its stall, Malcolm walked to the side of the door, and from the shadows, peered out into the yard. As the young monk held the horse's head, a slight, wiry man vaulted into the saddle.

Twenty years had not been unkind to Fergus, Lord of Gallo-way. There was a touch of grey in his once-black curls, and even over this distance, his face had developed a distinctly lived-in, craggy look. He didn't have an easy life, preserving his country, which he insisted on calling a kingdom, from England, Scotland, and, by all accounts, the turbulence of his own sons. Malcolm could sympathize. Everyone did their best for their family's position, but in luring Donald into his trap, Fergus had committed one betrayal too many.

Malcolm's fingers closed around his sword hilt.

But this was hardly the place to settle violent scores. Besides, if Fergus was here now, he was surely involved with Brian of Kingowan and with Mairead's captivity. Mairead had said Fergus knew somehow about her visits to Roxburgh. Had he informed the husband? Was he the reason Mairead was imprisoned?

Dear God, what if Fergus ran into Halla? He was one of the few Scottish nobles who had met her and could identify her unequivocally, even in her ridiculous male costume.

And what if Fergus had seen him ride in? Would he know Malcolm MacHeth now? His own wife hadn't, but it had been dark in the woods.

One thing was certain, everyone needed to be warned of Fergus's presence here.

HALLA, ONCE MORE wearing a tasteful, unostentatious gown of fine green wool, was shown to the separate women's quarters.

"We are your only guests?" she asked Sister Ursula. The woman was not a nun, but a lay sister who would see to their needs.

"The only females. We have a nobleman and a crusader on the other side." Ursula opened the door to a room containing a bed and a mattress on the floor.

"My wish is to be private," Halla told her.

Ursula shrugged. "I can serve you meals here in your room. And you may come and go from here without using the main entrance. Look." The woman pointed to the end of the passage. "Turn the corner and walk up the steps. The door remains locked at all times, but the prior will give you a key."

"That will be most helpful," Halla said warmly.

Ursula shrugged again as if she couldn't understand Halla's concerns. "The gentlemen are as concerned with privacy as you are. You are unlikely to meet them even if you dined in the refectory." She hesitated, then beckoned Halla once more to the chamber door, from where she pointed to the large tapestry at the near end of the passage. It depicted a somewhat gory hunting scene and seemed rather old and worn. "That divides the women's quarters from the refectory. You might occasionally hear voices, but the brothers are a peaceful lot. And the tapestry doesn't just hang. It's nailed in place."

Halla nodded. Against marauding invaders, it was hardly a defense, but in this place, it should suffice. "I am hoping to meet another guest here for a few days. A lady who has, I believe, been generous to this house."

Ursula's eyes widened. Isolated or not, they all clearly knew of Mairead's troubles. "She will be most welcome as always. Does the prior know?"

"Of course."

Sister Ursula bowed. "You are a good lady."

As Halla went into her bare chamber, she reflected that Ursula might not say the same if she knew that it was Halla's sons who had plundered the land only a few months ago with her blessing.

Closing the door behind her, Astrid said, "This is ridiculous! If we are separated from the men, how will we speak to Muiredach, or summon the men?"

Halla brushed that aside. "More to the point, why would a traveling nobleman and a crusader stay here when Kingowan is only a few miles farther along the road? And on the main coast road, too."

Astrid shrugged. "The crusader is probably a holy kind of a man who likes to feel closer to God. Or perhaps he's dying of some wound or disease contracted in the Holy Land."

"Perhaps." It was something else to be considered as she thought over their hastily developed plan to free Mairead. Halla lay down on the bed to think, while Astrid pottered with their few possessions and then went off exploring.

Halla thought about the man in the darkness who had helped

her last night. Kingowan itself had looked very quiet, while the places that should have been quiet, like the woods at night, and this hardly huge or wealthy priory, seemed unusually busy.

Astrid bustled back in high excitement. "Lady, come and speak to the man!"

"What man?" Halla asked, sitting up.

"Behind the tapestry. He asked to speak to my lady."

Halla frowned. "Is it one of our men? Muiredach?"

Astrid shook her head impatiently. "Of course not. Come, lady, it must be important."

Uneasily, Halla rose to her feet and followed Astrid from the room and along the passage to the tapestry at the far end. It stretched from the low ceiling to the stone balustrade that ran some five or six yards. Close-to, she could see the short pillars and arches that had been built upon it were now blocked off by the tapestry. The spars of the balustrade itself had been covered by a wooden board at the other side. At this hour, the refectory beyond it should be quiet, the monks busy with their work.

Halla stood facing the tapestry, feeling somewhat foolish as well as alarmed.

Astrid said, "Sir?"

"I'm here." Low and deep, the voice reverberated in Halla's memory with a swirl of excitement. The man from last night?

"I brought the lady," Astrid said.

Halla rested her hands on the balustrade. "You may speak."

There was a faint pause, then the same voice said, "Forgive the unorthodox communication. Since we both appear to value our privacy, this seemed the best way to warn you."

"Warn me of what?"

"That the Lord of Galloway is staying in this house."

Halla stared at Astrid in consternation. The one man in Scotland, practically, who would know her and betray her. Aloud, she said, "Why should you imagine the Lord of Galloway is of any interest to me?"

A faint breath of laughter was the only reply to that. She gave him a moment, but when he said no more, she prompted, "Sir?"

There was no response.

"He's gone," Astrid said. "What a strange man. He must be the crusader if Fergus is the nobleman."

"Hush," Halla commanded, dragging her woman with her back to their chamber, where she closed the door. "I think he is someone who helped me last night, so I'm prepared to believe his heart is good. Although how he can know Fergus is a threat to us *does* worry me. I'm not sure now we shouldn't flee back to Ross as soon as we can extract Mairead."

"It's a long way back to Ross. Do you really think we can outride men who know this country better than we do?"

They were her own words thrown back at her. "I trust no one anymore," Halla said ruefully. "On the other hand, Fergus being here, now that we know it, might just help us."

"How?" Astrid demanded.

"We need a distraction," Halla reminded her. "What better a distraction than the Lady of Ross?"

MALCOLM RESADDLED HIS own horse and rode out of the monastery gates. He wore a brimmed hat pulled over his face and carried his helmet tied to the saddle. His sword was at his back, and his daggers at his belt, although for the moment, his cloak covered them.

He was fairly sure he understood Halla's plan—to hide out in the priory for a few days while the Kingowan men pursued phantoms. She had to be warned of Fergus's presence, even if she used it, as he suspected she would, to supply the phantom. He would spare her that danger if he could.

As he'd hoped, he found fresh tracks leading to Kingowan that he imagined were Fergus's.

Mairead's husband, clearly, had ambitions to be a great man.

He'd built himself a substantial stone house, with defensive wooden ramparts all the way around. In time, surely, he'd turn it into a proper castle. Malcolm watched it from the cover of the trees, letting his horse chomp idly upon the grass and leaves it could reach. Some of the leaves were beginning to fade and fall as autumn deepened. It seemed a lifetime since he'd watched the seasons change in his own country.

A couple of men strolled around the ramparts in either direction, pausing for a few words whenever they met. One upper window was still shuttered, presumably Mairead's.

Malcolm was no saint, and Mairead was both brave and beautiful. He'd been tempted many times to take her in his prison cell. She'd been willing, eager even, but some chivalrous or fastidious instinct had held him back. She'd been his son's lover, for one thing. For another, she'd reminded him just a little of Halla.

Halla, whom he'd finally held in his arms once more, in the dark. Halla, who hadn't known him. He couldn't deny it hurt. But she'd come to Angus to pay her debt to Mairead, to pay *his* debt. He didn't know what it meant. His need to speak to her, to be with her, felt like pain. And yet something equally powerful held him back. Malcolm, who'd never in his life given in to trepidation, had the horrible feeling it was simple fear.

Movement at the house dragged him out of his reverie. Someone ran down the front steps as a horse was brought around. Fergus of Galloway was preparing to mount. Hastily, Malcolm threw himself onto his own horse and rode hell for leather through the trees, swerving around so that he could come at Fergus from the south before the Lord of Galloway could turn off toward the priory.

Perhaps it was the exhilarating speed of his ride, but his whole hand itched to draw his sword, to pay Fergus back for this petty revenge on a brave lady, to punish him for betraying Donald as he had. But he was no longer the reckless youth who'd plunged his country into war for a crown. And so, he merely pretended to be, slowing as he approached Fergus and snatching off his hat with a grin. He let his face fall as if he'd just recognized the Lord of Galloway, and hastily slapped the hat back on his head, spurring his horse back to a full gallop—though not before he'd seen the astonished recognition on Fergus's face. And a sudden start of fear. For that instant, Fergus thought he was dead. And Malcolm was fiercely glad.

Malcolm galloped on down the road, knowing he'd left Fergus only two choices: to pursue Malcolm on his own or to get help from Kingowan. After all, just by his presence in Angus, Malcolm was breaking the terms of his release. He'd promised to stay in Ross for a year.

Go to Kingowan. Go to Kingowan. As he flew past the house, he allowed himself to glance back over his shoulder. Fergus was galloping in his wake, not yet at the house.

"Be sensible for once in your miserable life," Malcolm muttered aloud. "You know you'll never beat me on your own."

"Is she as beautiful as everyone says?" Halla asked as they rode through the woods toward Kingowan. Deliberately, she kept her voice idly curious, but she couldn't bring herself to look at Muiredach in case he guessed her true interest.

"The Lady Mairead?" he said, equally casual. "Yes, if you like redheads." He paused as if suddenly ashamed of such grudging praise. "She is beautiful, even with the bruise, but I think it's her sheer vitality that is so winning."

Of course. There would have to be more than mere beauty to win Malcolm. "Beauty, courage, and vitality—that is quite a combination of charms. I suppose she has also wit and learning."

Now she did feel Muiredach's gaze on her averted cheek and knew she should never have brought up the subject.

"Wit, certainly," Muiredach said with a shrug. "If she has learning, it's less obvious."

Halla was relieved to glimpse the house at Kingowan through the trees and stopped to examine it as minutely as she could through the distance and the obstacles. She pushed nearer, narrowing her eyes.

"Something's wrong," she said at last. "I can't see any guards. It's a trap."

"Not necessarily," Muiredach argued. "They might have gone inside, or ridden out for any number of reasons."

"Do you want to call it off for today, lady?" one of the soldiers asked, apparently disappointed.

Slowly, Halla shook her head. "We have what we want—no guards to see what we do. We have to try. But at the first sign of trouble, I'll give away my identity and lead them north before doubling back."

"Then you're not going into the house in search of Fergus?" Muiredach said in clear relief.

"I doubt he's there. I expect they've all gone hunting."

"Hopefully leaving the Lady Mairead unguarded. So, lady, you'll wait in the cover of the trees while I climb up for her? Tomas can bring the maid to you—"

"Not quite," Halla said. "Someone has to be inside the house to make sure there is no attention on Mairead while you free her. We agreed on that."

"Yes, but that was before we knew the soldiers would be gone anyway!"

"We don't know that they've gone. I'll go in and give you the signal as agreed."

Leaving Muiredach clearly unhappy, Halla rode sedately down the road toward the house, accompanied only by one man-at-arms. Muiredach kept pace with her, using the woods and then the long grass as cover.

A servant opened the gate and let her in. "Please give my compliments to your lady, and ask if I might beg refreshment from her. My name is Halla, daughter of Gillebride, and I've been traveling a long way to meet my husband in Moray."

"The lady is not here," the servant said with a flicker of his eyes. Like most, he didn't like lying. He probably didn't care for what was happening to his mistress either. "But come and rest in the hall. The lord will be back soon."

Halla inclined her head graciously and urged her horse after the servant. When she dismounted, she bade Tomas stay with the horse for she would not be long, and asked the servant if he would kindly bring refreshment out to man and beast.

"I don't wish to tarry," she explained. "I want this dreadful journey over as soon as possible."

In the main hall, a rather slimy individual rose to greet her. Sharp-eyed and servile, he bowed low and introduced himself as the lord's secretary.

Halla again gave her name and story. "I am sorry to miss the lord and lady of the house. The king himself told me of their hospitality, so I hope they will not think ill of me for claiming it without their presence." Well, the king's words had been reported to her via Mairead and Adam.

The secretary immediately looked impressed by the mention of the king, but before he could inquire further, Halla asked if the lord and lady would return today.

"The lord has ridden out on important business of the king's," the secretary said with a smirk. "I don't imagine he'll be long. He's gone off to capture Malcolm MacHeth."

It was as well that the MacHeth name was so infamous. It probably provided reason enough for her blanched cheeks and the sudden tendency of her body to sway like a suddenly rootless tree.

"God save us," she got out, pacing away from him. "I thought that crisis was over. I thought the king freed Malcolm MacHeth and his people disbanded."

"Indeed. And he is meant to stay in Ross, not ride around Angus, threatening the king's servants."

"Is that what he's done?" It was a mistake, surely a mistake, the sighting of a threatening stranger at a time when every danger was given the surname MacHeth. Either way, she was here to free Mairead and mustn't lose sight of that.

"He won't be given the chance," the secretary said with a sneer.

"Forgive me," she said seriously, "but does the Lord of Kingowan have enough men with him to fight, let alone to capture Malcolm MacHeth?"

"Malcolm is alone, and my lord has his entire following with him."

It couldn't have been better, save for the dreadful fear clawing at her stomach that Kingowan truly was chasing Malcolm. To have him taken from her before they'd even met again…

But that was ridiculous. Malcolm had no reason to be here. Except Mairead.

Mairead was young and beautiful and brave, and she alone had comforted him in the final year of his imprisonment. No wonder he hadn't come home.

The pain of it, even half-expected as it had always been, weighed down her limbs. Yet somehow, she managed to lift her hand, as though in nervous fear, and push the shutter over the window, blocking out the chilly breeze.

The secretary's hand almost closed over hers as he gently drew back the shutter once more. "You have nothing to fear, lady," he said confidently.

She had hoped to have time and leisure here by herself to make the signal. As it was, she had to sit and accept the refreshment she had asked for, and hope that Muiredach had seen the shutter close, however briefly.

IN HER LOCKED and darkened bedchamber, Mairead paced like a caged animal. Last night's encounter with the strange if handsome harpist already felt like a dream. If it wasn't that Grizel had clearly had the same dream, she would have discounted it all as nonsense. As it was, she'd packed Grizel off to do the laundry as planned. Only moments later, she'd heard some commotion both inside and outside the house. At one point, she was sure she heard Fergus of Galloway's voice, both eager and angry.

I was right. He has accused me of visiting Malcolm and no doubt arranging Donald's escape. I need to be away from here before they kill me.

But then she heard her husband's barked orders, sounds of rushing feet and clanking weapons from all over the house, and she was tempted to batter down the window shutter that Muiredach had rebarred. She was afraid Muiredach and his mysterious ally had been taken or were about to be. Her life was worth nothing now, yet for some reason, she felt worse for the harpist, who had no connection to her, no reason to help her. And yet he would die for her if she didn't manage to escape and somehow save him, too.

Her increasingly wild plans were interrupted by the sounds of men and horses leaving at speed and galloping north along the road to the coast. No one came to her door. She heard no screaming. Surely, if there was additional danger here, Grizel would have come back to warn her. No, this could be merely another distraction to allow Muiredach to climb up to her again.

Excitedly, she strained her ears, listening for sounds of his climbing. But she heard nothing. Eventually, she returned to her abandoned needlework—not her strong point; the stitches were ungainly, but at least it gave her something to stab. In spite of herself, her ears strained for sounds outside, or for Grizel's returning footsteps. Perhaps Muiredach had just been part of some elaborate plan of her husband's—or Fergus's, more like—to make her incriminate herself.

She was sure she heard a strange woman's voice at one point, but nothing more interesting until a rustling, tearing sound against the wall outside, followed by a grunt and a bump as if a boot had hit the wall. Mairead sprang to her feet, her heart beating hard.

Muiredach. It had to be. She felt stupidly helpless, just waiting. She'd begun to understand what Malcolm MacHeth had contended with for over twenty years. Some men in his position might have assuaged such feelings of powerlessness by exerting bodily control over Mairead. God knew she wouldn't have minded. But Malcolm was different. Even if the bond with his wife had loosened, he'd never have taken her, just *because* he no longer controlled the rest of his life.

The bar was wrenched off the shutters, which flew open with a little too much enthusiasm. Muiredach wobbled precariously until Mairead threw herself forward and seized him by the shoulders, and the two of them almost fell back into the room.

"God, have I hurt you?" Muiredach said anxiously, perhaps because her shoulders shook beneath him. She slid her arm down from her face to show him that she was laughing, and his handsome face broke into a grin, not entirely free of admiration. His face was only an inch from hers.

"Well," she said, just a little breathlessly, "comfortable as this is, don't we have a wall to climb?"

"You could let me catch my breath," he suggested.

"Not in this position. What if my husband came in?"

Reluctantly, it seemed, he eased off her and drew her into a sitting position beside him. She was almost disappointed. "Where is your husband?" he asked evenly.

"I don't know. I think he left with a lot of the men an hour and more ago. I wondered if that was you distracting him."

"We never got the chance," Muiredach said. "Fate must be on our side. What are you taking?"

Leaning back, she tugged her cloak from the bed and swung it around her shoulders before spreading her arms.

"You travel light," he observed.

"I do. But I also have a box stored at the priory."

He nodded, giving nothing away, and stood up to peer out the window. "I think we'd better go. Are you sure you can manage this?"

She twitched one eyebrow at him. "It's not my first time. Why do you think I chose this chamber?"

He insisted on going first, presumably to break her fall if necessary. Mairead swung herself out the window, loving the blast of wind against her face. However, it wasn't the easy climb she'd found it previously. The ivy, which wasn't so very old or well established, had been damaged by Muiredach's previous ascents and descents and tended to break and move.

More than once, Muiredach seized her scrabbling foot and shoved it into some tiny crevice. All the while, she strained her ears for any sign that she'd been seen, or that her escape from the room had been discovered. But for the most part, she concentrated so hard on her climb down that she didn't even see the man holding two horses until she slid the last few feet to the ground and ended in Muiredach's arms. Over his shoulder, an armed stranger gazed at them with interest.

"Muiredach," she whispered. "Run!"

"No need," he replied with irritating nonchalance. "He's with us." Muiredach turned, jerking his head toward the house door, and the man nodded.

Muiredach led her around the house and through a kitchen garden to the outer wall, which stood as high as his head. He took a run at it, throwing himself halfway up and scrambling up the rest. Throwing one leg over, he sat astride it and reached down to help her. However, Mairead had been used to doing things alone, and by this time, she merely hauled herself up the last few inches and smiled at him before dropping down the other side. She thought he laughed as he jumped after her. Exhilarated, she was happy enough to seize his hand and run with him for the cover of the trees, almost like mischievous children.

Here, there was another bad moment when she came suddenly upon another armed man with Grizel, but since the maidservant merely hurled herself at Mairead with joy, she decided that he, too, was with Muiredach.

Muiredach untied one of the large, waiting horses and boosted Mairead into the saddle before mounting behind her. As his man and Grizel mounted the other horse, he seemed anxious, peering through the trees.

"Who are we waiting for?" Mairead asked curiously. "Your mysterious ally?"

"Yes." His shoulders relaxed suddenly, and he grinned. "Let's go. We'll head north first to mislead any pursuit, then double back."

"My husband rode northward," Mairead warned, urging her horse after his. "What if we run into him returning?"

"We keep in the cover of the woods." He was distracted, looking constantly behind him and through the trees towards the road. Mairead, slightly piqued by his inattention, although she knew she had no reason to be, watched his frowning face instead.

"Why?" she demanded as they slowed. The thud and rustle of other approaching horses made the question suddenly urgent. "Why are you helping me?"

Muiredach's lips curved up. Two horses broke through the trees, one carrying an armed man, the other a lady. A wink of sun glinted off the man's sword and axe and seemed to shine right through the lady's veil, giving her a blinding, golden halo.

"In truth, because *she* wished it," Muiredach said.

If the romance of the whole episode crumpled for Mairead then, there was no time to dwell on it. The lady moved forward, and Mairead saw, with even greater curiosity, that she was beautiful and elegant to the point of regal. As her horse picked its way toward them, the lady's gaze found and locked with Mairead's. Although her expression was clear and emotionless, it didn't mean there was none there. She just hid it perfectly. She was everything Mairead wished to be. And with the sudden thought came a glimpse of knowledge, even before the woman spoke.

"You must be the Lady Mairead. I am Halla. Of Ross."

There wasn't enough warning, there could never have been

enough warning for this. She had no control over her face or voice. "You?" she whispered. "You came all this way for *me*? Dear God, lady, you can't be here."

"I received the news first. My family owes you a debt that can never be repaid. We were fortunate to find your husband from home." The lady's eyes didn't blink. "Apparently pursuing Malcolm mac Aed."

Mairead threw back her head in distress. "He is here, too? This is madness!"

"Or some false sighting," the lady said with apparent indifference. "As I believe used to happen with my sons."

"Then he did not come with you?"

"Like you, I have grown used to traveling unencumbered by husbands."

Sheer emotion broke from Mairead in a choke of laughter. She hadn't expected to like the Lady of Ross. She wasn't even sure she did. "I have no words for my gratitude."

"Nor do I," the lady said graciously. "I propose we ride on to the next village, and let them see you going northward. And pray your husband is still halfway to Moray."

"There is something else," Mairead said, turning to ride beside the lady. "I'm sure I heard the voice of Fergus of Galloway in the house. He is probably with my husband."

"He was staying at the monastery," the lady said calmly. "Let us hope he has gone home."

"Part of me wishes he will still be there so we can kill him in his bed."

The lady shrugged. "His betrayal of Donald made it possible for you to free both my son and Malcolm mac Aed."

"You give me too much credit, lady," Mairead muttered.

"No," she said, spurring forward.

"Why didn't you tell me?" Mairead demanded as she found herself riding by Muiredach.

"Tell you what?" Either he was playing for time to think or he wasn't paying attention.

"That your ally is the Lady of Ross."

"Because I didn't think you'd believe me."

She stared at his profile, letting her horse find its own way to the road. "And you wanted to punish me for being her husband's lover?" she said boldly.

"I didn't know that you were. Until now. Rumor links you rather with Adam mac Malcolm."

Anger and something very like disappointment fought their way through her. "I see now that the lady is worth ten of a man who relies on stories."

He turned and met her gaze, his own mild, but surely veiled, just like the lady's. "Why should that surprise you? Stories are my life, or at least my profession. I am the lady's harpist."

✦•——❖——•✦

CHAPTER THIRTEEN

H ALLA SAW AT once that Mairead had not been expecting her. She supposed Muiredach had deliberately given her that advantage, though it didn't feel like one. Mairead was everything she'd feared. Beautiful, mysterious, fascinating…and young. Her bravery and loyalty had never been in question. How could Malcolm, imprisoned alone for twenty-two years, not have fallen in love with her?

Which, of course, made it more likely that he really had come south to rescue her, if not to be with her on some more permanent basis, and that it really was Malcolm MacHeth whom Mairead's husband pursued. Headlong flight in their wake would achieve nothing. Even if they captured Malcolm, what good could two men-at-arms and a harpist do against twenty or fifty men, or however many Brian of Kingowan had with him?

And so, ignoring the clawing fear in her stomach, as she'd learned to so long ago, she rode through the next village. The people working in the ridged fields all stared and waved at Mairead, who smiled graciously and put one conspiratorial finger to her mouth to plead their silence. Some laughed with delight, although some, inevitably, would tell her lord when he inquired for her.

A little later, they turned west and, avoiding settlements and woodsmen, rode hard for the priory. Erring on the side of caution, Halla insisted that she and Mairead and the maid enter alone via the women's private door.

Astrid all but fell on her neck in welcome, although she quickly remembered her manners and curtseyed with all respect to the Lady Mairead. Ursula, summoned to bring them food, smiled with delight at Mairead and promised her all the sanctuary she wished.

"Any sign of your male guests?" Halla inquired as the lay sister began to bustle away.

"I believe both are still out, my lady."

"The secrecy of my guest's presence is vital," Halla reminded her.

"I know. Bless you both."

"Who are they?" Mairead asked bluntly when they were alone.

"One is certainly Fergus. The other may or may not be a friend, but we cannot afford to trust him." The latter was as much instruction to herself as to Mairead.

Ursula brought dinner to the table in Halla's bedchamber and then hurried off to prepare the cell next door for Mairead. Without a word of instruction, Mairead's maid served the three other women.

After Halla had told the story of the day's adventure to Astrid, the conversation was not lively. Mairead appeared tongue-tied and uncomfortable, twisting the daggers in Halla's heart, for the only reason such a woman as Mairead would be uncomfortable was that she had wronged Halla.

But Halla would be no one's victim. And so, she regarded Mairead pleasantly as she ate the hearty soup before her. "You have made a big impression upon my family," she observed.

"As has your family on me," Mairead said at once.

"Did you really do all this, risk so much for love of my son?"

Mairead smiled, as though grateful for the safe ground. "Not entirely. I am one of those restless people who constantly seek excitement. I married Colban, your brother's captain, because my father bade me. I married Brian of Kingowan and carried messages to and from Malcolm mac Aed because your brother bade me. Having said that, there is very little I would not do for Adam mac Malcolm."

"Nor he for you," Halla said, knowing it to be true. Adam was nothing if not loyal.

Mairead met her gaze. "Is that why you came here to help me?"

"To prevent my sons from coming? Partly. But mostly because it was I who received the message first, while I was journeying southward within Ross."

Mairead smiled suddenly. "I like your style, lady. You travel light, and yet with your own harpist."

"Muiredach is as much friend as musician. He has become indispensable to me."

Mairead looked back at her soup and took another mouthful. It seemed Muiredach intrigued her, but she would ask no more, either because she misconstrued Halla's words or because she had too much pride. Or both.

⇶⋘

BY THE TIME Ursula cleared away their dinner, the monks were preparing for their supper. The women could hear the clanking of plates and the quiet, cheerful voices seeping through the tapestry and boards from the refectory. Since neither of the priory's male guests had returned, Mairead chose to go with Ursula to the chapel for Vespers. Grizel and Astrid, who appeared to serve the Lady of Ross, went with her.

"You have been with the lady a long time," Mairead observed to Astrid as they followed the lay sister from the women's quarters, through the cloisters toward the chapel.

"Since she was born, more or less."

Clearly, there would be no gossip to be had from that quarter. Instead of prying into Halla's life as she'd meant to, Mairead said, "Then you have never married?"

"I married a man of Ross. A good man. He died fighting for the sons of Malcolm mac Aed."

"I'm sorry," Mairead said. "I, too, was married to a good man once." Roaring, fun-loving Colban, first out of the boats to fight, and last to get back in, until he'd never come back at all. He'd burned bright and burned out, Mairead's first love whom she barely remembered. Perhaps because Adam MacHeth had blocked him out so soon. That, too, had been an intense affair, and yet it felt almost as much part of her childhood as loving, faithless Colban. It was his father Malcolm who could have been her great love. Who surely would have been, had it not been for the lady who had rescued her from the prison within her own home.

She tried to draw peace from the beauty of the monks' singing. She tried to concentrate on the meaning of the prayers. But inevitably, her gaze wandered, searching for dangers, for interest. As she glanced behind her, she saw Muiredach, watching her.

She couldn't help it. She stuck out her tongue and turned back, though not before she'd glimpsed the surprised laughter in his face. At least that made her smile. Until she remembered that he, too, loved the Lady of Ross.

Unexpectedly, Muiredach caught up with her again as they left the chapel after the monks.

"That was an impious gesture," he observed with mock loftiness.

"Only if it gave you impious thoughts."

It surprised a breathless laugh from him. "Actually, it did."

"Then I would suggest the impiety was yours alone."

"While yours was meant to be purely insulting."

"Purely," she agreed.

"How have I offended you, Lady Mairead?"

She considered. "By assuming."

"Assuming what?"

She laughed. "Take your pick. You don't know whether to despise me for being Adam's whore or his father's."

At last, she'd managed to shake him. Shock stood out in his eyes. He even caught her arm in some instinctive gesture to placate, or perhaps even protect. "No one could despise you after what you have done. As for the rest, God knows I am no arbiter of morals."

"But you love the lady. You feel for her."

"I worship from afar," he said with a hint of self-deprecation. "Like everyone else."

"And yet you're close enough for it to hurt more." The words spilled without permission, but she refused to bite her lip as he gazed at her, his perceptive eyes reading more, no doubt, than she wished.

"Is that how it is for you?" he asked curiously.

"I am no threat to her. I told Donald, so, but God knows if he'd ever remember to explain to her."

"Did you love Adam, too?"

"Passionately," she said with a sigh.

"Then I'm glad I returned his gift to you."

"I am glad to see him happy. With his wife of all unlikely people."

"You are a cynic, lady. Or try to be."

She took his arm. "You are so wise, Master Harper. Or try to be. Shall we take a walk?"

ALTHOUGH MAIREAD AND Astrid went to the chapel for Vespers, Halla felt too on edge to pray.

It was just after Vespers that Ursula reported the return of the crusader, so there was no question of any of the women attending Compline. The house quietened quickly after that as the monks sought their few hours of precious sleep.

Halla, listening to the deep silence beneath Astrid's gentle snores, found herself wondering if Malcolm's prison cell had been larger or smaller than this tiny chamber. Not for the first time, she wondered how he'd stood it, not for mere months or even years, but decades, and her heart ached. He could not be the same man she'd known, not now.

Rising from the bed, still fully dressed, she quietly left the cell and walked as silently as she could along the passage, past Mairead's door and Ursula's, around the corner, and up the few steps to the private outside door. Her fingers hesitated on the latch and then withdrew. Turning, she paced all the way back again.

Although it wasn't yet quite dark, she could no longer make out the colors or figures in the large tapestry. Anyone or no one could stand behind it. She knew that for everyone's safety, she should return to her chamber, and yet she walked deliberately past her door to the tapestry, where she paused, listening intently.

She imagined it moved ever so slightly; she imagined she heard someone breathing over the drumming of her own heart. She couldn't afford to believe it. Slowly, she walked the length of the cloth. Someone might have walked with her on the other side, or it might have been the echo of her own, soft footfalls. She stopped when the balustrade became a solid stone wall. No footsteps sounded, no voice spoke. And yet she imagined... No, surely, she *knew*.

Slowly, she lifted one hand and touched the fabric of the tapestry with her fingertips.

"Lady," came a breath from the other side.

Her heart almost jumped into her throat. Now was the moment to retreat before he knew for certain that she, that anyone, had ever been there.

And yet she murmured, "You are the crusader."

She could actually hear the sardonic amusement in his low voice. "No. It was a misunderstanding I chose not to correct."

Him. It was definitely him, not Fergus. "Were you...*helping* us today?"

"In my own small way."

"Why?"

There was a pause, as if for consideration. "Chivalry?"

"You make it a question," Halla observed.

"I suspect my motives are more selfish than chivalric, but at least the outcome is the same. Were you known?"

"Were *you*?" she countered.

"Only when I chose to be."

He didn't know her, didn't trust her. "I am not the lady you rescued today," she confessed.

"*I* didn't rescue anyone."

She closed her eyes, feeling her way. "Why are you here?"

"For you."

She squeezed her eyelids shut. If that was true, if he was—

"But perhaps your heart is given to another." He spoke lightly enough, and yet surely, he cared for the answer. He wouldn't otherwise have said it.

"I have no heart. It broke long ago."

"So did mine. But it's growing back."

"Practiced words from a man who saw me once in the dark in oversized boy's clothes. Run, before you realize you're talking to the wrong woman."

He didn't reply, and her hand slipped down the tapestry to the cold stone balustrade. She hadn't wanted to be right. She wasn't who he thought she was. She hadn't wanted to heap more pain on herself. He had indeed run, but at least her pride remained intact.

A movement in the growing darkness at last penetrated her misery, and she turned toward it with a gasp.

"Don't," breathed the blur, that was all she could see before warm hands closed over hers, pinning them to the balustrade, preventing her from facing him. "Please, don't."

"Why not? Can't you take the truth?"

The whole length of his body touched her, hemming her in.

Her face brushed the tapestry which smelled old and musty.

"What truth?" he breathed in her ear. "That you love another?"

"I've only ever loved one man in my life. I only ever will." She twisted her head around, to prove she wasn't afraid. "Why do you speak of it at all?"

"Why do you think?"

A beard scraped against her cheek, and then his mouth closed on hers in the darkness. Hot, hungry, dizzyingly tender.

Years, a lifetime fell away, and she knew beyond doubt. Her body, her every sense remembered. She couldn't help the tears flowing silently down her cheeks and into her veil, her lips. *Malcolm. My Malcolm.*

He freed her hands. One tug of his swept back her veil. The circlet which had held it in place tumbled to the ground, and his fingers threaded through her hair, holding the back of her head. And then his lips and his body were gone, and the veil fluttered over her face. When she tore it off, there was only a blur climbing back through the side of the tapestry which had mysteriously become detached from the wall.

Only then did she hear what he had. Approaching footsteps from the main passage. Snatching up the fallen circlet, Halla whisked herself the short distance to her bedchamber and closed the door behind her. She leaned against it, stunned, for several minutes until the footsteps had passed and gone into the room next door. Mairead or her maid, Grizel.

It was funny. Truly, it was. Her own husband had tried to seduce her in a monastery, with no idea of who she really was. She didn't know whether it was insulting or flattering. Considering the availability of Mairead in the next room, she opted for flattering.

She wished he'd taken her on the cold stone floor. She'd have let him. She wished there had been time. She wished she'd had the forethought to drag him with her into this cell and eject Astrid.

She closed her eyes and walked the two paces to the flickering candle. She blew it out and sank onto the bed, curling into a ball beneath the blankets. On the whole, it was as well none of that had happened.

CHAPTER FOURTEEN

"**I** DON'T LIKE this," Donald said grimly, pacing the length of Brecka Hall while he flung words over his shoulder at Gormflaith. He'd come home only a couple of hours ago to the latest news of his parents' separate departures and had personally questioned John, the Lady Mairead's man who'd begun this chase. "I don't like the timing, and I don't trust it. Both of our parents are walking into a trap. Separately!"

"You don't know that," Gormflaith said anxiously. Although she had needlework in her lap, she hadn't glanced at it since Donald came home. "He seemed very sure of keeping himself and our mother out of trouble."

"But still he left Ross."

"Someone has to rescue Mairead of Kingowan," Gormflaith said reasonably.

"Not our mother! Not *him*. Gormflaith, I don't think I could bear it if he were taken again. And if *she*—"

"You should have more faith in him," Gormflaith interrupted.

At least it stopped him pacing to turn and scowl at her. They'd all been brought up on legends of Malcolm MacHeth, but the truth was, they didn't know the real man well enough to have genuine faith in his judgment or his abilities. Neither of them felt able to say so.

"We don't even know if Mairead is truly captive," Donald

muttered.

"You spoke to her man," Gormflaith pointed out. "You know he speaks the truth."

"As he knows it, perhaps." Donald flung himself down at the table, his fingers tapping in restless thought until, abruptly, he jumped to his feet again. "I'll take the men south and find out what's happening."

"You can't!" Gormflaith exclaimed. "It would end our agreement with the king."

"Our father's just broken it anyway," Donald growled.

"I don't think we should rush into anything," Gormflaith pleaded. "Trap or not, we could make everything worse by blundering into the king's territories with an army!"

"But we have to know, be able to act if necessary."

"We need to speak to Adam," Gormflaith said, and Donald stopped pacing again to glance at her.

"Good idea. We'll leave at dawn for Tirebeck, and you may stay there with Cairistiona, if you like, while Adam and I go south."

"Perhaps," Gormflaith said doubtfully. "If we all still think that's best when we've discussed it."

IF THE SITUATION hadn't been his own, Malcolm would probably have found it laughable. Here he was, over forty years old and courting his wife of more than two decades in the heart of his enemy's territory. Worse, having failed to recognize him from the outset, now that she did, she would not admit it, nor even believe, apparently, that *he* knew who *she* was.

Perhaps she'd spent too long around that harpist and his silly songs.

By the morning, Fergus still had not returned to the priory. Malcolm rose with the bell for early morning prayers, dressed, and went to saddle his horse to see if he could find out what was going on. He was just leading the beast out when two lay brothers burst through the gates, yelling in utter panic, "The MacHeths are coming!"

Malcolm couldn't help grinning. *My friends, they're already here.* Hastily, he straightened his face once more and tried to look concerned. Still leading his horse, he walked across to the racing men, calling to them to stop their mad dash into the chapel.

"Wait, there," he commanded. "What makes you think so? Did you see them?"

"No, sir. Word from Montrose is that they're marching south and laying waste—"

"Reliable word?" Malcolm interrupted.

"Oh yes, sir."

"Because I heard the king had released Malcolm MacHeth and the men of Ross had all gone home."

"Well, if they had, they've come back again! The king should never have trusted them, should have captured the whole lot!"

The prior himself led the monks from the chapel and listened to the no doubt embellished tale of marauding MacHeths.

"They'll be heading for Kingowan," the prior said, frowning. "Where is Sister Ursula? Ask her to bring the Lady Mairead to me, at the lady's convenience."

Malcolm frowned. This wasn't right.

Abruptly, he tied the horse to stop it from wandering and strode across to the main guest quarters. Here, he all but ran into a tall man exploding from his cell with his tunic still half over his head.

The man stopped dead with surprise, his arms still up around his ears. Warily, he eased them down, letting the tunic fall into place. Malcolm could see him missing the weapon he'd failed to carry in his haste.

"Muiredach, I believe," Malcolm said mildly.

The man was handsome, with a sort of pleasing, ascetic look. Like a fallen monk who regretted his sin. But he wasn't afraid.

"Do you?" he said.

"I do. Harpist to the Lady of Ross."

The man just gazed at him, neither denying nor confessing anything. At least she had a protector with courage. "Who are you?"

"Malcolm mac Aed. It's time we talked to my wife and the Lady Mairead."

Muiredach's jaw dropped. His eyes widened like saucers and sudden color flooded his face. And yet still he wasn't sure. "I'll ask them to send someone to the women's house—"

"No need. Come."

Malcolm strode off toward the refectory. He didn't much care if Muiredach followed him or not. If he didn't, he wasn't worth having around. The refectory was deserted, those not about their business panicking outside while the prior tried to calm them down.

As he approached the tapestry, Muiredach caught up with him. Muffled women's voices could already be heard beyond it. They must have spilled from their respective cells to hear the news.

"Will they hear us through the hanging?" Muiredach asked.

"Yes, but what's the point?" Calmly, Malcolm lifted the edge of the tapestry he'd detached from the wall last night and swung his legs over the balustrade.

The voices stopped. Four women in various stages of dress stared at him, and at Muiredach, who appeared silently at his side. Halla, without veil or overgown, took his breath away. She stood at the door of the first cell, one hand against the jamb, as though holding herself up. Her golden hair tumbled to her shoulders, much as it had when she'd been a young girl, shining and glorious. Her beauty took his breath away, as it always had. And yet there was…*more*. Fine, fascinating little lines fanning outward from the corners of her eyes. Wise, mature eyes. Her gaze was rooted to his.

For an instant, he was sure something like fear flickered

across her face—Halla, who was never afraid—and then her eyelids came down and her head lifted, and when she opened her eyes, they were direct and clear and utterly unafraid.

"What do you want?" she asked calmly. As if they'd only parted an hour ago.

And the funny thing was, at the sound of her voice, he almost felt they had.

It WAS THE first time she'd seen him in twenty-two years. They'd spoken through barriers, walked in the night, even kissed in darkness, and she'd never seen his face. Not properly. Now, she couldn't look away, not even if her life depended on it, because he gazed only at her.

The strong, handsome youth she'd married had grown into an impressive man, tall as he'd always been, a little broader perhaps in the shoulders and chest. But she'd felt that power in him last night, close against her back, her hips, her legs.

His face was still Malcolm's face, though perhaps a shade heavier, a shade harsher, and without the bronze of a life spent mostly outdoors. No longer young, he had deeply etched lines around his eyes and mouth, and the beard she'd felt last night covered his lower jaw and chin. But his countenance was still firm and beautiful. And calm. Much calmer than she remembered. Her turbulent husband who had kissed another woman last night. Or thought he had.

Or had he?

Twenty years of ruling and commanding cut through her confusion to her rescue. Somehow, as she'd always done, she gathered herself through the doubt and pain and sheer, wild excitement and asked negligently, "What do you want?"

He laughed. And it had been so long since she'd heard that bright, uninhibited sound that it almost undid her. Fortunately,

Mairead chose that moment to be roused from her astonishment.

"Malcolm mac Aed!" she exclaimed, stepping forward as if she couldn't help herself. "What in God's name are you doing here?"

Malcolm spared her a warm glance and a smile that almost shattered Halla's fragile composure. He walked forward, his gaze clashing once more with Halla's as he advanced upon her. "I hear the MacHeths are coming."

She swallowed, covering her panic by standing as still as a stone. "We hear that, too. Did you bring them?"

"Of course not." He came to a halt in front of her.

They knew—Astrid and Muiredach and probably Mairead— they all knew that he hadn't come home, that this was their first reunion. White Christ, did he think so, too? Which of the women here had he imagined she was last night?

Her hand jumped when his warm rough fingers closed around it. She had to fight to maintain her polite unconcern as he lifted it to his lips and kissed it.

"How do you do, my lady wife?" he said softly and bent his head. In his eyes lurked all the old danger, impulsive and thrilling and, right now, terrifying.

There was no way to avoid it. A kiss of greeting was expected, especially after twenty years. She remembered. She remembered everything as his mouth took hers, firm and yet respectful in public. Secretly, utterly sensual. A mere moment from which she had to recover.

"I heard you were in Ross," she managed as he straightened.

"I heard you weren't."

So, he'd known. He'd followed her. Not come for Mairead… Or had he killed two birds with one stone?

"The question is," he said, retaining her hand as he turned to include the others. Did that hurt Mairead? The girl was more vulnerable than she pretended. *Aren't we all?* "The question is, are the MacHeths truly raiding in Angus, and if so, who is leading them?"

"Adam would not risk it," Halla said, dragging her thoughts together under her frown. "He would always see the larger need."

Malcolm lifted one eyebrow in a gesture so familiar, it hurt her. "Unless he's come for Mairead?"

"Love does strange things to a man," Muiredach observed, watching the Lady Mairead, who shrugged impatiently.

"Perhaps. But Adam's love, if it ever affected him that way, is all for Christian. He might and would act through loyalty, but never stupidity."

Halla found she could smile. "Well. You do know him."

"Up to a point," Mairead said ruefully. "What of Donald?"

"Impulsive enough, but not with Adam to rein him in."

"But if Adam's at Tirebeck," Muiredach said slowly, "and John the messenger is at Brecka when Donald returns from the north—"

"Gormflaith is there," Malcolm interrupted.

Before she could prevent it, Halla's eyes flew to his face. He had been to Brecka. He *had* come home. She couldn't think what that meant, not now, not with all her careful plans for Malcolm and Donald's freedom, for peace, about to explode in violent failure.

"Gormflaith is sweet-natured and loyal," Halla said. "But no one ever called her worldly. She could not hold Donald back if his heart was set on this. But why would it be? Donald is no fool. He would not bring an army south now."

"Even to save you?" Malcolm asked quietly.

She stared at him. "I don't know. I'm never in danger. It's always someone else." She turned back toward her room, tugging her hand to free it from his. "I have to find them."

"If they exist." Malcolm's grip tightened, holding her still.

"It could just be a rumour," Mairead agreed. "It happens a lot. Every brigand attack, any group of strangers can be accused of being MacHeths. To be honest, for the last year, you could all have stayed in Ross with your feet up, and the whole country would still have been afraid of you."

"I'll ride towards Montrose and see," Muiredach offered. "No one is looking for me."

"And if they *are* MacHeths?" Mairead retorted. "How will you stop them, Muiredach the Harper?"

Muiredach met her gaze without obvious offense. "I'll give them your ring."

To Halla's surprise, Mairead flushed. Something was going on between those two that might have interested her in other circumstances. For now, it was hard enough to deal with the vital matter in hand while Malcolm stood at her side, his fingers curled around hers.

Muiredach turned and seemed to address Malcolm as well as Halla. "Adam and Donald both know me well enough to understand that I would not lie. If I say it is your command, they'll go."

"And if it isn't one of them?" Halla said with foreboding. "If it's some rogue army of Ross men that we deliberately riled up to threaten the King of Scots? They might not have disbanded as they should and just gone on the rampage. Or they heard of Mairead's imprisonment. They must all know of your aid to us."

"We need to know," Malcolm said abruptly. "And we need to deal with it, whatever it is, before the King of Scots sends his army and disavows all our agreements. You and I, Halla, are far too vulnerable here. And Mairead is in enough trouble. We all go. Now."

He moved, just as suddenly as he'd used to, tugging her into her bedchamber and kicking shut the door. Halla's heart hammered. There was no lock, but no one would dare to come in. She looked up, giving away as little as she could.

A small, rueful smile teased the corners of his mouth. His thumb moved, idly caressing her palm. "I dreamed of our reunion a hundred times and more. Never was it like this."

She drew in her breath. "Well, as I recall, life with you was always unexpected."

There wasn't a great deal he could say to that, and he didn't. But the smile had gone from his eyes, leaving them serious as they searched hers. "Are we allies, Halla?"

The pain of that was like an arrow in her gut, depriving her of breath. All she could do was wrench her gaze free. "How can you even ask?" she got out before she bit her lip to silence.

His other hand came up, grasping the back of her neck, lifting her head once more. "You left Brecka. You left Ross."

You didn't come home! But she couldn't, wouldn't say that. Instead, she curled her lip for strength and raised her eyes to his once more. "I was about your business," she said with disdain. "As I always have been."

Those dark eyes hadn't missed much when he was a young man. Now, they seemed to turn her inside out, against all her silent struggles.

"You never used to hide from me," he said softly.

She hated him for the flooding memory, for the way her very bones melted as if she was still that young, devoted girl who'd withered away in lonely isolation. She lifted her chin.

"You are a stranger," she said deliberately.

His eyelashes flickered, his own trick of hiding. He might even have whitened, but there was no time for either regret or triumph. His hands dropped as though burned, and he turned away from her, already opening the door. "It would seem we both are."

MUIREDACH, WHOSE FEET were always on the ground, had realized long ago that his unrequited love for his chaste lady was only bearable because no one else touched her either. As they rode toward the main road, the Lord and Lady of Ross at the front of their little party, he was almost surprised that the sight didn't hurt him more.

Of course, it had been a very odd reunion. Ridiculously understated. Or at least it would have seemed so without the tension quivering in the very air between them. They pretended, but something worryingly deep and intense was going on beneath the surface, something that excluded everyone else.

"She is cold," Mairead said beside him, as though the words were wrung from her. She sounded more distressed than she'd been throughout her escape. "I never imagined she would be cold."

"She isn't," Muiredach said shortly. The lady, who wasn't frightened of anything, was afraid.

Mairead turned her head and looked at him. *"What do you want?"* she repeated. "After twenty-two years?"

"You understand nothing."

"I understand how much he's longed for this, and how much she's hurting him."

"She's hurting *him?"* Muiredach edged his horse closer to hers, only just preventing himself from seizing her bridle as anger pushed discretion into the wind. "She fought every day for him, sent her sons to fight for him while she waited in agonies of anxiety. She ruled his earldom and kept every man, woman, and child loyal to him in the teeth of the king, and Norman soldiers and every other threat that reared its ugly head. She planned his escape and Donald's, and when she heard it had worked, she made a feast for him, a welcome home, a triumph. And he didn't come."

Mairead frowned with brief confusion. "What do you mean, he didn't come?"

"He sent the men with his sons and went off by himself as if she were nothing."

"But she isn't," Mairead said blankly. "She is everything. It broke my heart every day, but she is."

"Then allow her a little pride. For he shattered it with his carelessness."

Mairead shook her head with surprising vehemence. "Not

carelessness. Never that."

"Then what?"

She shook her head. "I don't know. It's as if...captivity damaged him, and then so did freedom."

She looked away as the party slowed, peering through the woods in the direction of Kingowan. There, no doubt, soldiers again walked along the wooden parapet, watching. They would know by now that Mairead had gone. Probably, they had given up on finding Malcolm MacHeth or fled before his marauding army. If it existed.

"They are strangers," Mairead said abruptly. "They need time to remember each other, learn what each other has become."

"And if they don't like what each other has become?"

Mairead laughed. "Then perhaps you and I have a chance after all."

Chapter Fifteen

Although they asked whenever they passed through settlements or met any travelers, no one had seen the MacHeths. Most had heard they were in the region, though, and were waiting and praying with dread to be spared.

Theirs was not a huge party liable to draw much attention on the road. Nevertheless, Malcolm used Halla's house guards as scouts, whether they traveled on the road or in the cover of the woods. He occasionally rode off alone in one direction or another and returned minutes later. Once, he even dismounted and passed the reins to Halla. She took them without a word, quite naturally, and watched him sprint through the trees.

"Where is he going?" Muiredach asked in tones that implied his lord need not go so far merely to relieve himself or any other trivial purpose.

"Scouting," Halla said. "We only have the two men, and it isn't always enough."

"Is such excessive care necessary?"

"He thinks so. It was how we survived several invasions after the Battle of Stracathro, and how we eluded capture, fighting only when we had a chance of winning."

"You hid with him?" Mairead asked in surprise.

Halla smiled. Those had been strange, anxious, and yet wonderful days, full of as much euphoria as grief.

"Why do you think the men of Ross will do anything for her?" Astrid interjected. "Because she calls herself their lady, because she married their earl stripped by the king of his title? She marched with them, suffered with them, bound their wounds, and celebrated with them."

Even the memory was gladness and pain. Halla looked directly at Astrid. "So did you."

Astrid smiled. "Aye."

A few minutes later, Malcolm again emerged through the trees, took the reins from Halla, and mounted.

"No signs of raiding parties or soldiers, but there's a family just left the road as if they mean to camp. We should talk to them."

Although he'd spoken to the group in general, as indeed he'd addressed all his speech since they'd left the priory, Halla nodded. The huge, unresolved issues between them would wait until this greater danger was over. Which suited Halla well enough. She could find no words for what lay now between herself and Malcolm, but there was an odd contentment in riding by his side, searching out the threat together. Even if it drove them apart in the end.

In a small clearing, they discovered a man, woman, and two children around a fire. They all leapt up in alarm when the horses walked out of the trees. The man seized a knife from his belt and pushed in front of his family.

"There's no need for that," Malcolm said mildly. "We haven't come to rob you." He cast a critical eye over them. "Looks as if that's happened to you already."

"MacHeths," the man said with loathing, lowering his knife as he took in the presence of noblewomen with the soldiers.

"Where?" Malcolm asked.

"We come from a village inland from Montrose. We tried to fight, but they took everything, drove off our animals, killed nearly all of us. I took my family and ran when they set fire to what was left."

"The MacHeths did that?" Halla asked curiously. "I heard they had returned to Ross."

"So did we," the man said bitterly. "Either they hadn't, or they came back."

"How do you know they were MacHeths?" Malcolm asked.

The whole family stared at him as though he was stupid. Every act of brigandage could be blamed on the MacHeths. It was a tendency Halla had encouraged, on Adam's advice. The MacHeths were feared.

"They told us," the man said bitterly. "They were *proud* of it? Can you imagine being proud of being a *MacHeth*?"

Halla shook her head. "Inconceivable," she agreed under Malcolm's sardonic gaze. "And outrageous. Such men will be punished in the next world, though personally, I would like to begin it in this one. Who was the leader of these men, do you know?"

"He didn't introduce himself," the man muttered.

"One of the sons of Malcolm MacHeth, no doubt."

The woman spoke up. "No, lady, he was older than that. The sons are young, aren't they? This one was older, greying." She shivered, clutching her children to her.

"Malcolm MacHeth himself, then?" Malcolm suggested. "I believe the king released him."

"More fool he," the man said angrily. "What did he expect?"

"Who knows? The king is just a boy and doesn't understand. Describe this chief MacHeth to me? Was he a tall man? Fat, thin? Fair or dark?"

The man scowled, looking to his wife as if for inspiration. It was she who said reluctantly. "Not so tall. Slight, wiry, though bloody strong. He wielded that sword something fierce. His hair and beard were dark but greying."

"Not Malcolm or his sons," Malcolm said thoughtfully. "A rogue MacHeth army? Are there no soldiers out looking for them?"

The man shrugged. "Maybe by now. We saw no signs of

any."

"We'll find out who they are," Malcolm assured him. "And see that they're punished."

The man curled his lip. "Why, who are you? God Almighty? You going to bring back my brother and his children? My neighbors? My animals, my home?"

"No," Malcolm allowed. "But I'm not no one either." He spurred on to the other side of the clearing.

Halla urged her horse nearer the woman and bent from the saddle, her hand outstretched. "Alms for your losses," she said. "So that you might have something to start again."

The woman hesitated. Despite her poverty, she clearly had pride.

"For the children," Halla said, and the woman snatched the coins with a muttered word of thanks. Halla nodded and rode after the others.

"Could it be Findlaech?" Muiredach was saying.

"He was always wild and wayward," Malcolm allowed.

"But he would not act without Adam's blessing," Halla said.

Malcolm glanced at her. "Even for you?"

Findlaech was the boy, and the man, to whom she'd entrusted the care of her sons. He'd taught them to ride and to fight and raid, and to care for their men, and ended by being utterly devoted to his more difficult charge, whom he now served as captain. Between her and Findlaech had always been respect. And, on his side, a certain awe.

"I don't know," she admitted. Then she shook her head. "I doubt his common sense, to his face, but before God, Malcolm, what does he achieve by this senseless raiding of poor villages? How would that help me or you, or our cause? How could it possibly help Mairead? There is no reason for this."

Malcolm gazed ahead. "You're right. They're hardly hurtling south to free Mairead or search for you. They're just causing havoc, creating refugees and fear in the MacHeth name." He turned to Halla. "Are you thinking the same as I am?"

"Usually," she said without guarding her tongue. Then, hastily, before he could see her flush or even, perhaps, notice her slip, she urged her horse to a canter. "Let's find out if we're right."

Towards sunset, they came across definite signs of the raiding party—burned and abandoned settlements, the tracks of many feet, goats and sheep, and even the odd cow, wandering free and unwatched. And then the scouts reported armored soldiers riding inland.

"The king has demesne lands near here," Mairead said. "The soldiers are probably his men, looking for those MacHeths. Or at least going home after failing to find them."

"Men in armor are easy to avoid in this terrain," Malcolm observed. "Which gives us a chance to discover our raiders first."

"In the dark?" Muiredach asked doubtfully.

Malcolm considered. "Probably not. But we can probably get a little closer before we camp."

THE HOUSE GUARDS lit a fire and put up the tent where the women would sleep for privacy. By then, Malcolm had again disappeared into the darkness, no doubt spying out the land, and Muiredach had made a spit to cook the hares the men had shot earlier.

"Is he really the lady's harpist?" Mairead asked Astrid.

"You'd know if you'd ever heard him play," Astrid retorted.

"Actually, I did once," Mairead remembered. "Practically outside my window. He's good, I'll grant you." She raised her voice and called to him provocatively, "Will you not play for us, Muiredach?"

He smiled into the flames, for an instant reminding her of Adam, who'd seen God knew what in fires. "After supper, perhaps, if the lady wishes, and the lord does not object."

Mairead inclined her head mockingly. "Did he really teach

Adam mac Malcolm to play the harp?" she asked.

"And Donald and Gormflaith." Astrid turned her deceptively sleepy gaze on Mairead. "You find our Muiredach as fascinating as we do. Rumor says he's the son of an Irish king. Or perhaps an escaped slave."

"And what does Muiredach say?"

"To me? Nothing of that. Though he may have told the lady."

"He is very…devoted to her."

"We all are. And you have risked more than most for her."

In truth, the risks she'd taken had been for Adam, and for Somerled. And then for Malcolm himself. But she allowed there was something about the lady to inspire such devotion, even in Mairead, who had always been aware that if she had been able to make Malcolm's wife vanish in a puff of smoke, she would have done so.

Malcolm returned as silently as he'd left and sat down at the fire by Halla's side. Neither of them said anything. And yet Mairead saw, as she always should have, that removing Halla would change nothing for her. It made her throat ache, but for some reason, it was bearable.

Considering they were in enemy territory, surrounded by the king's men and not necessarily friendly raiders, the camp was surprisingly relaxed. They all ate together, although the soldiers took it in turns to stand and watch and listen, at least until the lady requested Muiredach to play.

Without a word, he rose and unwrapped his harp from its blanket. By the glow of the fire, Mairead found herself watching his long, strong fingers pluck the strings as he played. The movement and the music were strangely hypnotic, and she continued to watch his hands as he sang softly of long-ago magic and love and battles.

Only once did she raise her eyes to his shadowed face. His gaze moved on from hers almost at once. And a moment later, the song changed to one of quick humor and dance, which had everyone tapping their feet on the grass and swaying to the rhythm.

When it was finished, Malcolm said, "I see that you're more than worth your supper. My house is clearly honored by your presence and your music."

Muiredach inclined his head, almost like one great man acknowledging the compliments of another. Perhaps the notion of him being a king's son was not so far-fetched.

"For now," Malcolm said, "we should sleep. I'll watch the first few hours and then wake Tomas."

No one, even the lady herself, seemed to think of disobeying him.

⟫⟪

HALLA HADN'T BEEN dozing for long when Astrid's elbow dug her in the ribs. The woman had only been turning over in her sleep, but it jerked Halla's eyes opened instantly.

She faced the badly tied opening in the tent, through which she could see the almost-full moon and bright stars, some occasionally obscured by passing clouds. Beneath them, the campfire still burned. By its glow, she could make out the huddled, sleeping figures of her guards and Muiredach. She knew it was them because the still, sitting figure silhouetted against the flames was Malcolm's.

For some time, she lay still, just watching him, wondering how she felt and why it hurt. It wasn't so different from those early days when she'd first met him and he'd fascinated and provoked her in equal measure. Only she was no longer a child. And she no longer knew what Malcolm was.

Her heart beating hard, she rose carefully, taking her blanket with her, and slipped out of the tent, retying it behind her. He didn't move as she approached and sat silently beside him.

More than twenty years of words struggled to be said, and yet none of them would come out. She couldn't even look at him, although she heard his even breathing as if it were her own. She inhaled the very scent of him until her eyes stung and her throat ached.

He said, "I don't know."

Slowly, she turned her head to face him. "What?"

"I don't know why I didn't come home at once. I thought only of you, and yet I couldn't face you. Not as I was."

"How were you?"

He shrugged. "I didn't know. I still don't. I just wasn't…me."

She understood something of that: he'd got too used to solitude to be suddenly in the constant company of the rambunctious men of Ross. He'd been overwhelmed by sudden freedom, his sons, the lifetimes that had passed without him. Perhaps he'd even felt some weird loss of control. His own actions had got himself in prison, and yet he was suddenly freed by those of others, none of his own.

She swallowed. "I know. I knew it at the time. I just… I'd imagined you would still do it, for Ross and for Gormflaith, if not for me."

At last, his eyes lifted from the flames to her face. "I wasn't…*worthy*. And in my selfishness, I thought of others only as they affected me, not as I affected them."

Something caught in her throat. She didn't know if it was tears or laughter. "Worthy? When have you ever been *worthy*, Malcolm mac Aed?"

A breath of laughter stirred her hair, and then his hand on her nape dragged her up to meet his mouth. "Never," he muttered against her lips.

His kiss was rough and long and ultimately tender. She couldn't help touching his cheek, caressing, holding as her mouth clung to his. Strange and yet familiar, like him. This new, mature Malcolm, the echo of the youth she'd married and loved so much. And yet in his efforts—and hers—to marry up past and present, was there not hope of something even deeper and greater? His mouth promised so much…

As did his clouded yet tumultuous eyes when he finally re-leased her lips and drew back. Still holding her gaze, he rose, drawing her to her feet. Her heart thundered in her breast. But it seemed he was only kicking Tomas awake.

The man sat up immediately, his dagger in s hand.

"Your watch," Malcolm said, low and still holding Halla by the hand, walked away into the friendly cover of the trees. He didn't go far before he dropped the blanket from his shoulders and threw it on the ground.

"They will know," Halla said with difficulty. "They will all know."

"Do you care?"

She shook her head dumbly. There had been other nights under the stars, with companions sleeping closer by than this. When there had been no one in her world but him. But this was different, so very different that her whole body trembled as he laid her on his blanket and covered them both with hers.

"There were times, black times when I thought I would never hold you in my arms again."

"Did you close your eyes and imagine other women were me?"

"There was no point. They smelled wrong." His hands were beneath her gown, at once avid and worshipful, tugging aside her clothing and his own. The delicious weakness of arousal flooded her, frightening her because since he'd last lain with her, there had been no one else. She no longer knew if she was capable of giving or receiving pleasure except in dreams.

"But you took them anyway," she whispered.

"You don't care for that any more than I did." His hand found the desperate, raging heat between her legs, and she gasped. "They never stopped me missing you for a moment. But God knows it was a comfort I would never have denied you or blamed you for."

He moved over her, taking her face between his hands so that she couldn't look away.

"I couldn't," she whispered. "How can you even ask me that now?"

"You mean now that I'm finally taking you again?"

"Yes," she gasped as he entered her with slow, aching strength. This older, different, *bigger* Malcolm.

His whole body shuddered, and he dropped his forehead on hers as if in anguish. "Halla," he whispered. "Dear God, Halla."

She wrapped her limbs around him, one hand in his hair, the other flat against his hot, heaving back, and from sheer instinct, began to move her hips. And from then, there was no question but that nature would take its course.

Even so, she expected that first reunion to be quick and frenzied. It wasn't. Whether for her or for him or for them both, he made it slow and tender and somehow more deeply sensual than anything she remembered from their youth. Perhaps this was his moment of resuming control. She could never have begrudged him that, even supposing there was anything she could have done about it. As it was, it appeared she was still more than capable of both giving and receiving. Of loving this stranger who echoed her husband, who *was* her husband still.

With caressing hands and lips and the slow, deep strokes of his body, he brought her singing flesh to the edge of bliss, and then, watching as he strained, he pushed her over the edge and dived with her. She reached for his mouth with blind, delirious gratitude, but he didn't at once give her his kiss. Even through his own climax, it seemed he needed to see hers. And then he fell on her like a starving man on a feast.

At last, she lay with her cheek on his damp chest as he stroked her long hair across his skin. She rose and fell with his every breath. And at last, she could say it.

"I have grown too fond, too needful, of my own dignity. When you didn't come, I thought you'd gone with her, with Mairead. Even when I knew you hadn't, I couldn't bear the humiliation of your neglect. That is why I left Brecka."

He moved, turning her onto her back and looming over her.

"I know I hurt more than your pride, and for that, for all of it, I'm sorry."

She touched his cheek, his lips with her fingertips. "Shall we begin again, Malcolm mac Aed?"

He shook his head. "No," he said with unexpected ferocity. "Never. It's *all* us, even the twenty-two years apart, even the hate and pride and jealousy. I won't lose any of it."

Strangely enough, it was their second coupling that was frenzied and quick, like a sudden blaze of sunshine in a storm. His open mouth covered hers, muffling their cries.

As soon as their lips parted in satisfaction, he was asleep. She lay with him in her arms, smiling to the darkness and stroking his hair, his skin.

Malcolm, she thought in new wonder. *My Malcolm.*

HE DIDN'T SLEEP for long. His eyes sprang open, and she could see remembrance flash through them before he smiled and kissed her. Her heart beat faster as she imagined, welcomed a third loving. But he broke the kiss with apparent reluctance and began to pull her clothing back around her under the blanket.

"Go back to your tent and sleep," he murmured. "I'll be back before you wake."

"Where are you going?"

"To see what moves in the dark before dawn."

"I could come with you," she suggested.

"Don't tempt me. I'm quieter—and more observant—alone." Under her gaze, he struggled back into his clothes and drew her to her feet.

"You're loving this, aren't you?" she accused.

He grinned, suddenly, achingly, like the younger Malcolm, and kissed her hand. "I am now. Come."

Hand in hand, they walked the few yards through the trees to the camp, where Tomas still sat by the fire, regarding them stolidly.

"All well?" Malcolm murmured.

"Apparently," Tomas said.

Halla walked past him with dignity and back into the tent. She thought the other women were asleep. She hoped they were.

CHAPTER SIXTEEN

MALCOLM'S WHOLE BODY surged with energy, almost bursting with joy because he'd known Halla again. A new, mature, aware Halla, more beautiful, more passionate even than he remembered.

As he crept through the dark wood, he had to force himself to concentrate on his path and his surroundings, not on her. But he wondered if it would have been like this if he'd gone home when he should, with his sons and the men. She would have healed him then as now. But he'd been such a mess, he doubted he'd have made anything right for her.

Deliberately, he thrust aside such pointless thoughts and reined in the energy that urged him to run, crashing through the undergrowth like a one-man army. He followed the direction of the fading tracks he'd found at dusk last night. He was sure they would lead to the raiding party, though the distance was another matter, and they would be up and moving at dawn, especially if they were aware of the king's soldiers searching for them.

In fact, despite the delicious memory of the night, he found it surprisingly easy to stay alert. All his senses seemed to have been honed and sharpened by Halla's loving. He felt awake, alive, as if he'd walked through half his life half-asleep. He had every intention of solving this mess, whatever it was, and returning home to Ross with Halla, to his sons and daughter, and his grandson, and his people. And this time, he would be in truth the Earl of Ross, not a deprived and discontented would-be king. The young man who'd always wanted more had finally learned to value what he had.

The inexplicable sense of not being alone preceded the faint sounds of cracking twigs and brushing leaves, the almost silent movement of feet on the forest floor. No army—or at least not yet—but one man.

Malcolm stepped aside into deeper cover and waited, his sword drawn, his ears straining. Still one man.

He walked warily into Malcolm's view, a dark young man, his sword already in his hand. From his grip and the way he moved, Malcolm surmised he knew how to use it. One of the king's soldiers, he judged. He wore a helmet and breastplate, so he was prepared for an attack. Malcolm, however, didn't want to fight if he could avoid it. He didn't want the clash of steel to bring the rest of the king's men down upon him. On the other hand, he was understandably doubtful of the effect of stepping into the soldier's path and introducing himself, at least until he had the upper hand.

Malcolm tensed, slowly drawing his dagger. If the man would only make a further one-quarter turn, he could leap on him, his dagger to his throat. Then they could talk in a civilized manner.

Slowly, the stranger turned, searching between the trees, as if he, too, sensed another presence and was determined to find it before he moved on. Malcolm took one silent step forward and another. Two more and he could jump on his man, rendering his sword useless until he could disarm him.

On the next silent step, a twig snapped. From sheer instinct, Malcolm leapt back. Just as well, because his quarry moved with fantastic speed, spinning around and cutting a wide swathe with his sword that could have cut a man in two. As it was, Malcolm took the tip on his dagger to save himself a nasty gash and reached up to drag his own sword free. Silence was no longer an option.

"Who the devil are you?" the younger man demanded in French, cutting upward.

Malcolm met the blow on his own sword. "I was about to ask you the same question," he said, battering the enemy blade back and advancing. "But you seem a trifle jumpy."

"You mean you were skulking in the forest with a dagger and you don't want to kill me?"

"You never gave me the chance to find out."

The Norman soldier was quick and his dander was clearly up. And since they'd begun it, Malcolm had no real objection to a fight if he could avoid making it to the death. So, he kept pace and made it quick, watching for the tiniest opening. At the first hint of one, Malcolm seized it, thrusting inward against the Norman's blade and twisting up with such unexpected force that the younger man grunted and his sword flew through the air.

Malcolm lashed out with his foot, swiping the soldier's legs from under him, and his opponent landed in the mud, Malcolm's sword point at his throat.

"Yield, for God's sake. I have no wish to kill you."

"Then I do yield for any sake you like," the Norman said coolly. "You fight better than any man I've come across."

Malcolm lifted his sword. "I once found myself with a lot of time to practice." He reached down, and the young man, still somewhat wary, took his hand. Malcolm pulled him to his feet.

"Bernard de Brus," the Norman said. "At your service."

"De Brus?" Malcolm repeated. "Your family has the lordship of Annandale."

"We do. But I am a younger son and at present find myself captain of the king's garrison at Alyth."

"Congratulations," Malcolm said politely. "Then you are pursuing the raiders who've been attacking the villages from here to the coast?"

"We lost them yesterday evening. I'm trying to pick up their trail before they move again, or the rain comes. Which it will," he added with a glance of displeasure at the still-lightening gray sky.

"Inevitably," Malcolm agreed.

De Brus, as if suddenly realizing his openness was not being reciprocated by his erstwhile opponent, regarded him with a quick, suspicious frown. "And your interest in the raiders?"

Malcolm smiled faintly. "What makes you think I have one?"

"You asked me. And you've been following the same signs I have, in the same direction."

He wasn't stupid, the young Norman. "We met a family some way back who told us they were fleeing from the MacHeths."

"And you are?" de Brus pursued.

"Malcolm." The Norman was not going to be as easy to misdirect as he'd hoped. Another, riskier plan sprang into his mind. He began to mull it over while he met de Brus's gaze.

"Just Malcolm?" de Brus said.

Malcolm considered. He quite liked the Norman captain and didn't wish to lie to him. "Some have called me the Crusader."

De Brus's face cleared. "Ah. That explains a lot."

"Less than you might think," Malcolm murmured. "I have a suggestion, Captain. Why don't we combine forces to capture these villains?"

De Brus eyed him. "You don't name them MacHeths."

"In truth, I'm not convinced they are."

"They don't behave like MacHeths," de Brus agreed. "They're staying too long in the same area. Normally, they commit lightning raids and vanish, only to pop up several miles away."

"Exactly what I thought."

De Brus regarded him. Although he seemed to be trusting by nature, he was clearly no fool. But the crusader epithet had worked its magic. The man was disposed to trust him. "How many men do you have?" the Norman asked.

"Come and see," Malcolm invited.

THE CAMP WAS mostly packed away and the packhorse being loaded up, while the women stood around and broke their fast on yesterday's priory bread when Malcolm emerged from the trees with a Norman soldier.

Halla's heart lunged with the sudden fear that Malcolm had been captured. But an instant's observation showed that it was the other way around. Only the Norman hadn't quite grasped it yet. Both were still armed and conversing with perfect amiability.

Muiredach materialized between her and Mairead. "He's brought a Norman soldier here. One of the king's men."

"So it would appear," Halla agreed calmly, walking forward to meet them.

"He'll have his reasons," Mairead said to Muiredach as they followed.

She was right. Malcolm always had his reasons. Halla just didn't always agree with them.

The Norman, who appeared to be a personable young man, removed his helmet and bowed as they approached.

"This is Bernard de Brus," Malcolm said, "Captain of the king's garrison at Alyth. Sir, my wife, and this is the Lady Mairead of Kingowan, as you may know."

It was cleverly done, covering his wife's lack of name with one the soldier was likely to know. And Mairead's beauty was bound to help.

It did. Although he bowed again to Halla with great respect, as he turned to Mairead, he said, "I have seen the Lady of Kingowan before, though I can't hope she remembers me."

"No, you can't," Muiredach said unexpectedly. Mairead blinked at him in surprise. Muiredach himself looked momentarily appalled at the words which had seemed to spill involuntarily from his mouth. "She has a shocking memory," he murmured.

De Brus looked inclined to be amused. "And you, sir, are?"

"Muiredach."

De Brus glanced from him to Malcolm and back. "You don't look like a crusader."

"I'm not," Muiredach said blankly. "I'm a harpist."

"A harpist," de Brus repeated.

"Even crusaders need music," Malcolm said mildly.

"Indeed." De Brus looked around him. "Where are your men?"

Malcolm lifted his arm, encompassing the present company and the two men leading the packhorse toward him.

De Brus's mouth fell open. "You intend to capture a band of raiding MacHeths with two fighting men and a harpist? What conceivable difference could these make to my force?"

"You'd be surprised," Malcolm said. "If they *are* MacHeths, we won't need even two men."

De Brus glanced at him, frowning. "You have some kind of *hold* over the MacHeths?"

"Some," Malcolm admitted.

The frown deepened. "Who *are*—?" De Brus broke off, the dreadful suspicion arriving on his amiable young face with a jolt. "Oh no."

He reached for his sword so quickly that Halla had no time even to utter a warning. But Malcolm, it seemed, knew his man, and had a dagger at the Norman's throat before the sword was half out of the scabbard at his back. De Brus stilled, breathing heavily with fury and frustration.

"Don't," Malcolm said. "It would break all the rules of hospitality."

"You think to ransom me?" de Brus demanded with contempt, although he released his sword hilt and his arm fell back to his side.

"Would I get much for you?" Malcolm asked, as though interested. He sheathed his dagger.

"No."

"Well, we'll stick with the first plan."

De Brus turned his head, regarding him. "You shouldn't be here. If you are who I think you are, you're meant to be in Ross. And we had confirmation from Moray that you crossed into Ross more than seven days ago, so you're not still on your way."

"I left again," Malcolm admitted.

"With that gang of ruffians at your back?"

"No, I left all my ruffians in Ross. This was a purely personal matter." Malcolm's lips curved. "I had some trouble with an errant wife."

"He doesn't mean you," Halla told Mairead, watching as Malcolm untied her horse and glanced back at de Brus.

Malcolm said, "I need your word that you'll ride with us without trying to escape."

"Or harm us," Muiredach added.

"Quite," Malcolm agreed.

De Brus looked round the camp before bringing his gaze back to rest on Malcolm. "You've piqued my curiosity," he said. "So, I'll give you my word. But I need to send a message to my men."

"No need," Malcolm said steadily. "I suspect you'll be back with them by midday. Certainly before dark. You can ride my wife's horse. My wife will not," he added, "be on it at the time."

"She will be on foot," Halla said sadly, "dragged along by a leading rope."

De Brus paused, one foot in the stirrup, his face expressing shock.

Malcolm regarded her with veiled eyes. It broke her heart to realize he'd learned how to hide his smile. "Come here, errant wife," he said softly.

Halla obeyed, though not before eyeing up Muiredach's mount with clear speculation. Wordlessly, Malcolm lifted her into the saddle of his own horse, and she smiled, throwing her leg over the animal's back. Malcolm mounted behind her, his arms enclosed her as he gathered in the reins.

In spite of the uncertainty and the inevitable danger ahead, Halla couldn't remember the last time she'd been so happy.

HALLA'S CONTENTMENT SEEPED into him, adding to the strange, wondrous thrill of riding with her in his arms once more. It brought back a hundred memories of narrow escapes and wild rides, evading capture, rejoining troops, or just careering about for fun. Even in the midst of war, there had been such carefree moments of fun. They'd been so young, imagined they could do anything, and still somehow stay together in this happiness.

They'd been wrong. He'd been wrong. Too confident of his own charm, he'd placed his trust in a Norman knight, not so different from the one who rode beside them now, invited him to his hall. And the man had taken him as he slept, surrounding him with an army and whisking him south into Moray before Halla and the men of Ross knew he'd gone.

More than two decades later, he'd made love to her again, ridden with her again. There was hope in that. And secret joy.

Outwardly, his attention was all on finding the raiders. It didn't take long. As he suspected, when they rode into the shallow hills looking down on the Loch of Lintrathen, they could see a camp full of men. Some were practicing with arms, others swimming and splashing in the loch, or just lazing on the damp grass.

Leaving the horses drinking from a stream, they slithered downhill, closer to the camp, keeping low to be unseen.

"Well, they look like wild men of the north," de Brus observed, low.

"Wild, certainly," Malcolm agreed.

"And I'm sure they're speaking in the Gaelic tongue. I can make out odd words."

Muiredach said, "They speak Gaelic all over Scotland, except in Norman castles."

"And Lothian," Malcolm added mildly.

"Can you make them go home?" de Brus asked.

"Yes," Malcolm said. "But they're not MacHeths."

"How can you tell?"

"Look at their leader," Malcolm said. "Sitting on the chair outside the tent."

"A dark-haired man," de Brus allowed. "He could be their leader, from your report and others we've heard."

"Look again," Malcolm said.

"There's no point," de Brus said impatiently. "His head is down. I think he's asleep. I can't make out his face."

Malcolm sighed and stood up. Cupping his mouth, he yelled downhill, "Hello, down there by the loch! Are you waiting for me?"

Several of the men paused and stared up in his direction. However, someone had to nudge the seated man before his head jerked up, scanning the hills. He'd been asleep. Malcolm waved to him.

"Fergus of Galloway," Halla said. "I thought so."

"Your neighbor, I believe," Malcolm said to de Brus. "I trust you recognize him?"

THE BEDCHAMBER DOOR opened and closed, and the still air was instantly infused with a distinctive, unquiet presence. Christian didn't need to open her eyes to know it was Adam. She smiled as he lay down on the bed, wrapping his person around her curled back.

"Why are you abed at this hour?" he asked. "Are you ill?"

"Oh no," she said hastily. "Just a little tired."

"You're not hiding in here because you've had enough of my brother and sister?"

Christian twisted her head around to try to see his face. "Of course not!

"Because Donald has ridden to the border, taking all his men and a few of mine."

"To keep an eye on him?" Christian asked cynically and, as it turned out, quite rightly.

"Just in case," Adam said uncomfortably. "It's difficult to sit back and do nothing. Especially since word has come from Angus that someone is raiding there in our name."

Christian straightened her straining neck and frowned into the pillow instead. "Is someone trying to break the king's agreement with your father?"

"I suspect so. Which is why Donald mustn't make it reality. My father *will* come home."

"With your mother?"

"Yes," Adam said firmly. "So, you do not mind that Gormflaith stays with us for a while?"

"I am glad to have her. I like her," Christian assured him. As if in proof, she lifted his hand from her breast and kissed it. *Now,* she thought. *Now is as good a time as there will be.* "Adam?"

He mumbled something, nuzzling her neck.

"I would like to tell Gormflaith something, but I need to tell you first."

"Tell me what?" he asked, clearly more interested in tracing the line of her thigh as far as it would go.

"That we are going to have a baby."

For a moment, his questing hand simply carried on. Then, as if her words had taken that time to penetrate, he stilled. Very slowly, he withdrew his hand and used it instead to pull her onto her back so that he could see her face. His dark eyes were serious and utterly focused on her. But his lips were trying to smile.

"Truly?" he breathed.

"Are you surprised?" she asked. "You know you have given me no rest since the night you first came to my bed."

"I knew you were not barren," he whispered, his turbulent eyes devouring her with a suddenly frightening intensity. "I knew you would give us—*me*—children."

Alarmed, she seized his face between her hands. "Adam? Is it the visions?"

"No," he said, holding on to her hands and kissing her with infinite tenderness. "It's happiness."

CHAPTER SEVENTEEN

HERE WAS AN instant, when the voice calling from the hill first woke Fergus, that happiness surged, and he snapped up his head to find the source. It was disorienting, for surely this had happened before, gazing up at a boy, a young man, on a hill, with every expectation of fun and glory…

He jerked himself back to reality with a jolt, shielding his eyes from the awkward blink of sun which shone suddenly from between the thick grey clouds.

"God in heaven, it can't be," he whispered.

"My lord?" some irritating voice said beside him.

The man on the hill lifted his arm and waved.

Malcolm MacHeth, looking not a day older than twenty years old. Impossible. And untrue, for Fergus had seen him before only two days ago, still recognizably Malcolm, but no youth either.

Fergus shook himself awake, gripping the arms of his chair tightly.

Malcolm had found him again. Why? The last time he'd led him on a wild-goose chase from Kingowan, during which a message had reached him that Mairead had been "abducted." In other words, that she'd escaped while Fergus, Brian of Kingowan, and all his men were chasing the phantom Malcolm.

And now, it seemed, Malcolm was pursuing him.

Fergus stood, his keen eyes scouring the hillside and the loch and all the surrounding countryside, for signs of men. He found none.

Interrupting the stream of questions from Aidan, his young but capable captain, Fergus uttered a few terse orders and strode forward toward the hill, beckoning.

There was a pause. Fergus actually thought he wouldn't come, after all that. Then he moved and began to walk down the hill. Fergus smiled. Until another man rose and walked behind him. As tall as Malcolm, surely, and dark hair peeking from beneath a fine helmet. One of the sons, perhaps? Fergus's smile broadened. If he played this properly, they'd have a MacHeth back in prison, and Fergus would be back in the king's good graces. Providing no army of genuine MacHeths lurked in the long grass up there.

"Get two men up that hill," Fergus murmured to his captain. "Discreetly. If there's anyone else, bring them. If it's a large force, sound the alarm."

So far as he could see, Malcolm kept his attention only on Fergus himself. As they drew closer, he saw that the other man in the helmet, although young and dark and strangely familiar, was neither of the MacHeth sons and clearly no mere man-at-arms either. But it was the ever unpredictable Malcolm who concerned him most.

"Malcolm mac Aed," he greeted him, smiling as he approached. "It *is* you! I thought I'd seen a ghost the other day at Kingowan."

Malcolm lifted one sardonic eyebrow. He didn't offer his hand, let alone an embrace. "Who told you I was dead?"

"Not dead, but in Ross. The unkind might call it the same thing."

"If that were so, *you* were pretty active for a dead man when you last visited Ross. You made an alliance with my family, burned my daughter-in-law's home, and abducted her."

There was no point in denying any of it. As a youth, at least, Malcolm had always admired the brazen along with the honest.

"Be fair, my friend. She was not your daughter-in-law at the time. I was helping your sons rid themselves of a pesky Norman knight."

"Against their will?" Malcolm said wryly. "But I haven't come to quarrel with you on that score."

"Or at all, I trust," Fergus said pointedly. He wasn't crass enough to point out the numbers of his men, all now dressed and armed, and though not threatening, clearly ready to protect their lord from sudden attack. His two scouts were already riding up the hill behind his visitors. Fergus was proud of them.

But Malcolm's gaze didn't waver. "You think I should just forget that you betrayed my son to the King of Scots?"

Damn, he could be a chilling bastard when he chose to be. Even when he was young, even in the midst of horseplay, the easygoing charm could vanish into this same cold, hard stare for reasons Fergus hadn't always grasped. In truth, Malcolm had always been a dangerous man to cross. Easy to forget when he'd been incarcerated for so long. But then, Malcolm would be foolish to forget who held all the cards here.

"In truth, you'd be wise to," Fergus said bluntly. "So that I might forget you're here at all, against all the oaths you swore to that same King of Scots."

"You're on boggy ground there too, Fergus. Who gave you permission to ravage Scotland in my name?"

Fergus gave his most ferocious smile. "I'm keeping your reputation alive, Malcolm mac Aed, after you went so tamely home to Ross."

Malcolm smiled. "With my son. If I were you, Fergus, I'd hurry back to my own lordship—I beg, your pardon, *kingdom*—before the King of Scots hears who really led these attacks."

Fergus laughed. "Who will tell him, Malcolm? You?"

"Lord, no. I don't speak to the Scottish court. Yet. *This* man, on the other hand—" He stepped aside, indicating his companion with a mocking flourish. In truth, Fergus had almost forgotten about him. "I don't need to introduce you, do I?"

The young man bowed stiffly. "My lord. An unexpected...honor."

"Aye, maybe," Fergus said. He'd lost sight of his scouts on the hill for a few moments, but one was descending again. Reporting nothing, presumably, while the second man checked farther afield to be sure. He glanced at the silent man with Malcolm MacHeth. "Your face is familiar though your name eludes me. Who the devil are you?"

"Bernard de Brus," Malcolm said gently. "Captain of the king's garrison at Alyth. And son, as you know, to the Lord of Annandale, a friend to both the King of Scots and the King of England."

Fergus swore under his breath. No one would doubt this boy's word. But a flick of one finger was all it took to bring Fergus's men closing in on them. For many reasons, he was reluctant to kill Malcolm MacHeth, but Bernard de Brus was dead the moment his name was spoken. And the beauty was, Malcolm would be blamed for that, too.

In the sudden tension, Bernard's fingers twitched, curling and then straightening, as if he had to force himself not to seize his sword. Malcolm didn't move.

Fergus curled his lip. "You're pretty careless with other people's lives, old friend. Did you even tell him what he was walking into?"

"He knew you from up there," Malcolm said dryly, pointing over his shoulder to the hill. No one had yet raised the alarm, and the second scout was visible now, farther round the hill and descending. "I doubt many people ever call him stupid."

"Then let me be the first," Fergus snapped, swinging on the young soldier. "You do *know* this is Malcolm MacHeth you've so foolishly allied yourself with?" Beyond their heads, he saw that his second scout seemed to be dragging two people by a leading rope. Captives. It was a relief in some ways. He hadn't expected Malcolm to be quite alone save for a tame Norman lordling.

He flicked his attention back to the young de Brus, who

merely gazed back at him, giving nothing away. Fergus grinned. "Did he tell you no one would kill him, except in battle? Certainly, the king will not, nor would his grandfather or great uncles. Because, you see, despite their modern ideas of kingship, despite their rigid holding to primogeniture and intolerance of rebellion, they can't quite shake off the old ways, the old respect for one so close to the throne. Our two Malcolms would happily slaughter each other in a battle that compelled hundreds of their own people to die with them, but they would never stoop to assassinate each other and give the people a break from war. The trouble is, my friend, I doubt the protection extends to his sons, and it most certainly doesn't cover you."

Fergus never objected to getting his hands dirty. Although the mere nod of his head would have instructed the nearest soldier to cut the de Brus boy down, he reached for his own sword instead.

Which was when, without warning, an arrow whizzed into the ground at his feet.

"What the—" Fergus stared at it, already knowing there was no point in leaping backward. He could be shot just the same. His gaze flew toward the hill, but no band of outlaws or soldiers streamed down it, only his own scout with his captives, rounding the foot of the slope in their direction. He swept his eyes to the left and found the first scout, still mounted, bow held high over the heads of Fergus's men, and a threaded arrow aiming straight at Fergus's heart.

Only, the scout was wearing a cloak now. Surely, he hadn't when he'd left? And the man's face beneath the helmet…was not a man's at all. In spite of himself, Fergus's heart rose into his mouth.

The lady whose son he'd betrayed controlled the arrow. Which must, he realized with sudden relief, have been a damnably lucky shot. Especially at this distance. She was coming closer, the horse picking its way forward without obvious guidance, though, more worryingly, the bow and the arrow remained steady.

Malcolm turned unhurriedly. There was a pause, then, "Not quite as we discussed, but it's true my lady wife is the best shot in Ross."

Fergus saw at once what he was doing and couldn't help grinning. "The Lady Halla is an archer now?"

"Always was," Malcolm said fondly. "I've always treated her with care since she shot me on our first meeting. I advise you to take similar precautions. After all, she's had nothing much to do for twenty years except practice."

"I take issue with that," Halla said clearly. "But the idea is correct. If anyone touches a weapon, Fergus of Galloway is dead."

Fergus spread his hands, taking a step nearer her. "Oh come. It isn't in your nature."

Halla pulled back on the bow. "You betrayed my son. Try me. Please."

A few dull thuds and the odd clash of steel sounded as those who'd already drawn weapons hurriedly dropped them.

"Captain," Malcolm said, "I think you have enough information. It must be time you rejoined your men before they can catch up with you here."

Bernard de Brus hesitated.

"It's important," Malcolm said impatiently, "to the king."

Fergus laughed. "To you, you mean. But even if he does go as you bid him, Malcolm, what then? Will you ride off, too, leaving the lady to threaten me alone, indefinitely? Do you think no one will shoot her as she turns and gallops after you?"

Malcolm shoved his Norman ally. "Go."

"I can't allow it," Fergus warned as Bernard began at last to lope off toward the cover of the hill.

"You have no choice," Malcolm said and leapt.

Dear God, Fergus had forgotten the sheer quickness of the man. Partly, of course, he did the unexpected and took advantage of your surprise so that you imagined he moved with supernatural speed. Halla's horse spun around, not restive, but guided by her so that Malcolm could leap up behind her. No one could touch her now without shooting Malcolm in the back. And clear as day, they meant to close in behind the Norman and protect him, too.

Sheer rage propelled Fergus after them. He hurled himself at Malcolm's leg, shoving wildly. "A challenge!" he yelled. "I challenge you, Malcolm mac Aed, to single combat!"

Malcolm couldn't even kick him without losing what was left of his balance and falling off. But at those words, Halla dug her heels into the horse's sides. Her accompanying instruction to the horse to gallop sounded frightened and was lost as Malcolm's hands closed over hers on the reins.

"Call them off!" he snarled at Fergus, presumably meaning the men who pursued Bernard de Brus with murderous intent.

"Then call him back and we'll discuss the terms of the challenge," Fergus panted, holding on to Malcolm's leg for dear life. "Halt!" he yelled at his own men by way of goodwill. It was the only way he could still win this.

Malcolm didn't need to call Bernard back. He was a chivalrous young fool and came anyway. Fergus was glad to notice him being met by the second mounted scout, who now cut his captives free in order to hold the more valuable de Brus. The freed captives, a soldier and a woman, rubbed at their wrists but made no attempt to run. The soldier, of course, would die for Malcolm mac Aed—sooner rather than later, if Fergus could arrange it.

Fergus's eyes widened as the woman pushed down her hood, revealing glorious red-gold hair. "Did you bring your whole damned harem?"

"No, I left my other six wives in Ross. What is this about, Fergus?"

No doubt he remembered, as Fergus did, who the winner of their play and practice fights had always been. But that was before he'd spent the last two decades in a tiny room in Roxburgh.

Malcolm said evenly, "You lured me here because you

thought you could finally defeat me? I see no point to that for either of us."

"There isn't one," Fergus said impatiently. "Not every action in the world is about you. I told Brian of Kingowan about Mairead visiting Roxburgh because I thought it would bring your son, your mad son, Adam."

Malcolm didn't bother defending his son. Obviously, they both knew Adam wasn't mad in any way that mattered. On the other hand, a flash of pure amusement passed over Malcolm's face that Fergus was at a loss to account for.

"Well, you were wrong. It brought my wife."

Fergus glanced from Halla, who still held her bow threateningly across her lap, the arrow still threaded, to Mairead, standing calmly by the side of the captured soldier. "What a strange friendship that is. The Lady of Ross never ceases to amaze me."

"The Lady of Ross," Malcolm said coldly, "does what is right. I believe you challenged me. Is it a verbal quarrel to the death? If so, I might concede, depending on the terms."

Fergus remembered the many, minor irritations of being with the young Malcolm MacHeth. Along with the exhilarating company and the fun had always come a sneaking, unworthy jealousy. Although Fergus ranked higher, in his own belief if, in no one else's, Malcolm had always assumed the lead, was generally right…and had married the exquisite Halla.

"If I kill you, I'll marry her," Fergus said, "according to the old ways. She will be honored."

He didn't look at the still figure of Halla. Malcolm didn't move much either. "I don't like your chances of surviving your wedding. Go on."

"If you win, you leave freely with your people, including my captives."

"And Bernard de Brus?"

"May go, too. If you win. No one interferes, no one fights but you and me."

Malcolm's gaze flickered to Halla and de Brus. Then he dismounted from his horse and handed the reins to the male freed captive, murmuring something without looking at him. Fergus didn't look much at him either, though he seemed faintly familiar. One of the lady's guards, no doubt, whom he'd met during his recent visit to Ross. Fergus didn't care. He'd just gambled everything on one fight. Foolish and yet curiously thrilling. His heart thundered with fierce excitement that amounted almost to joy. He might die. But he might just win.

As everyone fell back, forming an arena around them, Fergus drew his sword with a sigh of pleasure and faced his greatest enemy who had once been his friend.

THE WATCHERS ON the hill had seen the scouts break away from Fergus's main party and separate to approach the hill from two angles.

"Their helmets," Halla observed, "and their weapons might be useful to us."

The house guards grinned at each other, and one immediately crept off to the left. Tomas began to slope rightward before Muiredach caught his arm.

"You stay with the ladies," Muiredach commanded. *And you defend them with your life.* There was no need to speak that command aloud. All the lady's guards were prepared to die for her. Tomas's look of doubt was clearly more to do with his lack of belief in Muiredach's non-musical skills.

Well, it had been a long time. But some things were so ground in that they were never forgotten. Fergus's scout, dismounted now and creeping through the undergrowth with a dagger in each hand, and a bow and quiver across his back, never saw Muiredach coming. His own dagger pricked the back of the man's neck.

"Halt," Muiredach said softly. "Not a sound, or I'll cut your head from your spine. Drop the weapons."

From there, it was a simple matter to tie and gag him, take the rest of his weapons, and his helmet, and drag him back to their watching position.

Tomas regarded him with new respect, while Halla tried on the helmet and examined the weapons with interest. Mairead's expression was unreadable.

"Well," she observed. "For a harpist, you are certainly full of surprises."

"Don't be too impressed. He was distracted."

"Clearly," Mairead agreed. "Maybe you should go and beat up his friend now."

"Got to leave something for the soldiers," he said, and Tomas grinned.

One of the horses snorted, interrupting the momentary banter. Halla sat on its back, wearing the scout's helmet, his bow and quiver over her shoulder. "Keep out of sight," she ordered, and before anyone could recover enough to stop her, she rode down the hill toward Fergus's camp.

Muiredach groaned. Tomas swore long and fluently.

"What now, O Harper?" Mairead asked in her most provoking voice.

"Now," Muiredach said as the other captured scout was dumped unceremoniously at their feet, "I suppose I'd better be somebody's captive."

In the end, despite his arguments and commands, both he and Mairead played captive to Tomas, while the other guard stood over the captives and the remaining horses. Which was how they came to be in the thick of it when Fergus of Galloway challenged Malcolm MacHeth.

Muiredach, leading Malcolm's horse, and Mairead edged nearer to Halla as the combatants circled each other, the one tall and rangy, the other slight and wiry.

"Can he win?" Muiredach asked Halla in a low voice.

"Malcolm?" Halla didn't look at them. Her attention was all

on her husband, her expression unreadable. "He always used to."

"Before he was in prison for twenty years while Fergus honed his battle skills," Muiredach felt compelled to warn her.

"That's what Fergus is relying on," Halla murmured.

Tomas urged his horse next to Muiredach's, ready for whatever would happen next. If Malcolm died here, his blood would not be the last spilled today.

Fergus made the first attack, a sudden wicked lunge that looked as if it might actually hit home. A tiny yet despairing moan of fear escaped Mairead's lips. But it seemed Malcolm was quick, too, especially for his size, for his own great sword swung up to take the blow and immediately struck back, driving Fergus several paces back before he knocked up Malcolm's sword and circled again, sneaking in lower. Malcolm spun away, his sword crashing down on Fergus's as they faced each other once more.

The fight was riveting, all the more so for the stakes involved. If Malcolm won, he ruined Fergus's alliance with the King of Scots, at the very least. If Fergus won, no one doubted he would kill Malcolm and take his wife and his people. And then the MacHeths really would come. War between Ross and Galloway would be inevitable, with the King of Scots the only possible winner. Were Malcolm and Fergus really so blind that they couldn't see beyond their own petty anger and injustices?

Muiredach wondered why he ever expected anything different. It was just like Ireland. Malcolm was no better than Muiredach's own father and uncles and brothers in their relentless pursuit of power for power's sake.

And yet he had hoped that Malcolm would be different now from the boy who'd plunged his country into war twice for a crown. The odd times Halla had spoken of him had revealed a man who was rather more than that, a man for whom the crown was a beginning, not an end in itself. And Muiredach had wanted that to be true, for Halla's sake if for no other.

Yet here Malcolm MacHeth stood, willing to kill and die after finally, finally returning to the woman he didn't deserve.

Halla murmured to Tomas. "Take Bernard de Brus behind you and go while their attention is fixed elsewhere. Mairead, go with Muiredach."

Muiredach's gaze flickered to her in alarm. "I can't leave you here alone."

"I'm the only person here who's safe." Halla dragged her gaze away from the increasingly brutal fight—Malcolm had brought Fergus to his knees with a vicious kick, though Fergus fought back immediately, slashing at Malcolm's legs and forcing him back. There was blood. She caught Muiredach's eyes. "Why do you think he gave you his horse?"

"For his honor, we can't leave," Muiredach said bluntly.

"If you'll notice, Malcolm didn't actually agree to his terms. Which may be sophistry, but *I* certainly agreed to nothing. I am ordering you as your lady to take Mairead and go."

"Lady—"

She turned on him with hard, commanding eyes, a side of her he rarely saw. "Malcolm is here because of Donald. But this is a stupid fight, engineered by Fergus solely to save his alliance with the King of Scots after ravaging the said kingdom falsely in the MacHeth name. We owe him nothing."

"Agreed," Muiredach said impatiently. "But what of you if Malcolm mac Aed loses? What if he dies?"

A faint smile flickered over the lady's face and vanished. "Then there will be nothing anyone can do for me. I will kill Fergus. And you will still be safe."

Muiredach's heart ached. It almost sounded as if she were saying farewell. Her next words confirmed it.

"God be with you, Muiredach. You have been a good friend to me and mine, your value beyond words. Now, go."

Muiredach swallowed. Mairead tugged at his arm, her eyes huge and sad in her beautiful face. She'd do Malcolm's last, silent bidding; and she acknowledged the lady's right to stay with her lord. Muiredach saw at last that he had to do the same. And so, he edged away from the scene, Tomas and Mairead still with him.

At the back of the crowd, quite unguarded, Bernard de Brus stood stiffly, presumably catching only glimpses between the shifting crowd of the fight that was meant to decide his life or death.

"Mount," Muiredach murmured to him as Tomas reached down to him.

Muiredach all but threw Mairead into the saddle, then mounted behind her. Over the heads of the avid, yelling crowd, he saw that Malcolm was giving ground, only just fending off a relentless series of bone-jarring blows. In this fight, it was Fergus who undoubtedly had the stamina. He was playing with Malcolm, knocking him down again with a brutal blow to the head with his sword hilt.

With a silent prayer, Muiredach turned the horse and rode away, leaving his lady to her fate.

⇒⟫⟪⟸

MAIREAD, HER HEAD resting back on Muiredach's chest as they rode around the side of the hill out of sight of whatever mayhem was being committed, said, "I never imagined, when we freed him and Donald, that it would end like this."

Muiredach's heart ached for her. "It needn't be the end. People have been expecting Malcolm MacHeth to die for more than twenty-five years. Yet there he still is."

"You're being kind to me," Mairead said as if it surprised her. She twisted around to see his face. "We left your lady, too."

Muiredach's throat closed up. He urged the horse to climb.

"What now?" Tomas asked when they eventually arrived at the hollow dip in the hill where they'd left Astrid and the Grizel with the other guard and Fergus's two captured scouts.

"Watch and wait as we agreed," Muiredach said, his eyes straying below. The fight was still going on. At least Malcolm was still alive and Halla free. So far.

"He should just have ridden away when he had the chance," Mairead said furiously. "What was he thinking of?"

"All of us," Bernard de Brus snapped quite unexpectedly. "It's doubtful we would all have got out of there alive if he hadn't been given and accepted the challenge. Malcolm and I had to face him, to show him he was thwarted and force him back to Galloway. And of course, there was the matter of Malcolm's son. But what in God's name possessed you to follow us?"

"The lady," Muiredach said wryly. "She didn't believe Fergus would let you both live, so when we captured the scouts, she decided to even the odds. We couldn't let her go alone."

"And now we've left them *both* down there alone," Mairead said in a small, hard voice.

"As it should be," Astrid said harshly, wiping her eyes with a violent sweep of her arm. "I always knew they would die together."

"But Adam mac Malcolm never told you so, did he?" Muiredach retorted. "It's hardly written in stone. Nothing is."

"Sh-sh." Bernard lifted his hand and lowered it hastily, palm downward in a hushing gesture.

They stilled, and Muiredach heard at last what the Norman had. Soft hoof falls, the snort of horses too close for comfort.

"Wait," Bernard commanded, already crawling around the side of the hill toward the track they'd taken barely an hour before. Without a word, Muiredach followed him.

Through the cover of scruffy bushes, Muiredach glimpsed the approaching horsemen, heavily armed and armored and bearing the lion insignia of the King of Scots.

"Yours," Muiredach breathed.

"Mine," Bernard agreed, beginning to rise, his mouth already open to call to his men.

Muiredach yanked him back down. "Wait, what do you intend to do?"

"Ride down there and save your friend Malcolm MacHeth and his lady."

"Then your men will know Malcolm MacHeth is here and not in Ross as he should be." Muiredach thought the words aloud, debating with himself what was best.

Bernard grinned. "He came in search of his wife. Trust me, the young king's chivalrous soul will understand." He shook off Muiredach's detaining hand. "We don't have a choice, harper. Not if we wish to save them."

Muiredach stood up with him. "The lady will annihilate me for disobeying her."

ALTHOUGH PHYSICALLY SMALLER than some, Fergus of Galloway had never been an easy opponent. Even as boys, Malcolm had to work for his victories. Then, of course, they'd been playing for nothing but honor and their own self-importance. Today, Fergus fought desperately to save all his hopes and plans from collapse. Malcolm knew he was fighting for his life, and Halla's. Not that he believed Fergus would harm her. But Malcolm understood now what his absence had done to her life. He desired, overpoweringly, not to do it again.

"You cheated," Fergus panted, pounding him. "You sent them away."

"Halla sent them," Malcolm got out. "What did you expect? She's been their lady in fact, not just name, for twenty years. They obey her." He didn't bother pointing out that none of Fergus's men had tried to stop them going.

"And *she* obeys *you*," Fergus retorted, lunging once again.

Malcolm parried. "I wish."

Death was easier, of course, a voice whispered in his mind, trying to distract him as he decided which blow to accept and which to avoid. He didn't have the endurance any more to dance and dodge and still be able to fight in half an hour, or an hour, or however long this took. Death at least was certain. It was his imprisonment that had kept Halla prisoner, too, unable to move on.

But he didn't want death. More than ever after last night, he yearned for more of this new, mature Halla, to have the chance of a life and love with her. With his children and grandchildren, gifts he hadn't appreciated as he should when he was young.

But now, he knew. And God help him, he would *not* die for Fergus of Galloway.

Faster than he should have been able to turn it, Fergus's sword swept down in a killing blow. Malcolm's balance, the position of his sword was too wrong to ward it off, and so he allowed himself to fall, taking the massive blow on both forearm guards instead, grimly hanging on to his heavy sword at the same time.

It was a risk. If he'd used only one arm, his wrist would almost certainly have shattered beneath Fergus's sword. But using two distributed the force just enough. He wasn't afraid of the pain but of numbness that might prevent him from fighting back. He heard the effort in his own sudden roar as he slid his arms free, already turning his sword as he leapt to his feet. His forearms, his wrist, all moved, shrieking with agony as he knocked Fergus back with the flat of his sword, following it with a cut to the side, and as Fergus doubled up, he sent him flying with his knee.

Malcolm leapt on top of Fergus, tearing the sword from his weakened grasp as he lifted his own high and prepared to plunge it into Fergus's heart.

"Malcolm." It was Halla's urgent voice, tugging him from the red heat of battle.

He couldn't, shouldn't look up, and yet he did. She sat still upon the horse, the bow and arrow still in her grasp. She'd turned the horse so that he gazed at their profiles.

Beyond them, he saw what Halla had. A movement on the hill beyond the tense, gasping crowd. A stream of horsemen in full armor, riding toward them at speed. Bernard's men, it seemed, had found him after all.

Fergus's arm twitched, snatching at the dagger in his belt.

Malcolm dropped the sword point over Fergus's heart. "Don't."

Fergus tried to laugh. "Or what? You'll kill me?" But his hand fell away.

Malcolm lifted his sword again, still holding Fergus down with his knee while he talked rapidly. "The king's men are coming. De Brus's. Do what the MacHeths would do. Melt."

He rose to his feet, dragging Fergus with him. By then, the Galloway men had finally seen the attacking cavalry and were reaching for horses and weapons. Fergus uttered a few terse orders, throwing himself onto a horse that seemed to materialize by his side.

The horse pawed the ground, anxious to be off. "Why?" Fergus said between his teeth.

Malcolm curved his lips. "So that you'll still owe me."

Fergus's horse erupted into a gallop after his men toward the covering trees on the western side of the loch. As he rode, he hurled a word back over his shoulder at Malcolm. It sounded like, "Bastard."

Something very like laughter caught in Malcolm's hoarse, panting throat. And then Halla slid from the horse, all but dropping into his arms.

"Where are you hurt?" she whispered. And nothing in the world had ever been sweeter or more terrifying than the fear and care in her voice.

"I don't know. Nowhere. I'm fine."

"There's blood."

"There's always blood."

"Malcolm—"

He tightened his grip on her. "Don't make me lean on you." He saw the acknowledgment flash in her eyes. That great men were never hurt. They must always, always appear strong enough to lead, even when half dead with exhaustion or injury, no one could know.

She tried to draw back, but he held her now a moment longer, using the excuse to kiss her long and hard, like a lusty and victorious soldier.

"Now honor is satisfied," he breathed into her mouth and released her, turning to meet the slowing flow of men from the hill.

"Fergus was right," she said.

"About what?" Malcolm asked.

"Bastard," she said and mounted her own horse unaided.

This time Malcolm could laugh with genuine joy as he grinned up at Bernard de Brus and offered his hand.

"I see we weren't necessary after all." The Norman seemed disappointed.

"You might have been. At all events, I'm grateful." His roaming gaze found Muiredach and Tomas unexpectedly among the soldiers. "Where is Mairead?" he asked with sudden alarm.

"Safe where we left her and Astrid."

"Then I think," Malcolm said, trying not to sway as he dragged himself up behind Halla, "that it's time we went home."

CHAPTER EIGHTEEN

AVOIDING SETTLEMENTS SEEMED a good idea until a more serious wind sprang up and the rain came on as if it meant to stay. Malcolm dismounted and led them along the Clunie Water toward Doldencha, but well before the village, he began tearing back foliage and peering beneath tree roots until, with a grunt of satisfaction, he halted.

"I knew I'd been here before," he said. "I sheltered in this cave once with my brother."

The cave was big enough to shelter all of them. Even better, it was clearly well used by travelers, who'd left a pile of dry firewood. The house guards tied up the horses where they could crop leaves and grass, and then built the fire at the cave mouth, which was a trifle smoky, but dried out the damp clothes and kept them warm.

They ate the last of the food from the priory and settled down to sleep—except Mairead, who, still wide awake after the day's adventures, didn't feel remotely tired. She told Tomas she would take his watch and wake him if she heard anything or if she began to feel sleepy.

Gratefully, Tomas lay down beside his fellow on the other side of the cave, leaving Mairead to gaze into the fire's glow, and through the smoky cave mouth to the dark river. She could hear the rain splashing into it, and pattering onto the ground above. It was a pity she couldn't smell much more than smoke and burning wood, for she loved the sweet scents of wet land.

Behind her, in the cave, all was silent, save for the low murmur of the Lord and Lady of Ross talking together, until even that died away. Mairead smiled into the glow of the fire. It was strange how glad she could be for Malcolm, and even for Halla, and yet still ache with yearning.

A movement behind her made her glance around. Muiredach, stretching out from his bedroll on the cave floor, dropped a blanket around her shoulders, then dragged his own with him as he pulled himself over beside her.

"Why aren't you asleep?" he murmured.

She shrugged, gathering the blanket gratefully around her. "Why aren't you?"

"I was watching you," he said unexpectedly.

She glanced at him. "To see if I'd fail in my watch duties?"

"No. I was wondering why you smiled."

She smiled again. "So was I."

"Then…" He jerked his head to the back of the cave, where Malcolm and Halla slept very close together. Or at least, she assumed they did. She hadn't looked. "…their reunion does not hurt you?"

"Not as I thought it might. It seems…right." She held his gaze. "And you, Muiredach the harpist?"

"In the ten years I've known her, I don't believe she ever loved anyone but him. Her friendship just gave me a reason to stay. I like her family, her home."

"Perhaps that is what we each truly desired. Home. Where *is* your home?"

He smiled, so clearly used to not answering that she was sure he wouldn't. "Across the sea in Ireland. Or at least, it was. My family tore itself apart for power over a tiny kingdom far smaller than the earldom of Ross. I grew tired of being a pawn, a weapon in their quarrels, and so I left." He smiled deprecatingly. "I was no loss to anyone, being always more poet than soldier."

"And yet it was you who took down Fergus's scout."

"I was trained as a prince. Even I couldn't forget all of it."

"You intrigue me, Prince Muiredach."

"If you call me that again, I'll have you imprisoned in the tallest tower."

"What happened to your father's kingdom?"

Muiredach shrugged. "Swallowed by its Norse neighbors. Inevitably."

"Don't you desire to go home and win it back?"

"God, no," he said fervently.

She smiled faintly. "There can't be many men who would rather be a musician than a king."

His eyebrows lifted. "And what would you be, lady Mairead? If you could choose?"

"I have chosen," she said lightly.

"You've chosen sides," he argued. "That's not the same thing. How would you make your own life, if you could?"

She looked away. "What is it to you, harper?"

"You intrigue me, too."

She couldn't stop her gaze from sneaking back to his. The glow from the fire emphasized the sharp lines and hollows of his cheeks. Physically and otherwise, he was an attractive man; she'd always been aware of it. "I think," she said, "that I would travel and let the adventures find me. Then I could choose them as I wished, or move on."

"You're traveling now," Muiredach pointed out.

She searched his eyes, her heartbeat quickening. "Are you offering me an adventure, harper prince?"

His lips quirked. "Perhaps." He leaned over, giving her time to draw back if she wished. She didn't. She let him kiss her. It was sweet, exploratory, and full of possibility. Of hope.

She drew back to look into his face. "I will not lie with you."

"Ever?"

Her breath caught on laughter. "That is a long time. Not this night."

"Then I'll settle for another kiss."

She gave it freely, and that was even better. "You are indeed full of surprises," she murmured, just a little shakily.

"Does that mean you've changed your mind?"

"No. Would you really make love to me within the lady's hearing?"

"No, I'd take you outside and make love to you in the rain."

Involuntarily, she tightened her grip on his tunic. Something deeper than mere desire leapt at his words. She couldn't deny she was tempted. Her heart was thundering so loudly now, he must have felt it.

"Then it's as well I've already said no."

"Truly?"

"Don't you care that I am still married?"

"Do you?"

She sighed. "I have the comforting—or at least convenient—idea that I was never truly married in the eyes of God because I never meant it. I did it for a greater good, I feel He would understand."

"At worst, imprisoning you is grounds for breaking the contract," Muiredach opined.

"I was never an obedient wife," Mairead said. "I never wanted to be."

Muiredach took her hand from his tunic and kissed it. "I like you as you are."

"That's one of the sweetest things anyone's ever said to me."

"I don't believe that for a moment."

She laid her head on his shoulder. "Maybe I like you, too."

She must have fallen asleep like that. She certainly never woke Tomas. She guessed Muiredach did, for when she did wake, she lay beside the harpist, each wrapped respectably in their own blankets. The relentless patter and splash of rain had stopped. At the cave mouth, the fire had gone out but was still smoking gently in front of Tomas, who sat there yawning silently as the first light of dawn seeped in. Mairead felt oddly peaceful. The new day seemed to bring hope.

THEY MADE A more sluggish start that morning than they'd intended. The men-at-arms walked to Doldencha and brought back fresh bread and eggs, which Mairead and Grizel cooked over the revived fire. Only once their fast was broken did they pack everything up and prepare to leave.

Everyone else was outside, saddling and packing the horses, when the lady said abruptly to Mairead, "What will you do, now?"

"I don't know, yet. Go back to the Isles, perhaps. The Lady Ranghilde has always been kind to me." Mairead finished rolling her bedding back up and reached for the dried reeds to tie around it.

Halla said curiously, "Would you reconcile with your husband? If you could?"

Mairead curled her lip. "And play the contrite, forgiven wife? I don't think I could, supposing he ever truly forgave me, which he wouldn't. I don't blame him. I wronged him and misled him, even if not in the way that he imagines. He will repudiate me. After all, I never gave him children."

The lady took a deep breath. "Between you and my family is more than debt. Come home with us to Ross."

Mairead glanced up quickly and the half-tied reed sprang straight again. "To your hall?" she asked carefully.

"Of course. In the first instance, at least."

Mairead met her gaze and read there no malice or fear. She recognized and admired Halla for what she was: a strong, independent woman with a streak of responsibility that Mairead lacked. And yet she was conscious now of a wish to be like her, not for Malcolm's sake but for her own. In other circumstances, Halla could have been her friend, which made it all the harder.

"Lady, it could not work," she blurted. "I believe you know nothing improper ever occurred between your husband and me. And you probably know that was his choice, not mine. My presence would make you uncomfortable in the end. And your inevitable suspicion would hurt me as well as you. I thank you for your generosity, but I can't live in your hall." With unnecessary force, she finished tying the reed and rose to her feet.

"We should be friends, Mairead," Halla said. "For what you have done for my family, I have no words."

Mairead shook her head, blinded by sudden, foolish tears.

Halla laid one hand on her shoulder. "For your own safety, come with us into Ross. Wherever you go after that, within Ross or without, is your choice."

"Thank you," Mairead muttered. Briefly, she touched Halla's hand on her shoulder and walked away.

"Muiredach is a good man," Halla said to her back. "And more suited by birth than you might think."

Damn her, did she see everything? Mairead glanced over her shoulder. "The truth is, lady, right now I don't want Muiredach or any man." Not even Malcolm MacHeth. She caught the faint flicker of amusement in the lady's eyes that said, *Liar,* louder than any words. She was the lady.

Mairead gave a slightly crooked smile and walked out of the cave with her bedroll. Muiredach took it from her before she'd even registered his presence and strode away with it to tie it to her saddle. She followed, hoping in spite of herself to catch his eye. Because of their unexpected closeness last night. Because of his kisses.

He turned and boosted her into the saddle, turning away immediately to seize the reins of his own horse. No words, no secret touches or smiles, or even looks.

Mairead leaned forward and stroked her horse's ears, leaning down to whisper in them, "I think I've been spurned."

The horse twitched its ears and snorted.

"That's what I think," Mairead agreed.

Muiredach gave no indication that he'd heard.

⫸⫷

SKIRTING THE MOUNTAINS, it took them three days through the foothills before they reached the River Ness and crossed into Ross. Almost immediately, they were met by a relieved Donald and his following.

"Where the devil have you been?" Donald demanded, throwing himself off his horse to kiss the hands of his parents. "Did you attack Angus without us?"

Malcolm raised one eyebrow. "Who? Your mother and me, three women, two soldiers, and a harpist?"

Donald grinned. "All MacHeths. Or honorary MacHeths." He bowed to Mairead. "So, who knows?"

"We'll tell you all about it on the way home," Halla said. "Where is your sister?"

"At Tirebeck with Adam. Lady Mairead, delighted you've finally made it to Ross."

"I'm afraid," Mairead said lightly, "I'm going to leave again."

"When? For where?"

"I thought I'd take ship for the Isles."

"Stay a few days at least," Halla urged.

Mairead shook her head. "I can't, or I might never leave. But I hope I might visit you one day."

"Make it soon," Halla said. "My hall is yours. In the meantime, Muiredach will escort you to the coast. You'll find hospitality wherever you go."

"There is no need for Muiredach—" Mairead began.

"There is every need," Muiredach interrupted her. It was almost the first thing he'd said to her in three days, but she let it go since they were hardly alone.

Farewells were not as easy as she'd imagined. She'd grown to appreciate Halla's quiet humor and learned company. In fact, it came to her that those were also traits she'd always admired in Malcolm. Perhaps, in him, she'd always seen a friend and not a lover after all. For the first time, she began to understand her own loneliness since her parents had first sent her away to live among the violent, roaring islesmen, and then among the superficial, conniving courtiers who'd surrounded her second husband.

No wonder the MacHeths, Adam and Malcolm, had ensnared her, combining as they did, learning and laughter with their violence. And sheer differentness.

But at last, she rode free, aware of both sadness and relief. Muiredach rode in silence beside her. Behind them, followed the two members of Halla's house guards whom she'd come to know. Tomas still carried Grizel with him. Mairead wondered if the girl would stay with him. Perhaps she should give her the choice.

She opened her mouth to ask Muiredach's opinion before she remembered they weren't on speaking terms and closed her lips once more.

"Oh, damn it, Muiredach," she broke out at last. "I'd rather no company than this company! Go back to your lady and show *her* your long, superior face!"

He actually looked surprised. "Why would I do that?"

She sighed. "Muiredach. I know you overheard what I said to Halla." *I don't want Muiredach or any man.*

There was a pause, then he turned his head and looked at her. "You think I'm sulking."

"Aren't you?"

"No. I'm keeping out of your way until you realize you miss me."

"Until?" she scoffed.

"I realize it may be a long wait."

"Well, you're used to that," she retorted.

Annoyingly, he didn't look remotely hurt. "Are you trying to quarrel with me?" he asked with interest.

"Maybe. For what it's worth, I was trying to throw the lady

off the scent. If there was, if there *is*, anything between us, it is too new and vulnerable for other people to poke at. Especially the lady."

At the instruction of his hands, his horse walked closer to hers. "If you wish, we can make this journey last several days."

She smiled, gazing straight ahead. "If *you* wish, you could sail with me."

"To the islands?"

"I'm not wedded to that idea. We could go anywhere."

He reached out, his fingers covering hers on the reins. She turned her hand, gripping, before slowly turning to meet his gaze. His eyes were intense and excitingly warm.

"It isn't raining," he observed. "But I could take you into those trees. If you wished."

Blatantly, Mairead lifted their joined hands to her lips. "I do wish," she admitted, just a little shakily.

CHAPTER NINETEEN

"T HIS IS WHAT my homecoming should have been," Malcolm said as their horses walked together up the Peffery river bank. "If I had been capable of thought, I would have known it the first time."

Halla gained the top and pulled up beside him as Donald and most of the men poured over the river behind them. "If *I'd* been capable of thought, I would have known to meet in private first." She smiled faintly. "Where we first met, perhaps, by the waterfall."

"So that you could shoot me?"

"Just to remind you who truly rules Ross."

"I used to dream of coming home," Malcolm said. "Riding up to the gates of Brecka, with Donald on one side of me and Adam on the other, even if I couldn't see their faces. And then you would be there, and our daughter, to greet us."

"This is close," Halla said. "Send a man to Adam at Tirebeck. He'll come and bring Gormflaith back."

"Or I could go and fetch them. See where our son lives with his strange, brave lady. Donald and I had time at Roxburgh. Adam is more…enigmatic."

"I'm afraid he will always seem like that."

"Even to you?"

"Yes, even though I watched him struggle to become what he

is. But he is always worth every moment you spend with him. Go to Tirebeck."

"Come with me."

Halla hesitated. She had a better plan. "No. Make this time for Adam and Gormflaith. And then bring them home. We'll plan a feast when you do. Donald and I will go to Brecka and wait for you."

He considered her. She wondered if he were doubting her, gauging her motivation. She hadn't yet learned to read his face when he chose to close it.

"One night in Tirebeck," he said at last. "And then we'll ride for Brecka together."

"Then go." She held out her hand, and he took it and kissed it, still watching her face. Her fingers clung to his lips. How ridiculous that she'd miss him for these few days. Until very recently, there had been twenty years and so many more miles between them.

He lowered her hand but didn't at once release it. His eyes, warm and serious, continued to hold hers, causing her heart to beat and beat. There had been no repeat of their one night of intimacy in the wood, and now she could think of little else.

"We are more than we were before," he said softly. "And I think…what we have between us could be more, too."

"Perhaps," she said huskily because emotion choked her and wouldn't let her say more. Her fingers twisted, clasping his. "You will come home."

It wasn't a question. But he answered anyway. "I will come home."

And then her hand was free and cold, and he was riding away from her again. Two days, no more, and they would be together at Brecka at last.

Or perhaps there was a better way.

Tirebeck, like so much of Ross, was full of ghosts for Malcolm. People who seemed half-familiar ran in from the fields and from the harbor, just to trot beside his horse. Children peeped from doorways and from behind their mother's skirts as if they couldn't quite believe that Malcolm MacHeth, their earl, was real.

Rhuadri of Tirebeck had been his friend and follower. He'd survived all the battles of the war with the King of Scots and then, while Malcolm was captive in Roxburgh, had burned his hall down around himself. Because his unfaithful wife had left him for one of the king's soldiers, taking their daughter with her. It was this girl, Rhuadri's daughter, now grown to womanhood, Malcolm's daughter-in-law, who welcomed him back to Tirebeck. She didn't banish the ghosts, but somehow, she made them friendlier.

His son, Adam, however, emerging from the hall behind her in a rough leather tunic, looking wild and unfocused, was, surprisingly, less than welcoming.

"Where is my mother?" he asked bluntly.

So, quite focused then, after all. "On her way to Brecka, if she isn't there already," Malcolm replied. "She wants me to bring you back there with me. Is Gormflaith with you?"

At that moment, Gormflaith came flying round from the side of the hall, more like some peasant urchin than an earl's daughter, to greet him with uninhibited pleasure. And his heart lifted all over again. His daughter had the gift of happiness.

"Come inside," Christian said warmly.

Adam stood aside, still watching him in a way that was almost unnerving. And yet as they sat down close to the fire—for the first chill of winter seemed to have sprung into the air—Adam poured him wine and sat down with him. It was impossible to tell if his son was pleased to see him or not.

"What happened?" Adam asked, and so Malcolm told them about his adventures, how Halla rescued Mairead while he led the Kingowan men on a wild-goose chase, and about the false MacHeths raiding with Fergus of Galloway.

"We scared them back to Galloway," Malcolm said, "and the king will hear the truth."

"How?" Christian demanded.

Malcolm smiled. "With the help of a new friend. A Norman lord from the south."

"De Brus," Adam said unexpectedly, although Malcolm hadn't spoken the name. His gaze fixed on Malcolm. "What did you think of him?"

"That he was very young and honorable and loyal."

"For a Norman?" Adam suggested.

Malcolm smiled. "Perhaps. How do you know him?"

Adam's brows lifted in surprise. "I don't. But I know it is his family, not ours, who will be the future of Scotland."

Malcolm searched his enigmatic face. "You don't say anything without a reason, do you, Adam? Why do you tell me this? To be sure I don't start another war to win the kingdom for myself? Or to urge me on to it?"

"Would you?" Adam countered. "Would you rise again?"

"That would depend on many things. Would I fight again to win the crown?" He gave a crooked smile. "I don't need prophecy to know that ship sailed long ago. Though it's galling to know my chief claim to fame in the histories will be for spending half my life in captivity."

"No. There is greater power in mystery. People will wonder about you, about all of us."

Malcolm regarded him. "You spend a lot of time making the unpalatable palatable for people, don't you?"

For the first time in their short acquaintance, Adam looked disconcerted, dragging his gaze free as though ashamed of being found out. Malcolm clapped him lightly on the shoulder. "It's a kindness in you I admire, Adam."

His son's lashes flickered upward, revealing his eyes to be unusually clear. "It isn't always kindness," he admitted.

"Manipulation?" Malcolm guessed.

"Sometimes." Adam stirred uncomfortably. "I wouldn't presume to manipulate you. I wouldn't try."

"I know. But you don't need to coddle me either. I might regret the loss of the fine destiny I once believed to be mine, to be ours. But it seems…I've discovered there are things I care for more. Things it is right to care for more."

Adam nodded as if he understood that perfectly. He probably did, but for Malcolm, the concept was still new and fascinating.

ADAM AND CHRISTIAN kept a warm and hospitable hall. The Norman knights Malcolm remembered sat among Adam's native followers, quite at their ease. Malcolm found time to speak to Findlaech, whom he last remembered as a wild, spindly boy. Now he was a fierce and solid man who knew his sons better than Malcolm did.

"I know what you've done for my family. No words or gifts can repay it, so I won't try. But whatever you need, I will give."

By then, Findlaech had had a few cups more than he should. "I began wanting to make them worthy of you," he admitted. "And ended trying to be worthy of *him*."

"There are worse ambitions," Malcolm allowed. "You helped shape my sons into fine men."

"Into warriors, perhaps. They are their own men."

That was undoubtedly true. Malcolm hadn't expected to enjoy being with Adam quite so much as he did. Quick and mercurial and undoubtedly strange, he fascinated his father. But he was also entertaining company, witty and quick-tongued enough to cover those moments when he didn't quite seem to be there. On the journey, Malcolm had been relieved to see the men accept him with more than a little pride. Now he saw there was at least as much affection. As if Adam knew, from instinct or study, how to bind by charm. As Malcolm himself had always known.

Only after Christian and the women had retired, and some of

the men had fallen asleep where they sat did Adam say, "You don't believe in my sight." Leaning forward, he poured wine from the jug into both their cups.

Malcolm considered. "I've found it hard to *like*," he amended. "Belief is something else. I believe in your intelligence and your grasp of the world and our place within it."

"How?" Adam countered. "You barely know me."

"I heard a lot. In prison. And then there was Mairead, who thought so highly of you. And I spent more than two weeks in constant company with your brother, which was…illuminating. But you're right. We barely know each other. Tell me about it."

"The sight?" Adam's gaze drifted away. He raised his cup and drank, almost as if avoiding speaking. Only when it was empty did he lower it and refill it. Donald had said he never spoke of it, so Malcolm was prepared to be deflected. Then Adam began to talk. "It can come upon me any time, sometimes all the time. I can't see what's here for dreaming of what has passed. Or what will come."

Slowly, Adam raised his eyes to his father's, as if he needed him to understand this. "Each battle, each raid I survived were all miracles in their own way. Without Donald, without Findlaech and some of the other men, I would be dead many times over. I only killed de Lanson because I was dreaming the moment of his death at exactly the same time. I thought…I always knew I shouldn't live long with this gift. I just had to survive a little longer to bring you home. Beyond that, I didn't much care."

Malcolm stared at his son. There was no question now about belief. He had no idea how anyone could live with what Adam did, let alone make it work for him as he had. To be fighting blind… For an instant, fear for his son paralyzed him.

"Your mother knows this?" Malcolm managed at last. White Christ, how had she gone on with such knowledge, such fear? The depths of his son's loyalty, his courage, staggered him.

"She suspects." Adam stirred. "The thing is, I *can't* die now. I have Cairistiona. And soon, we shall have a child."

Malcolm reached up, grasping his son's shoulder, half in congratulation, half in promise. For Adam's words weren't so much a warning as a plea for a break in the constant warfare which *would* kill him in the end. He had less chance than anyone and surely, he'd used up all his luck.

"You're the seer," Malcolm said quietly. "What do you see?"

Adam smiled. "Now? Peace. Mostly, peace. For a little."

THEY SET OUT for Brecka the following morning in the rain and mist, which finally cleared at midday, gradually revealing patches of moorland and hill and gently steaming lochs, until the whole sky was finally blue and the sun shone down on the glory that was Ross in the autumn, all red and brown and gold, glistening from the earlier damp. Now even the streams sparkled.

They made better time, then, pushing the horses because Malcolm wanted to reach the hall before nightfall. Although he treasured every new moment with Gormflaith and Adam, every inch of him screamed out for Halla. Not just to be with his complete family at last, but to hear her voice, touch her, make her his in the peace of their own bedchamber.

In the end, they rode down on Brecka so quickly that the house guards began to close the gates in panic before they realized it was the earl himself. Malcolm wanted to laugh from pure happiness, because now, at last, he was coming home. His mind, his body, his whole being sang with anticipation.

Donald and the household stood outside the main hall to welcome them. Donald had little Adam in his arms, bouncing him. It was a precious sight. Along with the child in Christian's belly, it spoke for the future of the MacHeths. Reining in his horse and dismounting, he looked in vain for Halla.

The people cheered as if this was indeed his first homecoming. Malcolm acknowledged it, raising one hand and then throwing his gloves in the air.

He seized Donald by the shoulders and kissed the laughing baby, who seemed quite unperturbed by the noise. "Where is your mother?"

Donald stopped smiling. "Um…she's gone."

Blood sang in his ears. The bottom fell out of Malcolm's world all over again, leaving it black and empty.

Revenge, he thought blankly. *She's done it for revenge to show me how it felt for her when I didn't come home.*

Dear God, hadn't he acknowledged it enough, apologized enough? He'd been so sure she understood, that he was forgiven. That they'd passed such silly matters and found the beginnings of something rich and exciting. Yet it seemed he didn't know her at all, for she'd undoubtedly gone, either to punish him or because, in spite of everything he'd persuaded himself to believe, she no longer loved him.

There had been no need to pretend. That had been simple cruelty on her part.

But even as the thought struck him with unpalatable self-pity, he recognized that none of that was Halla. She would shout at him, verbally annihilate him, hit him, shoot him. At a pinch, now she was so dignified, she might hunch her shoulders at him. Cold cruelty was not in her nature any more than the cowardice of running away.

Relief flooded him so hard now, as he walked into the hall, that he had to sit down on the nearest bench.

He fixed Donald with his gaze. "Gone where?"

"I don't know," Donald replied. "But she said you would."

Malcolm stared up at him, his brow slowly clearing. "She said that?"

"I think it's a game," Donald said, grinning, clearly entertained by the idea of his parents playing at anything at all. "But we're not allowed to join in."

"Whom did she take?" His gaze fell on Astrid, lurking guiltily by the old bedchamber door. "Please tell me she didn't go alone."

"She took her two younger women and two of the men."

Malcolm nodded and stood up. "Then I'd better go and fetch her."

"It will be dark in an hour or so," Gormflaith said in clear alarm. "Wait until first light."

"I am quite used," Malcolm said, "to traveling around Ross in the dark. It can't have changed that much."

"No, but your memory can," Gormflaith said bluntly.

Malcolm blinked. "I don't know whether you're wise or insulting. Bring me some wine and food to carry, and I'll bring you back your mother, if not tomorrow, then the day after."

FOR ONCE, THE weather was kind. Although it was a cold night to camp out, it was dry and clear. Halla's people clearly thought her mind had been overset by the return of her husband. Aideen, her youngest attendant, tried to talk her into returning, and then, more urgently, to stay with them in the tent by the foot of the waterfall.

But Halla, feeling like the defiant young girl she'd been all those years ago, insisted on climbing up the hill by herself and building her makeshift shelter and a fire just beside the rocky ledge where she'd first seen him.

She wasn't afraid. She'd only brought the men and her women to stop everyone else from worrying. But she needed to be entirely alone, just for a little. She suspected one of the men had sneaked up the hill to see that she was safe and warm, but if so, he didn't stay.

She lay down in her tent, huddled happily inside her blankets. Tomorrow she would walk down the hill, eat with her people, and then come back up here to wait for him. She knew he would come. And they would talk, say all the things that needed to be said to marry past and present and make their future together. And then she would seduce him.

She smiled, for it was a good plan, and she wasn't blind to her luck. How many women fell in love twice with the same husband?

Through the canvas, she could make out the glow from the fire, warm and comforting in the darkness. She fell asleep to the relentless rush of the waterfall.

PRESENCE. SHE WOKE to the knowledge of another's presence, even before she remembered where she was and heard the sounds of someone brushing against the canvas. Or an animal, more likely, a wild cat or a fox, or even a wolf.

The problem with sleeping so far from her people was, of course, that she couldn't call for the men to deal with predators. She'd known that, which was why she'd brought a dagger. It had been Malcolm's, a gift from Somerled when she'd married him.

There was definite movement by the door. She could make out no staring yellow eyes in the darkness as she felt very slowly for the dagger in her pack. The bundle moved as she touched it, her fingers scrabbling desperately now for the weapon as the thing at the door rushed upon her.

She almost sobbed as her fingers closed at last around the dagger hilt, but before she could draw it free of its scabbard, something thudded beside her body—a human knee?—and a hand closed over hers on the weapon, prying her fingers free in spite of her frantic resistance.

"What is it about this place," a voice breathed in her ear, chilling her very blood, "that turns you so murderous?"

The scream died in her throat. She lay very still, staring into the darkness. She could make out no more than a blur.

"Malcolm?"

His answer was a kiss that took her totally by surprise, pressing her into the blankets as his body covered hers.

"Who else would it be?" he muttered into her mouth.

She struggled to free her trapped arm and threw both around his neck, all the details of her plan forgotten in the sheer, overwhelming joy of his presence. "I knew you would come."

"I'd cross the winter seas just to be alone with you for an hour, a minute."

She kissed him, tears she hadn't known were there trickling down her cheeks and into her hair. "You came too quickly. You must have ridden all night."

Her fingers threaded through his hair clutched convulsively. "It is right, isn't it?" she said with sudden anxiety. "We do need this reunion, just you and I, before we join our children and our people?"

He moved, hauling at the blankets separating them until he, too, was beneath them. "It's what we should have done when I first came home. Just as you said." His breathing was too fast and uneven. "Do I have to take my boots off?"

Laughter fought through her tears as she welcomed him with passion. No words were necessary after all, but they came anyway in whispers and sighs and gasps. As he crushed her mouth beneath his, she surrendered to him utterly, not just her body and her love, but the earldom she had ruled so long in his name.

Her lord had come home.

CHAPTER TWENTY

A MONTH LATER, the first serious snow fell on Brecka. It was as well winter had come late that year since the earl's entire family had spent the last four weeks progressing around Ross, staying a night or so in each of his halls, or in those of his most important followers, showing the returned lord to his people, while the lord himself assessed his domain.

By any standards, Halla had done more than well. She'd worked miracles, transforming his war-torn earldom back into a place of prosperity and peace and law. She had always possessed patience for the everyday, and mundane, responsibility for the needs of the people, and wherever they went, Malcolm recognized the benefits she'd brought them, despite the earldom's supposed isolation. She traded timber to the north, she'd brought regular markets to Rosemarkie and Tain, and delivered justice without discrimination. His pride in her swelled with wonder.

Although this progress was a tiring if necessary duty, Malcolm found himself enjoying every bit of it. The wit he had been able to practice only on the more amiable of his jailers, and latterly, Mairead, broke free. He bantered with his larger-than-life family and charmed his people who had stood by him so long and so loyally. He renewed some old, half-forgotten friendships, including that with the Bishop of Ross's son, Symeon, now bishop himself, and made new ones with sons and daughters and grandsons. So much had changed, and yet so much stayed the same.

Finally, they rode back through the gates of Brecka in the bright, fast-falling snow, which clung in white layers to their clothes. Trails of breath streamed out from both horses and riders. The household—no longer just Halla's well-trained people but his—ran out to welcome them, seeing to the horses and ushering them into the clean, warm hall, already set up for dinner. Delicious smells from the kitchen assailed Malcolm's nostrils as he saw Halla gaze quickly, critically around her before nodding once to her women, who smiled as widely as if God had just blessed them. His Halla ruled with a rod of iron, a rod no less respected for being used with such a light touch.

Gormflaith danced off to her own bedchamber while Donald yelled for his son. Adam ushered Christian to his old bedchamber to rest before dinner. Malcolm opened the shutter on the nearest window to watch the snow and smiled.

"Winter in Brecka."

"You are content?" Halla said, coming to stand by him. She had removed the snow-covered, fur-lined cloak. Beneath it, she wore a heavy gown of deep, dark green wool over an undergown of a paler shade, which was visible at the hem and sleeves and neck.

"Do you not know that I am?"

For answer, she threaded her fingers through his in silence and they watched the snow together.

"And when the snow is gone," she said at last. "When spring becomes summer and even that begins to fade to autumn?"

He knew what she was asking. "Then I will make my peace with the King of Scots as I promised. He will recognize me as Earl of Ross, and the only wars I fight will be his."

There was a pause. "Will you hate it?" she asked.

It was a subject he'd often considered. "It will go against the grain," he admitted. "But no, I won't hate it. I fought and I lost long ago. That is another life. *This* is what I value."

She didn't need to ask what *this* was. She rarely did, although they were still learning the new as well as relearning the old about each other.

"Lord?" It was the priest, Halla's chaplain, whom he'd charged with reading any and all letters which came for him while they were away, and deciding which were important enough to send after him.

"Father Patrick," Malcolm greeted him. "How are you?" He eyed the fat sheaf of parchment in the priest's hands. "I see you've been kept busy."

"But not as busy," Halla said sweetly, "as you're clearly going to be. Welcome home, husband."

Although there was just the family and household for dinner, an atmosphere of festivity seemed to fill the hall that evening.

"I miss Muiredach," Gormflaith said suddenly. "We need music."

"Well, he taught all three of you," Halla responded. "Earn your supper for once."

"I've forgotten all that he ever taught me," Donald said at once. "I always sounded as if I was playing with my feet anyway. Adam can play."

Adam clearly could. He wasn't Muiredach, but he had a light touch, and the music seemed to smooth the frown between his brows. Christian was smiling as she watched and listened, forgetting to eat. Findlaech and Adam's other men grinned and nudged each other, half-proud of their strange young lord, half-amused by this un-warrior-like talent, as if they'd forgotten about it or hadn't known in the first place.

"Will Muiredach come back?" Gormflaith asked.

"I don't know," Halla replied. "I hope so. I hope he will bring Mairead with him."

"Really?" Gormflaith's clear interest changed abruptly as the music suddenly paused.

Adam still sat with the harp against his shoulders, but his fingers were falling away. His eyes were unfocused and yet rapt.

Without fuss, Gormflaith arose and went to him.

"My turn," she said calmly.

Adam's head snapped up to look at her. There was another pause. "So it is," he said, and stood to make way for her.

It was a tiny incident, troubling no one, but reminiscent of a few Malcolm had already noticed. Adam's brother and sister covered his social lapses so seamlessly, they'd clearly been doing so all their lives. And yet they obviously felt no shame in Adam. It was merely done from habit, for the sake of those who might not understand or who might even fear Adam's oddity. Adam's wife, too, accepted, as did the men. Malcolm felt ridiculously proud of all of them.

Gormflaith, his lively, beautiful daughter, played the harp much as she did everything else, with great vitality.

"She will ensnare him," Malcolm foretold.

"Who?" Halla asked.

"Harald Maddadson."

"You wrote to Orkney?" Halla said quickly.

"And heard back. He'll sail to Ross with the first spring tides."

Halla sat back, regarding him. "And if you don't like him? Will you still give her to him?"

Malcolm raised his cup and smiled into it. "No."

He sensed her relief at once. She'd kept Gormflaith with her too long to part with her to an unworthy man. She would always remember her own churning emotions when she'd first arrived in Ross and shot her betrothed with an arrow. A woman's lot in this world was rarely by her own choice. And yet somewhere, surely, they both trusted Gormflaith's own unshakeable opinion of Orkney's earl.

Malcolm leaned forward to catch Adam's attention farther along the table. "What did you see?"

It was surprisingly easy to ask now.

"Some good things," Adam said vaguely. A smile flickered across his face. "Congratulations."

"On what?" Malcolm asked, surprised.

A sound that was not quite laughter escaped Halla's lips. Beneath the table, she took his free hand and placed it on her belly.

Malcolm's breath caught. "Truly?"

"It's too soon for me to be certain, but Adam is rarely wrong."

A shiver ran through Malcolm, bringing with it a rush of as much memory as hope. They were all part of him: his father and mother, his brother, his wonderful children and grandchildren, and beyond. And the strong, beautiful woman who sat by his side now in reality, as she had always done in his heart.

He raised his cup to the hall. "The MacHeths!"

The echo was rousing, deafening, and Malcolm, who'd turned a kingdom upside down for a throne, couldn't have been happier with his lot.

EPILOGUE

Ross, winter 1205

AGAIN, THE OLD man smiled into the flames, because he liked to remember, and that *had* been the beginning of the long peace. A time for living, prosperity, and…fun. On a selfish note, he would not have survived many more battles, would not have had his long, happy life with Cairistiona, or fathered so many children.

Likewise, his parents would not have lived their final years together, with another son, his brother, to seal their enduring union. Malcolm had become Earl of Ross in law as well as in fact, and so had Donald, and Donald's sons in effect. But not young Adam…

Before the grief, just one of many, could take him again, an echo of harp music and the flash of a man's ascetic face in the fire, reminded him that Muiredach the harpist had come home at last, too. After two years of wandering, he had returned with Mairead, and they had raised their family of poets and warriors in Ross. Wisely, Mairead had never returned to the king's court, though Muiredach had accompanied the earl and played for the man who had once been the enemy.

Those struggles that had been so important in his youth, loomed so much smaller now. And yet, they had brought his father home, and if Malcolm had worn no crown, he had made a peace where life could thrive.

Of course, the visions reminded him, it had not *all* been peace. The MacHeths were still the MacHeths, and the growing clan was unruly. But they had been good years, and there was still time to prepare for what would inevitably come. If he did not lose himself in the dreams.

As the visions faded to mere flames, he realized his young granddaughter sat on the stool by his feet.

"Do you really see pictures in the fire, Grandfather?" she asked, without looking up.

He nodded without speech.

She swallowed. "So do I. Sometimes."

"I know."

"Are they real?"

"Real to you, though they might not *be*. They might never have been."

"Then some are the past?"

He nodded again. "For me."

"Do you know the future? What will happen to us?"

Don't look. Never look. If you have a choice… A wave of mighty emotion swept over him. He did not want this gift, this curse, for her. "It's not written in stone, child. The future, like the present, is what you make of it."

She leaned back against his legs, and he touched her hair, liking the frisson of prescience, no longer powerful enough to shock him.

You will have a good life. As mine was good.

Historical Note

The Chronicle of Holyrood tells us that in 1157 Malcolm MacHeth was reconciled with the King of Scots and it makes sense that this event is somehow related to the capture of Donald MacHeth at Whithorn the year before. Since there is no evidence as to what happened in this intervening year – we know that Donald was imprisoned at Roxburgh, but not for how long – I have compressed events to make a faster moving story that might just have happened.

Although we don't actually know what became of Donald after his capture, we do know that Malcolm was released and that he was certainly Earl of Ross by 1162 at the latest, for the king addressed a document to him no later than that year, using the title, and he was certainly accorded it in his obituary in 1168.

I like to think the years following Malcolm's release were happy and peaceful years for the MacHeths. They seem to have taken no part in subsequent uprisings in the 1160s involving Fergus of Galloway and Somerled of the Isles, which were both put down with relative ease by the King of Scots. I've hinted at Fergus's fall from royal favor at the end of this book, a possible reason for his conflict with the king. Fergus was forcibly retired to Holyrood Abbey, where he died an unlikely monk in 1161. It's tempting to imagine Malcolm MacHeth leading some of those forces against him, in the name of the king.

We also know that at some point in these years Malcolm's daughter Gormflaith (or Hvarflod) did indeed marry Harald Maddadson, Earl of Orkney. I believe the marriage was a happy one for when the king demanded he repudiate her as a condition of peace between them – no doubt because the daughter of Malcolm MacHeth was still regarded as a symbol of opposition to the Kings of Scots – Harald refused.

Of later MacHeths, we know very little. One Adam, son of Donald, who was captured by the king in 1186 (and his followers brutally burned to death) may have been a MacHeth. And one Kenneth MacHeth, of whom more in the next book, led another rising in 1215.

Finally, Malcolm's encounter with a minor member of the de Brus family is entirely fictional (as is the position I gave Bernard de Brus with the king's soldiers), although it's likely that as a nobleman of Scotland, Malcolm would have come to know the ambitious Norman Lords of Annandale whose descendant would become the great King Robert the Bruce.

Mary Lancaster

About Mary Lancaster

Mary Lancaster lives in Scotland with her husband, three mostly grown-up kids and a small, crazy dog.

Her first literary love was historical fiction, a genre which she relishes mixing up with romance and adventure in her own writing. Her most recent books are light, fun Regency romances written for Dragonblade Publishing: *The Imperial Season* series set at the Congress of Vienna; and the popular *Blackhaven Brides* series, which is set in a fashionable English spa town frequented by the great and the bad of Regency society.

Connect with Mary on-line – she loves to hear from readers:

Email Mary:
Mary@MaryLancaster.com

Website:
www.MaryLancaster.com

Newsletter sign-up:
http://eepurl.com/b4Xoif

Facebook:
facebook.com/mary.lancaster.1656

Facebook Author Page:
facebook.com/MaryLancasterNovelist

Twitter:
@MaryLancNovels

Amazon Author Page:
amazon.com/Mary-Lancaster/e/B00DJ5IACI

Bookbub:
bookbub.com/profile/mary-lancaster